TELL ME YOURS, I'LL TELL YOU MINE

Stories

by Kristina Ten

STILL HOUSE PRESS

PRAISE FOR *TELL ME YOURS, I'LL TELL YOU MINE*

"*Tell Me Yours, I'll Tell You Mine* is a joyous, incisive, inventive, and vital run of stories. I'd put it right alongside Terry Bisson's *Bears Discover Fire and Other Stories*, but with the distinct possibility that you might see some of Kelly Link's stone bunnies on the next page turn. You'll read this with a nervous grin, and then you'll read it again, just to see how Kristina Ten pulls some of these magic tricks off."

Stephen Graham Jones, author of *The Buffalo Hunter Hunter* and *My Heart Is a Chainsaw*

"Never have I ever tasted such a delicious cocktail of nostalgia and dread. Reading these stories feels like saying Bloody Mary into the mirror: in Kristina Ten's expertly crafted world, your own reflection becomes a monster. Fans of Kelly Link and Karen Russell will adore every darn second of this book. I know I did."

GennaRose Nethercott, author of *Thistlefoot* and *Fifty Beasts to Break Your Heart*

"In *Tell Me Yours, I'll Tell You Mine*, Kristina Ten transports us back to the schoolyard . . . just not the way we remember it. Infused with horror and heartbreak, these stories play at the edges of realism, dip in and out of the fantastic, and showcase Ten's incredible range as her characters navigate girlhood and womanhood, the immigrant experience, and the indelible marks that our histories leave on our futures. This collection delights from start to finish, each story a fresh take on our oldest fears."

Gwen E. Kirby, author of *Shit Cassandra Saw*

"Kristina Ten's *Tell Me Yours, I'll Tell You Mine* is an audacious debut, displaying a comfortable command across a variety of genres. These stories mix the creepy with the touching, the grotesque with the beautiful. My heart ached for some of these characters, pounded in fury for others. Ten is a writer to reckon with."

Nathan Ballingrud, author of *The Strange* and
Crypt of the Moon Spider

"Imagine you're playing a game, one of the oldest and best-loved in your collection, a game you've always found completely pleasurable, completely absorbing. This time, though, midway through the first round, the rules seem to bend and turn inside out. You no longer recognize the board, you realize, and what's with these playing pieces? Where did they come from? Did you move that one just now and forget about it, or did it move itself? The game is still pleasurable, still absorbing, but unfamiliar suddenly, and slightly threatening. That's what reading Kristina Ten is like. Her stories are marvels, and page after page they found new ways to surprise and discomfit me."

Kevin Brockmeier, author of *The Ghost Variations*

"The stories of *Tell Me Yours, I'll Tell You Mine* delight in trickery. Its collective narrative voice is somehow one of comfort, of solace; it might even evoke feelings of nostalgia—if you were raised in *The Twilight Zone*."

Joe Vallese, editor of *It Came from the Closet*

for the last one awake at the sleepover

CONTENTS

KEEP TABS ON YOU

In the man's story, all the women are paper dolls. The kind someone might get as a gift from a nostalgic aunt when what they really wanted was a crisp twenty.

The paper-doll women stand with their legs together and their arms bent at the elbows. They are thin from one side and thinner from the other, and their faces are set in a pleasant, close-mouthed expression that never changes. Their features are very, very flat. The man likes this about them.

The man has six currently, all with different hairstyles. A fine assortment, he thinks, though he is always looking to grow his collection.

Each woman comes with her own pack of paper clothing, and each item has tabs that allow the man to dress her up. It was easy enough to learn: align the garments with the body, fold the tabs over to hold them in place, and *voila*.

Sometimes, he buys extra clothing packs for the women he likes most. Other times, he makes them share.

There are Elegant at the Office packs with belted pencil skirts and designer purses. Back to School packs with heavy-looking satchels and cheerleader poms. Picnic in the Park, Born in the U.S.A., Mermaid Princess, Historic Miss.

The women are hourglass shaped and so is their clothing. Underneath, each wears a white bra and briefs with drawn-on frills. These are not removable, are flush with the women's skin. This the man doesn't like.

To keep things interesting, he unfolds the tabs on their clothing and arranges them in creative positions, then slides one body over another, appreciating how they are same-sized and perfectly smooth, the whole matter frictionless. He is not always careful, and some of his women have creases to show for it.

As for the women, they loathe him, of course.

Aerin, the one with the curly blonde hair and the dark sense of humor, can produce a sailor tattoo on her arm if she concentrates hard enough. She knows the man finds these unsightly, and the next day will just cut it out of her with embroidery scissors, replace it with a square of peach construction paper.

But it is worth it.

And he has done worse.

To Mara, who had straight black hair and a quick wit. To Jeanine, who dared to stand with her legs a centimeter apart instead of held tight together.

It doesn't take much to vanish a paper-doll woman. The flame of a lighter. The stream of a faucet. A working knowledge of origami and a hot glue gun.

But it doesn't take much to destroy a man either, especially one so fixated on abundance. The more women he collects, the more paper-thin edges, each sharp enough to carve.

Doesn't take much. Only takes time.

A thousand cuts. Slow, slow, slow.

There is no pulp to the man, the women know. When they cut, he'll be all nerve endings and supplication. And when he screams, they will smile, their expressions still not changing.

THE DIZZY ROOM

Mom and Dad all but forced the games on me. It's hard to believe now. All you hear about these days is how kids don't want to play water balloons anymore, don't want to do sack race, how every year there's an increase in reported grass allergies, and how in just a couple generations we as a society are going to forget we ever knew how to climb trees. Everyone has those apps that track screen time. Everyone's tried that thing where the whole family stacks their phones in the middle of the table for a weekly distraction-free dinner, or "DFD." And those First Baptist nutters who were always shouting about computers being the tools of the devil? Well, everyone who once rolled their eyes at them is starting to think maybe they were right.

I was ten when we got our first family computer, a Dell Dimension our next-door neighbor was offloading so he could upgrade to a newer model. He dropped it off one day in the original box and we spent the better part of an afternoon sifting through the tangle of cables and user manuals while my dad explained that the tall, heavy rectangle was the *real* computer, and the thing I probably *thought* of as the computer, the thing with the screen, was actually just the monitor. Everything was the ugly beige of a pure white sheet of paper left too long in the sun, a color I haven't found replicated anywhere since, though some of the tech companies, with their retro nineties' nostalgia lines, have tried. My dad held his breath carrying it to the guest room, where he set it down gingerly, one corner at a time, on my mom's old sewing table. We never had guests anyway, and the only other furniture in there was this horrible lumpy futon that even the cat refused to sleep on. So it didn't take long for us to rename that nine-by-nine square of peach shag the *computer room*—as in: no drinks, no snacks, no dirty hands in the computer room.

The Dell smelled like burning plastic from the second we plugged it in, and it raised the temperature of the room a full ten degrees. It was achingly slow and loud and alien, and constantly contracting viruses, which my mom's humorless, brainy friend George, an IT guy at the community college, came over to fix multiple times a month. Sometimes it would power down for no apparent reason, like it had grown weary of this world's insatiable demands and was, in a kind of workers' strike, putting itself to sleep. All in all, I thought the thing was absolute magic.

The first game we installed was *Wesley Whale and the Case of the Missing Conch Shell.*

The computer came with *Solitaire* and *Minesweeper* already built-in, and I didn't think I would ever tire of them. I could've kept clearing those numbered fields, dodging those jagged little bombs forever. But then my parents got the call from school and any games deemed *noneducational* were taken right off the menu.

My English skills weren't developing as quickly as everyone had hoped—everyone being my grade's guidance counselor and language arts teacher, as well as Severn Elementary's ESL coach, a soft-spoken, ponytailed woman named Ms. Arnold, who made us sit in a floor circle and who all the kids teased for having a boy's name for a last name, though I could tell deep down they were infatuated with her and wanted desperately to impress her, so eager were they to show off their hard-practiced "th" and short "i" sounds. One day in the middle of social studies, I was called down to the main office. There, my parents furiously folded their hands this way and that in their laps while the aforementioned everyone told us that if I didn't improve, they'd have no choice but to hold me back from middle school the following year.

This baffled my parents, who had picked up English at a miraculous rate in the two years since we'd moved from Volgograd. I'd heard them quizzing one another each morning through the vent that connected my bedroom to theirs: common, promise-to-be-useful phrases like "Do you have this garment in a different color?" and "Yes, I would like a sandwich with soda and fries."

Kids are supposed to be able to learn faster than adults, aren't they? Languages especially. Something about their brains being more elastic, more receptive, more willing to rewire certain circuits to make way for new information to flow. Mom and Dad told me about the first conversation they ever had with Ms. Arnold, shortly after we came to the States, during an open house for parents considering enrolling their kids in the fall. She said her favorite thing about her job was that children's minds were like sponges: at my age, they were ready to absorb anything. She had this anecdote about a student who'd become obsessed with the word *dickweed*, the punchline being that the thing about sponges was they tended to pick up the dirty stuff, too.

If the other kids' brains were like sponges, turns out mine was like a block of crumbling Styrofoam.

Wesley Whale was an animated purple narwhal, a bumbling, sleepy-eyed character who was always getting his tusk stuck in shrubby kelp clusters and the holes of sand dollars. His mouth was a long strip of white with no lines to separate the individual teeth, which I didn't resist at the time but I now find terrifying, and thick eyebrows he would waggle while you contemplated how to answer a question or make your next move. He had a sidekick, a wimpy orange fish with fins like a mohawk, not an exotic tropical variety but the boring kind you get at the county fair for two dollars a pop. Together they drank milkshakes and shot slingshots and visited an underwater store that sold cowboy hats, owned by swaggering Manta Ray Jay.

If it all sounds fairly asinine, it wasn't hard to figure out why. When I dug the game box out of the trash, those enormous bubble letters—AGES 5 TO 7—mocked me from one of the flimsy cardboard sides. Sure, I wasn't exactly at the fifth-grade reading level, but I could understand that much. The game had a vaguely environmental angle, something about imparting to young children the importance of saving the Earth's vulnerable coral reefs. But what it boiled down to was Wesley and his unnamed sidekick swimming around while you typed the English words for all the things they passed. If you managed to enter the words correctly, you'd go on to the next level, where the blue background darkened slightly to indicate the three of you had moved to deeper water. If you messed up even once, though, you were back to square one.

The thing with the blowhole was either a *whale* or a *dolphin*, the thing with the sails a *ship* or *shipwreck*. *Beach* or *shore* or *sand*. *Octopus* or *squid*. Any of those or some other word I'd never learned or couldn't remember. Even if I got through the rest of the words, I'd find myself stumped at the thing that looked like—but couldn't be—a bed; one shell the mattress and the other an ornate, squiggly-edged headboard. Between them, on a plush pink cushion, the perfectly round, opalescent pearl.

The school made the games seem pretty much mandatory, part of a Get Back on Track plan that would also include an extra one-on-one ESL session with Ms. Arnold each week, but my parents insisted I try to think of them as home*fun* instead of home*work*. They were called games, weren't they? Just more sophisticated versions of the ones I already loved. Besides, my mom said, she'd seen me beat *Solitaire* a hundred times. Wasn't I tired of watching those cards tumble in their predictable patterns, their cheery, bouncing parabolas, like gymnasts rehearsing the same old routine?

But the new games weren't exciting, nor were they relaxing, and most of the time, like with Wesley Whale's oyster, I felt like there was no way I could win. The guidance counselor had prescribed an hour a day, but my parents were like the kids in Ms. Arnold's class, so anxious to impress—to be the good immigrants, quick studies—that often I would spend entire afternoons in front of the screen, the mouse warm under my fingertips, my eyes dry and blurry and threatening to vibrate right out of their sockets.

Computer games were expensive back then, too. That much hasn't changed. During our new monthly check-ins at the main office, during which I mostly zoned out and counted the flecks on the ceiling tiles, I would occasionally hear my dad drop a name like *GameStop* or *RadioShack*, suggesting these were the places where he bought his daughter her language-learning games. But we weren't exactly an MSRP family. Everything we bought we bought secondhand, or more often third or fourth, at a deep discount if we couldn't get it for free. My mom found her beat-up Singer on the curb outside an out-of-business JOANN Fabrics, and all my games came from the bargain bin at the neighborhood Goodwill.

They were all loose variations on *Wesley Whale*, cheesy concepts with bad graphics that I would've made fun of mercilessly if they didn't always end up getting the best of me. There was the one where you walk around the zoo and type the English words for all the different animals, the one where you walk around a shopping mall and type the English words for all the different toys. Playgrounds, archeological digs, theme parks, outer space. There were the ones that took you through Bible stories and the ones that starred popular Disney heroes. The ones laid out like board games where you had to get from beginning to end by typing the English words for jobs, buildings, household objects, all while—like some sick bonus challenge—navigating trouble tiles that would instruct you, if you landed there, to GO BACK TO START.

The worst one was called, I don't know, something like *Mindy Lulu Has a Boo-Boo*, in which a little girl visits the doctor's office for the very first time. She has pink freckles and eyes too big for her head, and when she enters the pale yellow room she promptly takes her clothes off. You're playing the role of doctor, and to level up you have to type the English words for all her body parts.

I figured out *eyes*, *mouth*, *neck*, *armpit* all right. But I always got stuck on *belly button*.

That was the worst one. The girl on the screen couldn't have been much younger than I was, and still, through the eyes of the doctor, I felt pervy, intrusive, as the game slowly crawled its way down, down. I imagined the doctor's hands out of frame, powdery from their gloves and aluminum cold.

Now, the best one? The best one was Dizzy Game.

••••

It wasn't called Dizzy Game in any official capacity. The box it came in was a plain, dull black, dented at the corners and unmarked except for half a dozen stickers on the back, the order of which was evidence of increasing markdowns: green, then yellow, then red, Goodwill's lowest, last-call price. I turned the box around and around, looking for the usual reassuring mascot flashing a thumbs-up-you-got-this, or a manufacturer name like The So-and-So Learning Company. But there was nothing, and no title either. I called it Dizzy Game because that's how it made me feel the first time I played it: queasy and out of breath like I'd just chugged a whole liter of Welch's, then gone straight for the park's loopiest coaster, and there was no end, no air brakes, no bored attendant in sight.

The first thing I noticed: the contrast was *jacked*. Not that color saturation was amazing in any game those days, but with this one I could barely make out what was on the screen. It was all grey shapes over grey shapes, larger grey shapes shifting in the background, lighter or darker by marginal degrees. I messed around with the gamma settings for a full ten minutes before I got it even close to workable. Then my eyes adjusted before my brain did.

When the greys gave way to a clear, vibrant image, I was mesmerized. The graphics were crisp and fast-moving, impossibly detailed—a shocking departure from the pixelated animation of campy characters like Mindy Lulu and Wesley Whale. I hadn't thought the Dell capable of it. Once my brain caught up, though, I crashed back into disappointment. Because the scene before me was a grocery store, which meant I knew how this one went: walk around, try to conjure up the English words for *eggplant*, *onion*, all the different kinds of produce. I sighed and settled into the computer chair, an instant backache with peeling leather upholstery and only three working wheels, which my mom had gotten in a howling deal at a recent sidewalk sale. I pulled the keyboard forward and prepared for another long afternoon of failure.

Wiggling the cursor, I drove my character—a stock boy in a green apron and collared shirt—ahead. Immediately, my hand cramped around the mouse and my stomach lurched.

The ground in the game wasn't the gleaming colorless vinyl I knew from all the times I'd accompanied my parents to Food City, where they let me steer the cart like a racecar through the aisles. Instead, the floor was slippery, gelatinous, made of coils of gauzy hair one minute and wet cobwebs and still-burning lava the next, then suddenly it would harden into these bizarre, spiky formations, like if coral reefs could survive on dry land. But that wasn't the sick-making part. What did it for me was this: the depth perception was all wrong. I couldn't tell how far back the aisles went, or how close anything on the shelves was. Sometimes it felt like the faceless customers milling about the store were miles in the distance. Other times I thought they might reach out and grab me through the fragile barrier of glass.

I hit pause and laid my forehead on the sewing table, trying to get a grip, breathing evenly to the rhythm of *kids' game, kids' game*—it was only a kids' game, for God's sake. But after a few minutes, something dragged my eyes back up toward the screen. Call it the effectiveness of the Get Back on Track plan, or the addictive nature of video games. Call it the work ethic our immigrant parents instill in us—people have, people will. Call it whatever you want. What matters is, pretty soon, I was hooked.

The funny thing about Dizzy Game was that it behaved just like your average teacher-approved, Scholastic Book Fair "edutainment" for the first fifteen minutes or so. After that, it went totally whacko.

Where the cabbage, spinach, and leeks should have been, there were bins and bins of tiny, milk-white larvae. They squirmed under the misting system, growing plumper and shinier beneath its measured spray. The juice cartons were uncapped and overflowing with some sludgy tan-pink liquid, and behind the deli counter, a fellow employee—an older woman with a hairnet and an apron that matched the one game-me was wearing—carved thin strips off a disembodied nose as tall as the slicer itself. It wasn't all that over-the-top, horror-show stuff either. In the frozen food aisle, a dog with a big red flower for a head lolled contentedly, drool sliding down the length of its bottom petals.

It made me want to ask my parents if we could adopt a puppy. The cat was getting so standoffish anyway.

Aside from the initial contrast issue, Dizzy Game was virtually glitch-free. But my favorite thing about it was that, as long as I played, I was more or less guaranteed to win. The game didn't ask me to type the words out myself, sending me back to the start the second I screwed up. Instead, it typed each word *to* me, while a voice—a pleasant, silky alto—spoke it aloud through the egg-shaped speakers. Each word was typed and spoken three times, while a message on the screen prompted me to repeat it. The game could *hear* me, and all it wanted was for me to practice. If I got a word wrong, it would gently correct me, and I'd try again.

I wouldn't realize until much later that our Dell Dimension didn't have a mic.

Those days, I sprinted to the computer room every afternoon, skipping the pointed "So how was *school?*" talk with Mom and the dino nuggets she'd laid out on the counter for my after-school snack. She looked confused at first, peeved even, but I knew she and Dad must've been relieved. Today, people buy into the idea that computers are the tools of the devil. But back then, this was me showing initiative. This was me devoting myself to becoming an A-plus American.

The computer room got so hot sometimes, I could open all the windows and still sweat through my T-shirt into the cracked leather seat.

Dizzy Game's grocery store had this huge pastry wall, only where there should've been cinnamon bundt cakes and day-old donuts, there was row after row of oversized fishhooks.

I reached game-me's arm for one of the fishhooks, barbed once on the curved point and twice more along its metal shank. It was weird the way I felt when I looked at it. It didn't register as something designed to pierce a prize salmon on some wholesome family fishing trip, but as something I knew—with a heady, buzzing certainty—I would one day extract from the meat of a human eye.

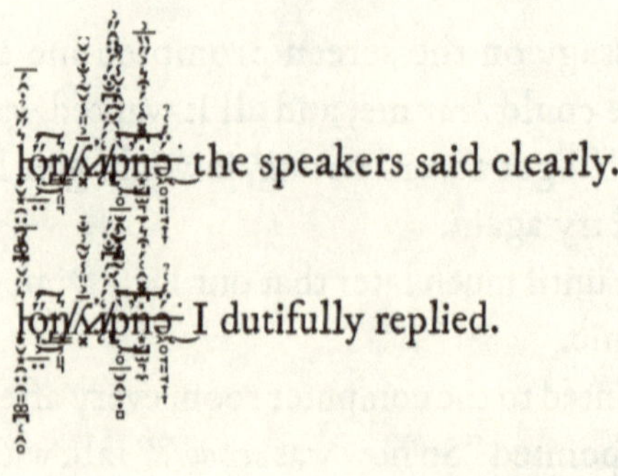

the speakers said clearly.

I dutifully replied.

••••

Could it have been that I didn't realize it at first? That I thought Dizzy Game was just teaching me a more advanced version of English, a level I hadn't yet reached in the dumbed-down games, or in ESL with Ms. Arnold twice a week? Maybe I assumed that after we mastered conjugation, definite and indefinite articles, homophones and animal idioms and phrasal verbs, we'd have a whole unit dedicated to this other aspect of the language, the slithering and guttural register that ran your throat raw. After all, English is notoriously difficult for non-native speakers to learn. It has so many rules, and as many exceptions to them. I was new to it then. There was a lot I couldn't have known.

Or is it more likely that I *did* realize it, that it didn't even take me that long? I was falling behind in school because I was at a major linguistic disadvantage, not because I was stupid. Would you believe I had a strong early suspicion, but I was willing to push it aside? Because I was *good* at Dizzy Game—new-high-score-every-time good—in a way I hadn't been good at anything in years. It was patient with me, forgiving, and playing got my parents off my back. More than off my back, it got them on my side. Now they joked at the dinner table that my English would get so textbook, pretty soon I'd be qualified to teach language arts, and I could take sour Mr. McNamara's job. In the computer room, *Wesley Whale* and the others formed a sad tower under the futon, reaching for its wooden frame like a grey hand through a cemetery plot. Like the pathetic, dead-to-me things they were.

One day, my dad came in, wheeling our unwieldy Hoover behind him. I paused the game but didn't swivel around, sitting stock-still so my head would stay blocking the screen. If he thought I was acting suspicious, he didn't say it. That's standard preteen-girl stuff anyway. I would do the same thing later with my instant messages, which were dull stuff, not the least bit damning, but which I gleaned from the other kids simply weren't the sort of thing parents were meant to see.

I heard his knees creak as he knelt down. He tapped one of the plastic cases.

"Finished with these already, Uly?" he asked in English. I caught the smile in his voice.

Eager to get back to the game, I grunted an affirmative over my shoulder. He laughed, scooping up the discarded CD-ROMs. He always said he was trilingual, fluent in the nonverbal language of disinterested daughters.

Had I made a habit of speaking Dizzy outside the computer room, no doubt things would have turned out different. But the words in the game were so specific, so peculiar—*fishhook, coagulate, mammon*—so not the stuff of everyday conversation that, honestly, they never came up. How often did the discussion turn toward coagulation in your elementary assembly hall?

Either that or I *had* spoken Dizzy, but only once, and that's all it took for me to learn my lesson. It would've happened during recess. I would've been sitting in the shade of the tallest jungle gym tower, watching this kid Jacob run fast laps around the geodome climber. Jacob was always doing that kind of thing, treating recess like some one-man military training camp. He was a loner like me, only for him it was by choice; I got the sense he wasn't trying to make any friends at Severn that wouldn't later follow him to Annapolis or West Point. He had a camo-print backpack that he never took off, not even during lunch or paint days in art class, and I remember he was wearing it when he sprinted straight toward me on the jungle gym that day.

He veered right at the very last second and proceeded to do twenty back-and-forths on the horizontal ladder, crossing his feet at the ankles so they didn't touch the wood chips. Then he scrambled up and sat next to me, on the other side of the tower's bright yellow support beam, and started examining his monster calluses. He took them between his fingers and squeezed, so by the time he was done, his palm looked like the back of a stegosaurus. He seemed proud, like the kind of kid who would appreciate me appreciating them. So, without thinking, I murmured:

I know "calluses" now, but then the Dizzy word was the only thing I knew to call them. Jacob must not have seen me after all, because he *freaked*—leapt to his feet and immediately lurched backwards off the side of the structure. It wasn't far down. He got four stitches on his hand and later bragged to the class that he didn't really need them, but his mom said it would put her mind at ease.

After that, the same part of me that knew I had to keep my dad from seeing Dizzy Game on the screen also knew I couldn't speak the words again to anyone. It wasn't any of their business, for one thing. And it would be a betrayal, I decided, to have been taught—no, to have been *chosen* to be a *student of*—this precious tongue, just to go indiscriminately passing the code sheet around. Every time I thought about it, I was overcome by this tingling sensation, like spider wasps in the bloodstream, that those outsiders, those foreigners, they wouldn't get it anyway.

Like spider wasps: 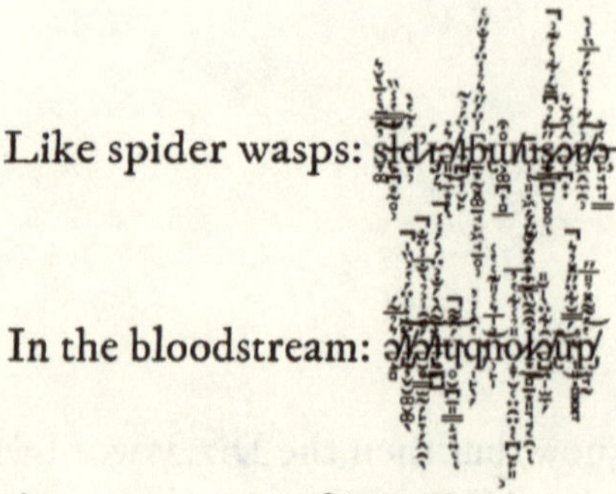

In the bloodstream:

I'm rusty, you see? But I've been practicing.

••••

Wrapped up in their own lives though they were—my mom worked as a receptionist at Twin Skies Real Estate, my dad for a local carpenter who specialized in beetle-kill pine—my parents weren't oblivious to my preference for Dizzy Game. Preference isn't quite it; I'd reached a point where I refused to play anything else. They promised to keep an eye out at the Goodwill, in case it had a sequel. Often these kinds of games did, and I'd played a lot of them. *Wesley Whale and the Case of the Stolen Starfish. Wesley Whale and the Case of the Crystal Bay. Wesley Whale and the Case of the Buckaroos of Brackish Cove.* In the last one, the narwhal's mohawked sidekick was replaced by a surfer-dude-voiced shark in aviators.

They never did find a Dizzy Game 2. What would they have looked for, anyway? Another unmarked box over an unmarked sleeve, and when you pulled the disc out, the strangest thing: its thin silver film bubbly and peeling, like no way it should've worked when you slipped it in the drive. It didn't have the right colors either. All the other CD-ROMs glinted rainbows when you tilted them left and right, threw psychedelic patterns on the walls if they caught a stream of sun through the window. Dizzy Game, though—it's like it swallowed the light.

Didn't really matter about the sequel, though. Something in Dizzy Game's software caused it to upgrade automatically, so it never ran out of levels. Not that I'd call what it had levels, exactly. What I mean is that it didn't have an end.

The computer room got so, so hot sometimes. I'd sit there roasting, stripped down to a tank top and my day-of-the-week underwear, which I grabbed from the drawer at random, ignoring the embroidered words at the hip that for so long had meant nothing to me, and so always ended up wearing the wrong day. I'd beg my parents to let me take meals in there, but they were fanatical about keeping crumbs from getting stuck in the keyboard. So sometimes I'd pretend I wasn't hungry, even when the pangs felt like my stomach was buckling, twisting itself into a pretzel just so it'd have something to eat.

When we first got the Dell, our old cat—the one we always joked was too good for the futon—liked to curl up on my lap while I stacked *Solitaire* decks. Later he stopped coming into that part of the house entirely. He took to padding nervously at all hours in a corner of the living room, wearing circles in the carpet around our fake bird-of-paradise plant.

These days, you can't go a week without stumbling into an article linking video game violence to adolescent aggression and overly stylized characters to unrealistic beauty standards among impressionable teens and tweens. Even the most innocent titles come stamped with warnings about carpal tunnel and tennis elbow, eyestrain and poor posture and this curve of the neck people outside the medical profession have taken to calling gamer's hump. And they're probably onto something—I'm not saying they're not. But it was hard to think of Dizzy Game as having negative consequences, because, the thing was, after I started playing, things got *better*.

Better for all of us, I mean, not just me. Once I installed it, the Dell stopped contracting viruses—or, rather, it would look like it was about to get one, then the screen glitched out for twenty or thirty seconds before magically ironing itself out. His IT services no longer required, George took on the project, in his off-hours, of teaching my mom how to drive, and she'd slip in from their outings looking happier than she had in years. Dad, for his part, got a fast series of promotions after two of his coworkers put in notice, one after a bad fall off a wraparound deck and the other following a gruesome accident with the company's massive circular saw. Even though it meant that guy had two and a half fewer fingers, and even though it meant Dad was spending less time home with us, we couldn't see it as anything but a stroke of luck: another month's rent covered, another bill paid off. I was even glad about George, since Mom needed the company, even though he was too serious for my liking.

The only one of us who had a bad break was the cat, who'd stopped eating and had progressed to yanking up large swaths of fur around his paws.

As for me? I was blowing the Get Back on Track team's benchmarks out of the water.

Because at the same time Dizzy Game taught me its singular vocabulary, it helped pretty much everything else fall into place. It was like when the final Lego piece clicks in, and all at once you see not just the castle before you but everything that has the potential to be there, if only you pick up the expansion packs: the moat and drawbridge with horses, the princess waving from her turret in the clouds. Suddenly I was light-years ahead of everyone in Ms. Arnold's class. Hitting the "th" in the happy birthday song? Piece of cake. Maneuvering through different "e" vowels? Sweet, no sweat. I was acing every reading test, every science lab, every question about Mesopotamian burial practices. The guidance counselor was talking about nominating me for this elite math camp and bumping me up to algebra in the fall.

The other kids could tell when school stopped being such a slog for me. They hadn't wanted to associate themselves with the fall-behind kid, or invest time in a friendship when I'd just be held back a year while they moved into a new building across the street. Then a switch flipped, and I became one of them. I got more invitations to pool parties and arcade Saturdays during the spring of fifth grade than I had the entire time we'd been in the States. In these shiny, unfamiliar environments, my cheap stirrup leggings and too-big, too-worn T-shirts felt shamefully out of place. Friends who took pity on me let me borrow their trendy plaid jumpers and velour sweatpants, one-shoulder tops with ambiguous phrases like WANT IT and FREE scribbled across the chest.

In the car, I groaned at my parents' ancient Russian CDs, with their shaky, operatic crescendos, and turned the radio to American Top 40. In the mornings, I pushed aside my usual bowl of kasha and asked my mom if next time she'd pick up a box of Trix. Wanted to trade my glass of kompot for Sunny D.

I was starting to fit right in, and my parents responded to my sudden acclimatization the same way they had to Dizzy Game: with a raised-brow skepticism that quickly gave way to an easy and resigned gratitude. Even with my newly packed social calendar, I always made time for it. An hour a day, right? Guidance counselor's orders.

When I was twelve, the same year I was voted seventh-grade princess at Severn Middle's winter formal, my grandma—Dad's mom—came all the way from her beach town on the Black Sea to spend three weeks living with us. I don't remember much about that visit. A few of the other girls had gotten inline skates for Christmas and we were spending most of our time at the Carl's Jr., whose back lot's center grass median made it the perfect, donut-shaped roller rink. What I do remember is Grandma unpacking her suitcase on the guest-room futon and me standing awkwardly in the doorway, working to wrap my head around what it would mean for her to occupy this space—*my* computer room, *my* Dizzy Room—for the next twenty-one whole days. Dad had bought a bunch of blankets full-price, special for her arrival, trying to trick the futon into being more comfortable than it was.

She didn't seem to mind it. She sat there pulling out one neatly folded blouse after the next, and after those, the gifts she had brought us from Sukhumi: lacy kitchen linens for my mom, Dad's favorite liqueur-filled chocolates. And for me, a small menagerie of delicate glass animal figurines, which I recognized as the kind she collected in her own china cabinet, and which I'd admired longingly when visiting Grandma's house when I was little.

I made a face without realizing it. The animals, though pretty, smacked of some other me, some buggy, outdated version I wanted deleted from everyone's memory. Still, I shouldn't have done that in front of her. Should've played the thankful granddaughter, let her call me the Russian word for bunny or kitten, and been done with it. This trip was the last time I would ever see her. So I could've at least done that.

But it wasn't my reaction to her gift that bothered her, and it wasn't the shirts I had taken to wearing, which that day, I remember, commanded in sparkly thread: CALL ME. What got to her was that I had more or less forgotten her language.

I was surprised myself. It had been a while—we'd transitioned to speaking English at home, another important pillar of the Get Back on Track plan—but I expected it to be one of those things that comes back to you when you need it. It shouldn't fall away so easily, I thought, being built as it was into my very sequencing.

She pointed at the first figurine, an owl, and said what I assumed to be the Russian name for it. Then she pointed to the next one, a walrus, and waited, tipping her head slightly forward. It was my turn. I searched the quicksand of my mind for Wesley Whale and his missing conch shell. There had been a walrus in that one, hadn't there? I struggled to recall how I'd *thought* it in my head before trying, and failing, to translate it to the keys. But I couldn't materialize it. Even as I try to think of it now, it vanishes into ghostly tendrils that don't take the shape of anything. To my grandma, I just said, "Walrus." She smiled and shook her head no, tapped the needle-like tusks. She'd had a smudge of pink lipstick on her front tooth all day, but we'd all silently agreed we'd better not tell her. I repeated, "Walrus," then, like some plea for forgiveness, worked my way down the line: "Walrus, camel," then expertly, "peacock, fox, owl." The smile slid from her face. The pink disappeared.

She shook her head again, appalled, and made the sign of the cross over her chest. She was rearing back like she might spit at me when my dad appeared in the doorway, fluffing a spare pillow.

That night, my parents told her to go on and leave it alone. That I was just growing up, and frankly it was about time I got used to my new surroundings—or so I gathered from their hushed, borderline-amused tones, the way they shrugged and steered her gently toward the living room sofa, where they'd flipped all the sun-faded cushions so they looked brand-new. Because they spoke Russian to her, I couldn't make out the details. Maybe it was just our crummy incandescent lighting, but from my snooping spot in the hallway, she seemed much older than she had earlier that day. She was pale, rubbing her forehead and worrying her lower lip. She looked like she'd seen the devil himself. She said something that, judging by my parents' shocked expressions, must have been a curse. Though I couldn't, and still can't, be sure.

She spent three weeks shuffling around in her house slippers, touring the local art and history museums, sweeping my dad's hair out of his eyes, then died on the return flight to Sukhumi. It wasn't one of those freak accidents you hear about: engine failure, windshield blowout, high-flying geese, so-called force majeure. Just a pulmonary embolism, somewhere over Sweden. Doesn't get more natural causes than that. She liked whole milk, fatty meats. She was old. Had looked so old, I remember.

••••

I never understood why I had been chosen; what it was about me the game had liked. Just that I was that person for eight good years, a glad and faithful student, and then, around the time I started reading for my college entrance exams, the game abruptly stopped updating. I remember the exact day it happened (a Tuesday), and the weather (first hail of the season), and what I had in my backpack (an SAT prep book). I even remember what I ate for lunch: two single-serving bags of Lay's Classic, which the school had deemed healthier than Doritos or Cheetos just because they didn't leave orange dust on your hands. I remember those things because I've been over them a thousand times, trying to work out if anything I did might've caused it.

I was devastated. I kept coming back to the game, quitting and restarting it, hoping there'd be something new for me there the next time. I begged my mom to have George come take a look, even though I didn't like him tinkering around in there; we'd gotten a new Dell the previous year, and I was beginning to suspect its operating system wasn't compatible. But George said he couldn't find a single issue. And the next week, for the first time in all that time, a virus popped up on the screen. The new computer came with an external mic—probe-y with a long beige neck—and the moment I saw it was the moment I realized our first Dell hadn't had one. It was an extra slap in the face that the game had picked then to withdraw. It was set up to hear me. It just wasn't listening.

For a year, I seesawed between fits of unfocused anger and a sadness so complete and siphoning I swear there's no word for it in any dictionary. All this, plus the new habit I'd developed of chewing my knuckles until they bled, my parents blamed on application-season stress.

Then one day I woke up and decided it had all been a misunderstanding; God knows I wasn't new to those. It *wasn't* over. Dizzy Game had simply taught me all it had to teach me, and now it was time for me to do my part. It would come back, no need to worry. When I was ready. When I'd proven myself.

Even now, I can feel it on the air sometimes. It'll be subtle, a whiff of cherry blossom that flashes me back instantly to that dribbling supermarket mutt with a flower for a head. Other times it'll be so overwhelming, I have to pull out the mini garbage can I keep under my desk at work, I'm so certain I'm going to empty myself out right there.

And when a coworker peeks over the wall of my cubicle and asks if I'm all right, I say yeah. And when they ask if I want to go to the boozy college tailgate, the *Simpsons* trivia night, the marathon of Spielberg war films at the local Cineplex, the illegal fireworks show, I say yeah. You bet I do.

I'm popular at work because I'm a good time. I'm *amenable. Insouciant.* I fit right in. I say all the right things. Yes to their silly little sins. Yes to everything.

"Count me in," I say. What I don't say is: "For as long as you've got me."

Because you're coming, I know it. You wouldn't have trained me then stranded me. Brought me into your world of greys on greys for nothing. Your game had a logic. It wouldn't make sense.

For my part, I'll be ready.

I try to make the cubicle as hot as I can, hot like we like it, though it's not easy with the three and a half short walls, the way one of the sales guys, who's always on his feet, pacing, insists on leaving a window open. But two sweaters and a space heater, and it almost feels like home.

I'll be—

I still keep your secrets, you know. That camo-print kid from Severn, Jacob? He looked me up a while ago, sent me a message about the word he'd heard me use on the playground. Said it had really changed things for him, made him think about the world differently. I looked him up, too, and you know what? He never went to West Point, and he's into some wild stuff these days. Was in the news for a hundred-page manifesto he staplegunned to a church door. About the word, he asked if I could repeat it. Just once, could I repeat it? He sent message after message: please, please, please.

Silly rabbit. Trix are for kids.

I'll be—

I wish I could say I knew the Russian word for it. It's right there on the tip of my tongue, like always, then it scurries back to the underside. Language-learning programs have advanced in leaps and bounds since the days of those old CD-ROMs, and sometimes I think about picking one up: Russian for Heritage Speakers 6.0. I could surprise my parents at New Year's dinner with their words for "Pass the soup, please," and "I'm sorry, I forgive you," and "Do you remember when we used to eat dino nuggets with kompot?" Of course, that would require me to go home for New Year's in the first place. Sit through the poisonous quiet of my dad's sparse bachelor pad, the happy clamor of the apartment Mom shares with George on the opposite side of town.

No. Better to stay focused. To prepare for whoever, whatever, you send for me.

Better to give the Dizzy word for it, then.

So you know that I'll be 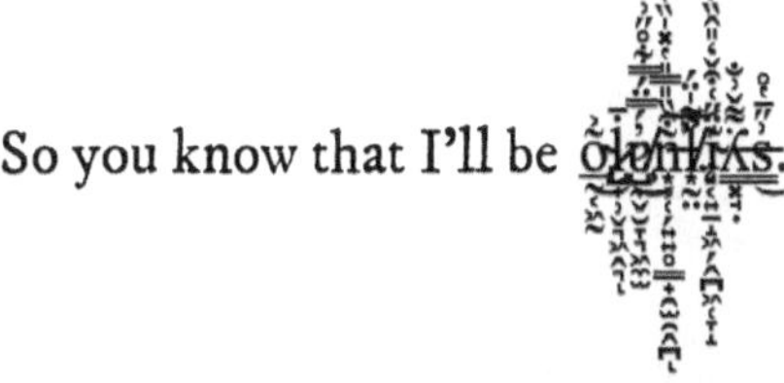

The English word? I think you know it. Wise and many-tongued as you are, I think you know it! But you prompt me. Oh, you test me! So for you, I will say it. Flawlessly, on the first try, and without hesitation.

The English word for it is *waiting*.

THE CURING

We stole the bottle of Elmer's glue in the pass time between lunch and free period, the orange cap a beacon on the art room's back shelves. Mrs. Chowdhury was out having her third baby in as many years, and the sub they'd hired to take her place spent most of his time in the lounge, flipping through motorcycle magazines and drinking neon-colored Surge from a borrowed *World's Greatest Teacher* mug.

This was before the jocks become the jocks, before the brains become the brains. Before everyone scatters on the last day of middle school and emerges from the roiling summer waters fully formed, as theater kids or stoners, or preps, skaters, goths. We were on our own, before the world was gracious enough to categorize us, let us in on the great secret of where we belonged.

If Mrs. Chowdhury had been there, she would never have let us take the glue, needing it for pop-up books with the sixth graders later that day, and probably having paid for it herself. But Mrs. Chowdhury wasn't there. And we had another project in mind.

Free period was meant to give us time to catch up on homework and study for tests, but nobody actually dared do any work there, for fear we'd be laughed out of those narrow linoleum halls. Instead, we spent the time killing time, and even that wasn't as straightforward as it sounds. Because like anything at that age, what you *did* became who you *were*. And before kids were old enough to get serious about travel soccer or bong rips or the high school production of *Kilroy Was Here*, what they got serious about was their free-period time killer of choice.

The Doodlers huddled around an open notebook, drawing copy after copy of what everyone called the "Cool S." Some speculated it was the original version of the Superman logo; others insisted it came from the name of a designer label that only the rich kids, children of doctors and lawyers, could afford. We all knew how to draw it, the "S": six vertical lines in two rows, then the diagonals to connect them. But no one, except the Doodlers, was *allowed* to draw it, not at school anyway. What we did at home was between us and our never-around parents and our staticky Bob Barker reruns and God.

The Doodlers would become the theater kids, or the goths, depending on whether they applied their burgeoning artistic talents to stage sets or eyeliner. The Casios—the ones who figured out how to spell words on their calculators, BOOBS and BOOBLESS and HELLO—would maintain their fascination with digital languages, going on to write lines of code for some of the most successful apps around. Then there were the Matchmakers, who pushed their desks together and played every true-love game they could think of. They'd be among the first to join OkCupid, then jump ship to Tinder and Hinge when those came about, no pool of potential suitors big or warm enough to satisfy them.

The Slaps spent all of free period striking these colorful slap bracelets against their wrists, pulling them off, then slapping them down again, again. The stiff bracelets, basically steel tape measures wrapped in fabric, were the only thing the monitors knew to confiscate immediately, and the banned bin in the front office soon overflowed with strips of zebra print, rainbow snakeskin, and peace signs. The Slaps would eventually become competitive gymnasts and world-class ballerinas, MMA fighters and bodybuilders covered in tattoos. They'd grown accustomed to their bodies being magnets for pain.

We weren't any of those things. We didn't have anything to do with those kids, and we didn't have much to do with each other, either. Except that we all spoke in variations of a funny-accented English. We had funny-sounding last names and carried funny-smelling lunches that swung from our fingers in plastic bags, and in these ways, we were the same.

Our parents were too busy to make friends with the other parents, too frugal to bid in the annual fundraiser auction, too tired to join the PTA. But they always made time to pack our lunches, the cafeteria alternative costing an absolutely-out-of-the-question two dollars per day. For Geetha, it was golden disks of rava idli with a ramekin of bright coconut chutney. For Christian, peppery beef with fried crescents of onions and shiny trees of bok choy. Tatiana, Anh, and Javi traded golubtsy for bun cha for cheesy tortas, while the cafeteria-lunch kids looked on, wrinkling their noses over their trays of rectangular pizza and cartons of strawberry milk.

After lunch, we went to free period, where the other cliques assembled around their calculators and MASH life-predictor charts, avoiding us completely. We sat with our backpacks on our laps, the sharp smell of spices and green-card lotteries radiating from us.

Until the day we stole the Elmer's glue, and everything changed.

It's funny how the glue game became our thing. It wasn't even one of the core group who came up with it. There was always one regular, born-and-bred American kid who hung out with us solely because they were the new kid in school, outcasted briefly by the rest of the population as if under some probationary period during which they had to prove themselves worthy or be left on the social fringes for good. Exactly one at a time. Once the next new kid showed up, the previous one cycled out, by then having gotten the lay of the land and found a better group to fit into. They cycled out fast, the new kids. Too fast to make much of an impression.

Except for Reid, a bowl-cut blond from Massachusetts who brought PB and J's in ziplocks and taught us everything we needed to know about making replicas of ourselves with glue.

He said everyone at his old school did it: smeared Elmer's glue all over their fingers and palms, waited for it to dry, then peeled it off carefully, so it came up in a single, translucent husk, intact and thin as eggshells. When we asked Reid why they did that, he said why not. When we asked if it was bad for you, putting all that adhesive directly on your skin, he shrugged.

"It's just something to do," he said. Then he swept his hair out of his eyes in that TRL way we knew the other kids would fall head over heels for, and we recognized that there was no time to waste. Sooner rather than later, Reid would move on.

We figured out which of our lockers was closest to the art room and planned to steal the glue the very next day. Because something to do was precisely what we were looking for. Because all we'd found at home were squashed tubes of heavy-duty fabric glue and wood epoxy, in off-limits drawers full of sewing needles and loose keys, and Reid had warned us against using anything stronger than Elmer's.

Anh stationed herself outside the teachers' lounge, ready with questions about Harley-Davidsons and crosshatch shading in case the sub got the idea that he should actually do his job. Christian and Geetha waited anxiously by an open locker. Tatiana played the wide-eyed lookout, not trusting anyone else to do it, saying for sure she'd catch the belt if her dad were to find out.

Javi watched the clock.

And Reid led the way.

••••

If you did it right, you'd have a glue version of your own hand lying flat on the pale wood of the desk before you, identical down to the whorls of your fingertips. Everything about it was ritualistic, addictive: from the solemn passing of the bottle to the group inspection of the glue's curing—Geetha always insisting it needed just a minute longer—to the lifting of the finicky edge at the heel of the palm. All of us enthralled, refusing to breathe.

Later, some of us would relish peeling our sunburns in the same way, brown and pink skin taking the shape of land and sea in the world map that stretched across our shoulders and backs. It would give us a proximate satisfaction. Those of us who would grow old enough to do it, anyway.

The free-period monitors weren't oblivious to our newfound interest. All of a sudden, the kids they could always count on to be shy and yielding were whispering furiously in the corner, their backpack straps tangling, forgotten, in the chair legs. But the monitors already had their hands full with the Slaps, who appeared every day with red wrists and a fresh collection of bracelets, undeterred by threats of the banned bin. It was as if the bracelets shot up from their lawns each morning with the sprinklers.

So we didn't give much thought to the monitors. It was the attention of the other kids that mattered.

They eyed us curiously: our palms covered in globby white paste, the finished products like the disembodied hands of ghosts. Javi, whose parents were even more religious than the rest of ours and lectured him constantly about the afterlife, jokingly called them spirit hands, and the name stuck. We high-fived each other with our spirit hands. We staged low-stakes thumb wars. We waved. Eventually, the other kids had to look away. It was code: everyone had their own time killer, and they'd already chosen theirs.

When the Casios got bored of spelling BOOBLESS in numbers, they discovered GIGGLE, EGGSHELL, and OHIO.

When we got bored of our flat spirit hands, we started spreading the glue all the way to the other side, across our nails and knuckles, down to the wrist bone. When we pulled the dried glue off, the three-dimensional hand it formed was the stuff of big-city sculpture gardens. We all agreed that, petty theft notwithstanding, it would've made Mrs. Chowdhury proud.

One day, one of the Matchmakers marched over and ran her finger over the creases in Tatiana's spirit hand.

"This is your heart line," the Matchmaker cooed. Her lashes were long, her irises milk chocolate, and Tatiana looked like she might lift off into space on the next word.

"See how strong it is right here?" The Matchmaker grazed a spot under the pinky, and Tatiana shoved her own hand into the kangaroo pocket of her sweatshirt, as if it was her real skin that had been touched. "Then it splinters off. That means—"

Another Matchmaker hissed loudly in our direction, and the palm reader gave us an apologetic look before returning to her part of the room. Tatiana spent the rest of free period staring at the upturned line on her spirit hand's palm, and when Christian presented his own still-drying hand for inspection, she didn't even look up, just muttered, "Uh-huh. Looks great to me."

Even on days when no one noticed us any more than they had before, it felt good to make more of ourselves, to see ourselves reflected in this small way we could control.

There weren't many Geethas in our town, or Anhs, or Javis. It was a relief to find that it could welcome—was even capable of holding—a few more of us.

Christian must've been on his thirtieth or fortieth spirit hand when he pushed away from his desk, his chin a terror-struck prune.

"It moved," he said. Anh, the bravest among us, pointed toward the open window and laughed. Reid, who hadn't made a spirit hand in weeks, listened for the number-two-pencil sounds of the Doodlers. He knew it was only a matter of time, and he already had one foot out the door.

Christian shook his head. "No. I mean, it *moved*."

He leaned back and instantly we understood what he meant. The hand, sheer and fragile as chiffon, was crawling toward the edge of his desk, as if powered by muscles and ligaments we could not see. Anh froze mid-laugh, the "O" of her mouth a deflating balloon.

Later, Christian would say he had a paper cut on his thumb that day, and the blood's what activated the glue for us in a way that Reid, with all his experience, had never seen before. Tatiana's theory had to do with the sun hitting the desk at exactly the right angle. The rest of us just figured that each of us, in our private inner worlds, had wished for it hard enough.

The spirit hand paused and drummed its fingers against the wood, pinky to index, as if thinking. It reached into Christian's unzipped pencil case and plucked out his treasured two-color BIC pen.

Then it did something none of us would have dreamed of.

It clicked on the blue ink tip and slowly carved an asterisk into the desktop, bold and obvious as the North Star.

••••

By the time we started making full spirit bodies, Reid was long gone, drawing that pointy "S" along with the rest of them until his hand cramped. We weren't bitter—it was the way of the new kids to not stay new kids forever—but we still joked that, had he stuck around with us, he would've had backup hands to spare.

The new new kid was Savannah. She wore basketball shorts that looked big enough to belong to an older brother, and she would never stop being angry, in all the time we knew her, about getting yanked out of her old school in Texas, all her friends now two whole time zones away. Savannah never did get in with the other cliques. She was with us till the end of the school year. Mostly, we saw her sitting in the gulch between the playground and the Shell station, flicking a lighter on and off, alone.

If Mrs. Chowdhury had been there, she would've stopped us before we took it any further. But Mrs. Chowdhury wasn't there, and Mr. Hockeborn was.

Mr. Hockeborn was the social studies teacher, and he was obsessed with the Second World War. Whatever the lesson started out as, he always found a way to work it back to the Allies and the Axis, the German casualties at Dunkirk—even when we were supposed to be learning about the branches of the U.S. government or the women's suffrage movement. Once, spiraled off on one of his tangents, he told the class that families used to send soldiers silk stockings stuffed with candies and safety razor blades and other necessities a man at war would need.

"Like a piñata?" It was one of the Casios, smirking, proud of his disruption.

"Not at all like a piñata." Mr. Hockeborn dropped his eyebrows in a look meant to remind us that we were talking about war. "Not at all."

He went on: "Some people today think the soldiers coveted the stockings because the shape—thighs, calves, feet—reminded them of their wives and girlfriends back home. Others say the men wore the stockings themselves, their wool socks having fallen to pieces from all the marching they'd done." He paused for dramatic effect. "And others think it's all just hokum. That the silk-stocking care packages are nothing but a myth."

That was Mr. Hockeborn's favorite word, *hokum*. When Geetha came home later singing, "Hokum, hokum!" her parents demanded to know what in God's name they were teaching her at that second-rate American public school, and threatened to pull her out if she ever said it again.

Christian's spirit hand came alive on a Wednesday, Mr. Hockeborn delivered the pantyhose history lesson that Thursday, and by Friday we'd come up with a plan: we would do the spirit hands on a grander scale, use the glue to make duplicates of our entire bodies. If silk stockings could be made to not look like clothing anymore—to look like *real legs*—then couldn't we do the same? After all, the soldiers' families had managed it approximately one million years ago, and today we had twentieth-century adhesive technology, and an unopened six-pack of Elmer's bottles Anh had swiped behind some absent-minded teacher's back. And we had the keys to Geetha's house, which had enough rooms for each of us to strip down to our underwear and spread the glue over ourselves in peace, without anyone seeing anything they weren't supposed to.

Like most of us, Geetha was an only child. Only Christian had a little sister, Megan, who was born in an American hospital and burbled her first words in English, and who he regarded as an alien because she didn't share any of his interests and instead spent hours every day smacking her unopened bubble wand toy against any hard surface she could reach. Megan wasn't old enough to go to school yet, and Christian swore his mom's body had a permanent lean to it from toting his sister to and from work.

Geetha's parents were never home. None of our parents were ever home, but Geetha's parents were not-home in the fun way, meaning she had her own fancy teal iMac in her bedroom and a friendly old labrador named Ollie for company and a pantry full of roasted chana we ate in fistfuls straight from the bag. Unlike the rest of us, Geetha even had a real babysitter when she was younger, but last year her parents decided they could try trusting her on her own.

Savannah had elected to spend her afternoon scowling at birds and rocks and whatever and whoever else dared to cross her, but the rest of us were there, at Geetha's. We kicked our shoes off inside the door, and Tatiana spent an inordinate amount of time straightening them out, so each shoe was next to its sister on the mat. She looked sheepish, but we didn't say anything: we knew by then how her dad was.

Anh dutifully handed out the bottles of Elmer's, and we disappeared into our separate rooms. It took a lot more time for a whole body's worth of glue to dry than it did a single hand, and Javi, who'd wound up in the clean, bare laundry room, was bored out of his skull waiting all that time without snacks or books or a TV. The dog whined piteously from the mudroom, locked out of every place with people. It was for its own safety—Anh said the glue was probably nontoxic, but Geetha wasn't willing to chance the day ending with a call to her mom's office, a trip to the emergency vet.

Once the glue had dried, peeling it off took a long time, too: maintaining that delicate, unbroken layer around the tricky ridges of our ears, the dimpling at the backs of our knees. By the time we reappeared in the living room fully clothed, our stomachs growling like they did all the time back then, the sun was ready to set. Geetha told us not to worry. Her parents would be playing squash with her mom's boss till late; there was a lot on the line, talk of a promotion.

The rest of us could only think of squash like the food—a pan full of sweet, fried cubes—but before Geetha could explain, our first spirit person emerged.

It was Tatiana's, taller than the rest of us by half a foot with a hooked nose just like hers, lips but no mouth, smooth valleys where there should have been eyes. From where it stood on the second-floor landing, it looked like it was blushing, reliving the Matchmaker incident or some other excruciating moment in Tatiana's life, though that was impossible: Tatiana hadn't mixed pink dye into her glue, so there was no way hers was a different color than ours. Her spirit person descended the stairs with Tatiana's familiar timid, halting walk, like it wanted to be sure it wasn't interrupting before it took even one step further.

Of course, it couldn't have been interrupting. It was what we were waiting for.

Soon, the others emerged: Javi's with his broad shoulders, Christian's with his fine cellist's fingers, Anh's so petite it reminded us how slight she really was, a fact her tenacity and brazenness had all but erased. Finally, Geetha's came out of her bedroom, the dried glue catching the light with the iridescence of a tightly woven spider web. The dog barked from behind the mudroom door, louder than ever.

Tatiana stood before her spirit person, disbelieving. When we'd left the rooms minutes before, the glue versions of us weren't stirring. Draped over the office chair and washing machine, they were no better than those promotional cardboard cutouts at the AMC, and so much worse for being featureless and flimsy. We didn't think the magic had worked.

Tatiana was barely breathing. "Remember when everyone wanted a My Size Barbie?"

Christian and Javi shrugged noncommittally. Anh and Geetha looked wistful. Even Geetha's parents, who could afford a litter of My Size Barbies, refused to buy one, because the dolls only came pale-skinned and blue-eyed, and were, according to Geetha's parents, utter nonsense besides. Nonsense, Geetha contemplated to herself now, being just another word for hokum.

The dog barked urgently, scratching at the door.

Tatiana stretched her arm out, letting her hand hover an inch from her spirit person's nose. "This is *so* much better than that."

On the other side of the room, the bottom of Geetha's spirit person's face ripped in a short horizontal line. It parted its dried-glue lips around the tear.

"Quiet!" Geetha's spirit person ordered, and the dog shut up.

••••

We thought we'd keep them in our bedrooms at home, but Christian raised the point that none of us were allowed to lock our bedrooms, and about half of us weren't even allowed to close our doors, so how exactly was that going to work? Then Javi's spirit person, as much a comedian as the real Javi, demonstrated it had no trouble working a lock anyway. Having freed Ollie from the mudroom, Javi's spirit person chased the old labrador in circles around the kitchen. The dog finally got so worked up it peed on the tile, sending Anh into titters while Geetha and Tatiana panic-rummaged through the cupboard of cleaning sprays.

Our only option, then, was to bring our spirit people to school. And like with anybody's first day of school, there was a heated discussion about what they should wear.

Tatiana wanted to dress hers up like a doll, in her best checkered dress with a ribbon around the waist. Anh scoffed: what did we think she was, the Bon-Ton? She could barely keep herself in clean clothes, much less outfit a whole other person. Christian reasoned that since our spirit people didn't have, um, well, *parts*, they didn't really need to wear anything, did they? He turned red as soon as he said it. Javi snickered. Geetha squirmed.

It didn't matter anyway. Didn't take long for us to figure out they couldn't withstand the weight of fabric. Geetha's spirit person collapsed under her lightest T-shirt, Geetha hurrying to pull the shirt off before the dried glue at her spirit person's wispy shoulders could split.

We were nervous about what people would think of them. We should've known better. Our schoolmates had always been self-absorbed and distracted, our teachers overloaded and under-observant. Too much grading, too many helicopter parents pestering them about why their son's clay pot hadn't been featured in the quarterly art show.

Actually, for the first few weeks, it was perfect. While our spirit people sat through math or language arts or phys ed, we did the things we'd always wanted to: pooled our change at the Shell for a hot pickle-in-a-pouch, wrote confessions in intricate cursive on the bathroom stalls. But there was only so much to do within walking distance of Corley Middle School, and when it all got old, we trudged back to class, secretly hoping we hadn't missed anything major.

But our teachers didn't mention participation points or makeup tests. They didn't even acknowledge our recent absence, just sighed and added extra names to the roll call. We'd never know which of us were real to them, and which of us nearly invisible.

So when the winter dance rolled around and Slaps were voted to every court slot for the second year in a row, Anh complained that she'd probably be popular, too, if she had any time left to curry favor. After, you know—she ticked off her obligations on her fingers one by one—getting straight A's, plus helping her grandparents at the store, plus babysitting her annoying buttface cousins, plus getting strong enough to carry the sousaphone in the marching band next year. She could use more hours in the day, she said, or just more of her in the same hours.

We allowed that Anh had what it took to be popular, but we weren't so sure about the rest of us. We agreed to test her theory because there was another obvious benefit to making additional spirit people: the more of them there were, the more places they could be. And even though we knew it was unlikely they'd fit in *everywhere*, we were positive this was the fastest way for us to find *somewhere* we belonged.

It would be like test-driving dozens of different lives at once. We'd find our place by summer break, and we'd do it without sacrificing our grades or missing a single cello lesson. And if by some miracle we became popular along the way, we'd find a way to live with it.

Geetha's mom got the promotion, and while her parents were out at their celebratory dinner at Tanino's, we knocked on wood and made three more spirit people apiece. When her parents disappeared for the weekend to a conference in Vegas, we made even more, the glue coming up faster and easier each time. We started racing to see who could get them done the quickest, Javi smoking the rest of us nine times out of ten.

Tatiana said it was no fair: Javi hadn't hit his growth spurt yet, and she had so much more glue to spread out and peel. Javi's spirit people did a victory conga line around the sectional. Tatiana's spirit people glared from their missing eyes.

Soon, the hallways at school were filled with our willowy spirit bodies, each the consistency of newly shed snakeskin and the color of fogged-up glass. And not true copies anymore, not really. Smarter than us. More agreeable than us. Better than us in every way. We didn't mind. It meant Geetha and Christian could pull ahead in line for valedictorian, finally edging out the leader of the Casios by a quarter of a point. It meant Tatiana could sign up for the newspaper like she'd always wanted, and write more articles than the rest of the staff combined, impressing the palm-reading Matchmaker, who happened to be editor-in-chief. Javi went out for almost every sport the school offered—except swimming and intramural dodgeball, things he acknowledged a person made of dried glue'd better not attempt. He set new records in all of them. And Anh? She got invited to her first sleepover party, and despite having to babysit her cousins that night, she could actually go.

None of this really happened to *us*, of course. But in a way, it did. Just like Tatiana felt the Matchmaker's touch on her own palm that day in free period, we felt everything our spirit people experienced. When one of them scored the game-winning point or got the solo in church choir, we were elated. We felt all their wins simultaneously. We had won, too.

And we felt the force of the work they put in. At the end of the day, exhausted from their cumulative efforts, we tumbled into our beds, heads feeling wrung out and everything sore and spent.

Observing our tired gaits the next morning, our parents squeezed our shoulders and consoled us. It had been like this for them, too, they said. People like us would always have to work twice as hard to prove ourselves half as worthy.

On their own, the words seemed angry. But the unchecked pride in our parents' voices betrayed them.

At school, the other kids didn't know what to do with themselves. While they were buried in their cootie catchers and pages of doodles, we'd become the biggest clique in school, seemingly overnight. It was impossible for them to ignore us now. We took up rows of desks in every classroom, had whole tables to ourselves in the cafeteria, were the first chairs of every instrument group in band. The custodians loved us because we cleaned up after ourselves— had been, as they put it, "raised right." The coaches loved us because we added significant numbers to the cheering section at home games.

We felt like superheroes. *Were* superheroes, with the special ability to split ourselves into so many layers. To keep it together while spreading ourselves thin.

We were so earnest, so disciplined, the other kids couldn't compete. Not that they didn't try. We caught the Slaps waving their bracelets around like they were wands. Then, the Casios tried to start a rumor that anything they typed into their calculators would come true. But they were all pretending, and everybody knew it.

One day, the Matchmakers even tried the glue game themselves, though this was strictly against the clique code. But they got impatient. Didn't wait long enough for the Elmer's to cure, and ended up getting their hands stuck to their binders and composition note-books. We laughed from our corner of free period: they didn't have the restraint, the diligence our parents had imprinted on us.

Whatever they did, they'd never be able to make the same magic we made of ourselves.

••••

Tatiana was in her bedroom learning how to kiss when we got the news. She wriggled on top of her comforter next to one of her spirit people, poking her tongue through the slit in its face to probe the empty air beyond. She pulled away, uncertain this was how it should feel. Her spirit person smiled, the glue around its mouth softened by spit. Tatiana settled for holding its hand, nearly weightless in her own.

On the other side of town, Geetha was frantically punching in Anh's house number, the beginning of the worst five-way call none of us could have foreseen. Downstairs, her dad was scrubbing the red spray paint off their garage door, fire in his throat.

"Ollie," Geetha sobbed, once we were all patched in.

It turned out the writing on the garage door wasn't the half of it. Geetha wouldn't tell us what it said, either, just that it was bad, *really* bad—bad enough that her mom had stormed off to work without even helping her dad uncoil the hose. Just that it said something about glue. Later, once she'd recovered from the initial shock, Geetha would do a scathing impression of her mother that day: "*We pay all this money to move again to this nice neighborhood, Anu. And for what?*"

But the garage door was only the mess they could wash away. The real mess, there was no getting rid of, no coming back to a clean slate from.

Whoever had spray-painted the garage door had also chucked a sirloin steak laced with antifreeze over the fence. Vomited-up chunks peppered the zinnia plot. It could have been two different culprits, of course—Geetha's parents hadn't installed cameras yet, so they couldn't be sure—but the family decided to believe it was the same person. It was better than entertaining the idea that there could be multiple people like that in the world, who were so hateful, who hated them so.

Geetha suspected Savannah: angry, lighter-flicking Savannah. But when we confronted her, she spat that she'd never do a thing like that. Her brother had died huffing spray paint back in San Antonio, and she had a soft spot for dogs.

The antifreeze was speculation, too, though the vet said he was 99 percent sure. Labradors love to put things in their mouths. They're bred for it: gently carrying the corpses of game birds back to their owners.

"At least Ollie was old," Christian said into the phone. He'd always been the logical one; he found comfort in sound reasoning, and he hoped Geetha might, too. But Geetha had learned to walk with her tiny hand balled tight in the scruff of that dog's neck, and it was the wrong thing to say.

Word got around, and the PTA held a meeting everyone admitted was probably long overdue. Students couldn't attend, but later, when the case went to the district court, the minutes from this and future meetings were made public and everyone could see.

For the most part, the teachers were okay with the spirit kids coming to school. They liked having full classrooms, packed assemblies, choir performances whose roaring crescendos vibrated pleasantly through the assembly hall. With attendance soaring to peaks they hadn't seen their entire careers, they felt their lessons must really be reaching the students—that the low pay and lost weekends were worth it; they must be doing something right. And if they could keep enrollment numbers up, wouldn't that mean the school would finally get some wider attention? Which might bring with it much-needed funding and, for example, teachers no longer having to buy their own supplies? Besides, as a rule, they got into teaching to *teach*. And the spirit kids were model pupils, so eager to learn.

For the most part, the administration had no strong feelings about banning the spirit kids.

For the most part, the parents wanted them dead. Today, their kids were getting beat out for concert solos and spots in the starting lineup. Tomorrow, it'd be placement exams. Then college scholarships. Then jobs.

Later, those of us who survived would read the published minutes with one hand over our eyes, the screen dimmed low enough that we could set it to black with a single click. We would want every opportunity to vanish those words when they became too much to handle.

Our hands would be smooth, untouched by any kind of glue for decades. At some point, one of us would hear from a shrink that glue peeling could actually be a useful strategy, a distraction from the urge to self-harm. Another one of us, during a family vacation in the sun-drenched wilds, would return to the campsite to find the kiddo absolutely covered in cactus spines, having tipped over backwards into a young saguaro. And since we wouldn't have health insurance at the time, the wife would tell us she knew a way to get the spines out, a trick from her childhood—all we'd need was a pair of tweezers and a bottle of glue—and we would say no, *God* no, and the wife would mistake our "no" for the screech of a gunned-down bird.

But we weren't those people yet, and some of us would never get the chance to be. We were just kids on a five-way call, desperate to get Geetha to stop crying.

Javi said the right thing. "We're gonna be grounded for *life*."

We all groaned, our spirit people huddling closer around our phones, trying to listen in.

It was a good enough diversion.

"You're right," Geetha said, less shakily, now that there was a pain we could all share in, one she didn't have to suffer alone. "Bet my parents accuse me of cheating again."

"Mine are going to call me lazy," Christian offered.

"Mine'll say I did it for attention," Anh sighed.

"Are you kidding?" Javi howled. "What d'you think my family's gonna say about me kicking it with a bunch of ghost-looking things? I'll be sentenced to church every day for the rest of my life!"

Tatiana's line was quiet. We knew—our guaranteed months of no after-school hangouts, no computers aside—that she had the most to lose. She'd been the most careful to make sure her dad didn't find out about her spirit people, folding them into her sweaters and dresses while she was home, and barring them in by shoving a bookcase against her closet door.

It was at that moment we realized we didn't know our parents at all: instead of being irate with us, or disappointed, or even confused, our parents were *impressed*. And they asked us to teach them the glue game, too.

We didn't ask them their reasons. Even if we weren't quite as smart as our spirit people, we still had some brains, and we figured our parents' motivations couldn't be far off from our own.

Everyone wants to be good. To be liked. Everyone wants to find a balance between what they want to do and what they *have* to.

So we told them to go out and get some Elmer's, and we showed them how it worked.

Tatiana's dad was the only one who didn't want to learn. He was too proud to ask that sort of thing of his adolescent daughter. It was probably for the best, since none of us could imagine that level of intimacy between the two of them. His giant, leathery hands, like bear paws, coated in glue, and him holding those hands still, rendering them perfectly harmless.

But he also didn't have the blow-up reaction we were expecting, and Tatiana's step was a little lighter, a little more confident, for a while.

The night we got together in Geetha's backyard to hold a funeral for Ollie, Tatiana told us she had a plan for the next time her dad got mad: she'd simply send one of her spirit people instead.

"Tati!" Geetha gasped, having reached her personal threshold for cruelty toward non-humankind. Or what we'd all agreed to call non-human, anyway.

"Huh? Would you rather it happen to me?" Tatiana crossed her long arms, a challenge. "There are a lot more of them, and I can always make more."

Javi hugged his knees. Anh hugged Tatiana. Christian grimaced, the one among us who could trace the twisted logic of a person enduring so much hurt—getting mixed up in ideas about what's owed and who deserves it—that they would readily inflict it on others.

"Anyway, I'll still feel it a bit. Happy?" Tatiana snapped, pulling out of Anh's arms. We'd never seen her like this. "It'll be better this way," she said. "At least glue doesn't bruise."

Christian considered, but knew better than to mention that Tatiana's plan couldn't work. Even if some teachers couldn't tell the difference between us and our spirit people, our parents, who had raised us from diapers, certainly would.

It didn't happen often, but this time his reasoning was off.

••••

There might've been a point when our parents would have been able to pick us out from a crowd of our spirit people, but that point had passed by the time spring break came around.

We blamed it on the news while we still could: there was a severe drought in Geetha's parents' hometown; sanctions against the countries where Christian and Tatiana were born, forcing hundreds of thousands to the brink of starvation. Border patrols, flash floods, corrupt cops, and drug shortages meant everyone had family to check up on, and, like always, their focus wasn't on us.

Still, when Anh walked in to find her grandparents playing tiến lên with one of her spirit people, it took her by surprise.

We pretended we could still tell the difference—that *we* would always recognize the real, original five—but gradually even this stopped being true.

Because while the school board held meeting after meeting, loaded down with motions to ban the spirit kids, to keep the spirit kids, to raise money to build the spirit kids their own school, we kept making more of them. We weren't waiting till we could get to Geetha's house anymore. We didn't care about having separate rooms, about the consequences of small-scale shoplifting for minors. From the home ec room, the guidance office, the Dollar General, we took it. Under the bleachers at school, in the locker room's communal showers while everyone was playing pickleball on the blacktop, we smeared the glue across our chests with a fevered, desperate urgency, blowing on each other's skin to hurry the dry. Like at any minute, this could all be over.

We sensed ourselves growing lighter and lighter, our bodies uncertain as crepe paper from the craft store. We'd been thoroughly distributed. We began holding onto everything as we passed it, brick walls and stair railings, so sure were we that the slightest breeze would blow us away. We felt ourselves losing substance before we got confirmation. *Insubstantial*, Geetha mused to no one in particular, being just another word for unverifiable. Unreal.

The fingerprints were a hot topic in the school board meetings; they made people uneasy. Those who were pro spirit kid argued that fingerprints marked us as individuals, and if the spirit kids had their own unique sets, it meant they were no less human than anyone else. Even identical twins have distinct fingerprints, they said.

When they filled the nurse's office with ink pads and

made the entire student body come in shifts to get their fingerprints done, we expected the results to be conclusive. We remembered those first ghostly, one-dimensional hands lined up on our desks in free period, the patterns of friction ridges an exact match to our own.

But pretty soon, the school announced that the spirit kids would stay put at least through the end of the year, which we took to mean they had passed the test.

Anh borrowed—her new word for stealing—a magnifying glass from the science lab, and examined the pads of her fingers beside those of a few of her spirit people.

"Yep," she said finally. We let out our collective breath.

They were changing, and the fingertips were just the beginning.

One thing among the many things that made our spirit people a wonder to us was the way you could see right through them—not totally, not with any real clarity, but as if you were looking through a pair of filmy eyeglasses whose prescription was way stronger than your own. When they leaned against our open lockers, we could discern behind them the shape of the string lights they'd hooked to the inside wall, the little notes they'd put up with magnets on the door. Notes to each other, we assumed. The messages weren't written in any of the eight languages in which we were jointly fluent, and we couldn't make heads or tails of them.

Then one day, the glue peeled off us without its usual transparency, clouded in places with shades of porcelain and copper and beige, and we looked down at our own bodies and saw the missing skin. The lesions were wide but not deep, a couple of layers at most, no worse than a road rash or a turf burn. But they stung profoundly, as if the wounds were more than surface. Tatiana likened it to growing pains. Geetha said it made her think of one of her uncles, who had a callus on his forehead from years of repeated contact with his prayer rug.

The next spirit people had hair on their arms and legs in large, irregular sections where it had been yanked up from our own. Our injuries weren't superficial anymore. Javi remained stoic as his scabbed into immense purple lava mounds that twinged and pulsed. Anh pulled her scabs up in the night, the skin underneath raw and weeping and, also, not exactly skin. The smell of infection wafted from her, cloyingly sweet—in the cafeteria we pushed away any desserts our parents had packed us.

We were mottled in our way, and the spirit kids were mottled in theirs, our raised parts and recesses lining up. We told ourselves we were the original images and they were our negatives. We told ourselves that, like anybody would.

Layer after layer, coating after coating, we gave ourselves up to our spirit versions. In science class, we learned about rock strata: how every layer tells you something about the period when it formed. Up came the calluses on Christian's left hand—the hours of practice with his mom clapping her hands like a metronome; the time the band's conductor got so frustrated he flung his sheet-music stand across the room and, barely missing Christian, slashed a third-chair oboe player on the chin. Up came Anh's freckles, which her grandma had been trying to disappear with gobs of bleaching cream since she was six.

Up came Javi's shin splints, along with the tendons that connected his calf muscles to the bone. The spirit people were unrecognizable with our smooth, stringy muscle on the outside. They tensed and released all over as they skipped over the cracks of the sidewalk, just like we'd been taught to; as they pumped their new legs, the playground's beat-up swing set wailing like a banshee.

Why did we keep doing it, then, factoring in all that it cost us? It wasn't a mindless compulsion, like some so-called child behavior specialists would later suggest. It was, like Reid had said at the start, something to do. A way to lay claim over our days, to be a part of something.

Then our spirit people came, and they were so clever, so beautiful and capable, and they seemed to fit in so much better than we ever had. On them, our peculiar features had been polished away, and their speech was news-anchor flat and unadorned by accent. Where once we had marveled at their resemblance to us, now we were grateful for the departures future generations had taken. We loved them, and we wanted the best for them. We were so proud.

We couldn't have anticipated how the other kids would come to love them, too, despite their parents' objections that the spirit kids were predatory, robbers of opportunity. The Matchmaker who'd once read Tatiana's palm now stood in front of one of her spirit people, asking to touch its exposed bicep. It nodded yes, its ropy neck muscles flexing. The Matchmaker lightly stroked its arm, then when it nodded again, worked her fingers into the spongy tissue. On the other side of the schoolyard, Tatiana tilted her head back and moaned.

Soon enough, everybody finds their place in the world. Our parents thought it was a choice they could make, that this country would be place enough for us. But they left parts of themselves behind when they came here, and it was just like us to follow their example.

Soon enough, we all find out what we're made of.

Would you believe that, at our centers, was glue?

We could have used it to stay together. But there came a point when we each had to save ourselves, or try.

There were those of us who would make it out of Corley with something left of our personhood. Not much, but just enough so we could rebuild piece by piece in the future: eyes with which to glare at the shrink when she assigned us our weekly "homework"; arms with which to steer our sniffling, cactus-pierced kiddo into the tent; lips with which to tell him this wouldn't hurt much. A lie.

And there were those of us who would be lost, our fading incremental, so day by day it was easy not to notice, until it was complete.

In the pass time between our final free period and the end-of-year assembly, we floated through the halls against the current, ghosts pushing against the material truth of all our past and future lives. The dried glue of us stretched, tore, and crumpled as it came in contact with the sharp edges of the kids who passed us: their skateboards and lunch boxes, their stacks of used textbooks. We kept moving, sticking to nothing.

At the end of the hallway, we reached toward the double doors that led outside, two thin rectangles leaking the afternoon sun. Our gossamer hands, in their last imploring, glimmered, penetrated by the light.

APPROVED METHODS OF LOVE DIVINATION IN THE FIRST-RATE CITY OF DUSHAGOROD

In the first-rate city of Dushagorod, your heart's desire is not hard to find. You might meet him one night in the rotating bar with a three-hundred-sixty-degree view of sprawling canals and skyscrapers, or at the neojazz cafe— you know the one—with the all-northern wine menu and the *ambiance romantique.* Or at the rare books store, the amateur rowing club, the school where you drop off your little cousin twice weekly as a favor to her mother, or at your own house, in which you can no longer set foot without being sprung upon by some Mr. Whateverovich in another one of your mama's well-intentioned setups. And if it doesn't happen organically, no problem. No problem! Because the proud people of Dushagorod practice a number of love divination methods: proven successes with no nasty stigmas, performed with skill and reverence, derived from ancient matchmaking wisdom. Three methods to choose from, to be exact. Three-ish, if we're being less so.

So if you're pining, carrot-darling, in Dushagorod, you needn't worry. You have every tool at your disposal, and you'll find your soulmate soon enough.

Unless you are Sofia Kuzmin, of course, in which case you are, regrettably, doomed.

Sofia Kuzmin has loose spirals of hair in a rusty brown that falls squarely between 6MB and 7LA on the Petrekian Color Match Matrix. She has a habit of chewing on the ends of said hair absentmindedly while concentrating on the task before her. She has an upper para-angle dimple on the right side of her face and a laugh that bursts from her lungs at an above-standard speed of ninety-eight kilometers per hour. She has bright, narrow, fretful, pea-green eyes that are constantly moving.

All of which matters not to the respected divinators of Dushagorod, nor to Sofia's parents, who have carted her to them dutifully month after month. Appearance and temperament, though logged in the spirit of due diligence, have little to do with the final reading the client receives. The reading the client receives depends strictly on: one, the reputability of the divinator; two, the quality of the divining materials she uses; and three, the client's talent in reciting the letters of the alphabet, "A" through "Z."

In the twelve months between Sofia's seventeenth and eighteenth birthdays, her tenacious parents took her to twelve different divinators of the Dushagorod Toggle Tab School. Twelve times they doused her hair in homemade cayenne pepper overnight tonic; twelve times they woke her at daybreak to prepare for the appointment ahead. "Enunciate!" they reminded her a dozen times over while she stood in front of the mirror, gargling saltwater and clearing her still-sleep-lined throat. *Ay*, *bee*, *see*—"Good start, So!"—*dee*, *ee*, *eff*—"Speak up now!"—*gee*—"Now stick the landing!"—*aytch*—"Again, more clearly!"—*aytch*—"Go on!"—*eye, jay, kay* . . .

One of three officially sanctioned methods of love divination, Toggle Tab's origins date back to the middle of the last century: little figure eights of metal uncovered by archaeologists and treasure seekers in what we now know were crude schoolyards. Excavated from layers of ash and dirt, the silver pull tabs glimmered in the sun, arranged in such peculiar formations that anthropologists quickly identified them as ritual items. The cans they had once been attached to were found in crumpled heaps in a neighboring quadrant.

Never mind all that. You can read about it, if you wish, at the city's excellent Culture and Heritage Museum. Now, the museum has received its fair share of criticism over the years, like most institutions constructed during the controversial Repop Period. But rest assured that any so-called propaganda surrounding love divination has since been removed, and what remains is a thoughtful, neutrally minded curation of Dushagorodian practices, then and now.

All of Sofia's Toggle Tab appointments were more or less the same. She walked up a staircase, or took an elevator, or one time used an elaborate platform-and-pulley system, to get to the third or fifth or seventh floor of a building—critics have called postwar Dushagorodian architecture "novel" and "intimidating"—where the door to the divinator's office stood slightly ajar between a pair of reclining armchairs. Then her parents would squeeze her hands reassuringly, her mother would sit in the chair on the left, her father in the one on the right, and Sofia would proceed, chest tight, between them, into the room where she hoped someone would illuminate her future.

Immediately she was assaulted by plumes of incense: rose and orange blossom variety, nose-hair-singeing strength. A small, suspiciously quiet bird perched contentedly in a cage—open—in the corner, and sheer scarves were draped over lampshades, painting the walls a moody, bruisy red. Such is the stuff of the Toggle Tab appointments, the most affordable Sofia's parents could find, their divining substance—soda cans—remaining widely accessible even as other materials grow less so. Though, like everything else, their cost has nearly tripled over the past year. To counteract any negative associations that come with cheapness, Toggle Tab divinators strive to give clients a *luxury* reading experience. Floor cushions positively teeming with tassels, an abundance for the senses.

They say the incense wards off ghosts. A harmless superstition.

Each time, Sofia lowered herself onto a cushion, placing both knees to one side, while the divinator, a severe woman with hair color, dimple placement, and laugh speed of no particular relevance performed the steps of the intricate ceremony.

"I will now procure the divining object," the divinator announced weightily. Sofia swallowed hard, eyes stinging from the fragrant smoke. The divinator pulled a can of pomegranate soda from the mini fridge behind her and, with an expert flourish, set it on the low table between them. Then she took the metal tab between her fingers and tugged it forward, opening the can with a tinny crunch.

The Toggle Tab method is simple, as are all state-approved love divination methods, for you needn't be a great scholar, a world-class thinker, to find your heart's desire. On this, all three Schools agree. Egalitarian, you see? *Ee, gee, ay, el* . . .

When the divinator toggled the tab forward, Sofia began: "Ay." She toggled the tab backward and Sofia continued: "Bee." And so it went: forward on "Cee," backward on "Dee." If the client reaches the end of the alphabet before the tab snaps loose, the pair take it from the start, reciting the alphabet again until the tab breaks off. The letter on which the tab comes free reveals the first initial of her soulmate's name.

Only for Sofia, it didn't quite pan out that way.

At her first appointment, the tab snapped loose at the exact moment she fell into a violent coughing fit, her nerves proving a poor combination with the stupendous quantity of incense. The second time, she failed to properly distinguish her *em* and *en*, so the reading had to be discarded. The third time, the bird swooped from its cage and snatched the tab clear off the can, so the divinator could not be sure whether its separation was the bird's or fate's doing. The fourth time . . . You get the picture. On more than one occasion, nothing happened at all, and Sofia and the divinator sat toggling and reciting for hours without the tab loosening one bit, until her father's deep snores could be heard through the office door and the sky in the window rolled onto its side, showing the city its black-purple back. It defied the laws of physics, and it defied the laws of the nine-hour Dushagorodian workday. So at last the divinator set the can aside and told Sofia that she was welcome to schedule another appointment if she pleased, but for now they were *fini*.

The Toggle Tab divinators agreed that, while every client's path to her soulmate is unique, some more direct and some winding, they had never seen anything like the potholed, sinkholed, dead-end street that was the ill fortune of Miss Sofia Kuzmin.

After each appointment, Sofia's parents were passed a cloth receipt with the results of the reading, sometimes in a slanting hand, other times stamped in block print or typed neatly in a serif font, and always that same dreaded word: *ILLEGIBLE*. Which to the Kuzmins looked an awful lot like *INELIGIBLE*. Unqualified for love. Not fit for it. Ruled out.

But Sofia's parents weren't ready to give up just yet, not on the eldest of their beloved Repop daughters, with her hair just like her mother's and her voice a wobbling, indecisive mezzo-soprano and her sense of humor rated a deadly Category 4.

"You get what you pay for," urged their prying neighbor Nastya, who reported that her own daughter had no luck whatsoever with the Toggle Tab method, then found her heart's desire within the first five minutes consulting the Dancing Rind. Now she and her husband—"L" for

Luka!—live in Dushagorod's most exclusive gated garden district, and they're expecting a child of their own before the year is through.

Long tempted by Toggle Tab as the economical option, Sofia's parents had to agree that the budget pair of boots bought twelve times winds up being a great deal more expensive than the superior pair bought once—a calculation worsened when the cheap boots make you sore, the way the dismal Toggle Tab results had disheartened Sofia, threatening to put her off the idea of marriage entirely.

So that's that, they decided. Next we march to the School of the Dancing Rind. They would get Sofia her legible reading, shut their eyes tight while they signed the bill, and afterward be free to allocate what was left of their funds and attention to her two younger sisters, soon to be of marriageable age themselves.

••••

There are far fewer Dancing Rind divinators than Toggle Tabs, the profession requiring more extensive and rigorous schooling, and Sofia was put on a waitlist so long that it was late summer by the time her appointment rolled around, and her hair had lightened to a brassy 7LA-2.

Even now, it is considered rude to show the dip of your elbows in a house of the Dancing Rind, so Sofia's parents shuffled her out of bed early once again and arranged on the coverlet every blouse she owned with long sleeves. For the next two hours, they picked one up, pressed it flat against her shoulders, cocked their heads one way and then the other, then flung the lousy, not-quite-right thing back onto the bed with a huff.

When they arrived for the appointment, Sofia was wearing one of her mother's old smocks, which was the appropriate color and modesty level according to her parents' copy of the Osipovan Decency Chart, but which puckered horribly at her chest and itched all over. On the way, they argued indiscreetly about money.

"You heard what Nastya said," her mother muttered. "Some girls are never going to get a clear reading with Toggle Tab. It's like they say: We've been trying to fit a pentagonal peg into a hexagonal hole. With Dancing Rind, even the tricky ones are just about guaranteed."

"Maybe," her father replied. "I'm still not happy about the price. What would possess a person to charge so much for three goes at an orange peel?"

Sofia's mother was right to shake her head at this. She didn't call him a thick-skulled horse's you-know-what, but she would have been right to do that. Oranges haven't grown within a week's train ride of Dushagorod in seventy years, and the tariffs on the crates brought in from the southern regions put the fruit at an absolute premium. Only the wealthiest residents of Dushagorod—even wealthier than Nastya's son-in-law with his pricy garden-district duplex—would do such a lavish, wasteful thing as buy oranges simply to *eat* them. More than 85 percent of the shipments go straight to the city's Dancing Rind divinators, whose interests lie primarily in the predictive powers of the juice and the peel.

There was once a marvelous exhibit at the Culture and Heritage Museum on Dushagorod's ruthless performance in the Bergamot Trade Wars, complete with a mock mass grave of dummy bodies topped, quite artistically, with a single bumpy-skinned bergamot. But as stated, much of the museum's more "graphic" content has been scrubbed for today's gentler audiences.

At the door to her office, the divinator presented her hands for the family's inspection; Dancing Rind divinators keep their thumbnails long and pointed, the better to slice the peel in one clean, intact strip. This divinator's nails were especially strong—auspicious. When she held them up to the window to demonstrate, hardly any light shone through.

Inside, there were no floor cushions, silk lampshades, incense cones in painstakingly hammered copper burners. No songbirds, mute or otherwise; no velveteen daybed the cheeky divinator could point to and say, "Di-*van*," before pointing to herself and saying, "Di-*vine*." No merry punchlines. In fact, after Sofia's parents nudged her over the threshold and she took in the room before her, her first impression was that she might've fallen into the burrow of some blind animal. The floor, ceiling, and all four walls were painted dark brown, a faint shadow's fall away from black.

There were no chairs, no tables. In the center of the room, there was an orange sphere: a rare, red-fleshed Cara Cara.

That the office was completely odorless didn't give Sofia much pause. Her parents had heard that any divinator worth their salt has the courtesy to use a scent-neutralizing spray, since the sugary, tangy bouquet their materials stockpile emanates can be rather off-putting to some.

Sofia stood quietly, hands behind her back, acutely aware of the fallow undertones of her hair, the mustiness of her mother's shirt, the half-moons of sweat waxing under her arms and at her too-tight collar—all the ways she interfered with the refined sterility of the space. The divinator smiled peaceably, pretending not to mind.

"Are you ready, carrot-darling?"

Sofia took a deep breath, nodded.

The divinator plucked the orange off the floor, bounced it twice in her hands, then pushed her right thumbnail through the rind in one deliberate motion. She spooled her nail around and around the outside, moving gradually downward, down and down and down and down, so that when she was done, she held in one hand a perfect, triumphantly unbroken peel, twisting around itself so many times it looked like a metal spring. In the other, she held the disrobed orange. Sofia, who had never seen one up close before, blushed and cast her eyes away—it felt so wrong to stare.

The divinator handed the peel to Sofia, who carefully reassembled it into its original sphere while the divinator proceeded to squeeze, with no few labored grunts, all the juice out of the fruit into a small pool between them. Then she bobbed her head at Sofia—"Lightly, but surely!" she instructed—and Sofia, having rehearsed this countless times with a narrow band of blue felt her parents had provided, tossed the peel into the air.

It fell with a *smack-splash* into the puddle of juice, and the two women leaned forward to read the shape it had taken.

While it requires a bit of finesse on the part of the thrower, and a bit more on the part of the carve-and-squeezer, Dancing Rind is, like the other methods, meant to be approachable, easy enough for anyone to manage. If you have two hands for the tossing, splendid. One will suffice as well, of course, and as an aside we hope you are benefitting from your P.O.P. Has a nice ring to it, doesn't it? Smoother off the tongue than "Post-Occupation Package." POP, POP! POP, POP! If you have *no* hands, ditto the package, and if you haven't yet received your prostheses, you're welcome to use your teeth. Only however you toss, it must be *you* tossing. After all, if the divinator does it for you, it'll be her soul-reading, not yours.

Lob the rind. Watch it fly in its smart, high arc. (The higher the arc, the closer to—!) The shape the rind takes when it lands represents the first initial of your soul-mate's name.

"Is that an 'M'?" Sofia asked hopefully, after some silence.

"No..." The divinator circled the fallen peel, crouching low then standing on her tippy-toes so she could take it in from every angle. "It's not an 'M.' It's not much of anything, I'm afraid."

"No, no," Sofia insisted. "Look at it from this side. It looks just like an 'E.'"

The divinator scowled. Dancing Rind is not really a reading-by-committee type of thing, especially when one half of said committee is a desperate, jilted amateur. Sofia wasn't the first of her clients to forget that.

Hoping to avoid the excruciating wait for another appointment if this one failed, Sofia's parents had paid up front for three consecutive readings. On the second reading, Sofia leaned so far forward that she and the divinator bumped heads: a silly blunder, and one that cost her dearly. In keeping with Dancing Rind customs, they both shut their eyes immediately so as not to catch a glimpse of the result. Quickly—as quickly as she could without sight—the divinator swept the void peel into the stockroom, where it would be burned by the divinator's assistant *tout suite*. Then they tried one last time.

"Just my luck," Sofia cried. "I swear it's the same shape as before! Are you sure you don't see the 'E'? The cursive 'E'? With a little swish in the middle?" Cursive or not—and mind you, cursive was removed from Dushagorod's standard curriculum years ago—the divinator didn't see it. And neither did Sofia, if she was being honest, for there was nothing remotely close to an "E" there. There was no part of the alphabet there, uppercase or lowercase. The peel was a loopy tangle with several tails, sharp turns giving way to a droopy center. It was like nothing the divinator had seen before, except for the twin peel she had seen just five minutes earlier.

Because Sofia was right. Her first and third tosses had fallen in exactly the same shape. The likelihood of which was—well, the museum has a whole section on throw statistics and probabilities, but for our purposes, let us say it was virtually impossible. The receipt the divinator delivered to her parents confirmed it, stamped twice in maroon ink with the same terrible word:

ILLEGIBLE.

And again: *ILLEGIBLE.*

That night, their house was a nest of angry hornets, a storm you turn your path from if you've any wits about you.

Sofia's parents were beside themselves. Her mother paced the length of the kitchen. "Twice illegible and once disqualified? What kind of reading is that?"

"I bet this is one of those scam artists," her father scoffed. "Nastya didn't mention them when she gave her glowing review, did she? Then again, she's biased. I mean the ones who don't even have real oranges but use that bioengineered stuff, whatever it's called. Greatfruit? Citrus X? It won't work unless it's a genuine orange, right?"

"That's right," her mother admitted. "That's right."

"Suck you dry all the same, though," her father continued, nostrils flaring. "Charge you as if they're doing the real thing, so when you finally figure them out, you've got nothing left to go back and do it the right way."

Sofia was slumped over the kitchen table, a girl in the shape of a crushed soda can. Her mother sat down in the chair next to her. Stood up. Sat back down, turned to Sofia.

"You said it didn't smell like oranges in there?"

Sofia didn't look up. "Right. It didn't smell like oranges."

"I guess that doesn't mean anything." Her mother chewed her lip, then stood up and started pacing again.

"They're not supposed to, any of them."

Sofia shrugged, busying herself with a chip of peeling paint on the table's surface.

Just then, her two sisters burst in through the front door, the first with 5Q hair in two tight braids, the second with 5QR hair tucked under a wide-brimmed cap, looking startlingly alike down to the degrees of their overbites—29.5 percent, 31 percent—and far more upbeat than the situation called for.

"Hey, So-So!" one called.

"How was the appointment?" sang the other. "Let me guess. Just so-so for our So-So?"

It was an old gag from way back at the beginning of Sofia's Toggle Tab era. The joke was that Sofia's appointments never went as well as anyone had hoped. Though "so-so" was perhaps not the right word for it anymore, suggesting as it did an outcome that was not good but not bad, either. If she had received an "X" or "Z" result, *that* would be so-so, since names starting with those letters are comparably harder to come by. But even that would've been some kind of success, would've offered some direction. With her long string of illegible readings, Sofia's circumstances had dipped well below so-so into very poor territory indeed.

"I should've just fudged it!" Sofia erupted. "I thought about it, too, when she looked away. The peel, the one from earlier, was burning in the next room, and the smell was so intense, and she looked away. For a second. And I thought I should reach out and kick it. Not even kick it, just *poke* it a little. Straighten out a couple of the lines and it could've been an 'M.'"

The room fell silent. Her sisters stopped laughing, and her father's jaw—B-type gonial angle, chin projection grade C—dropped open, but he said nothing. Her mother took three fast strides toward the table and grabbed her daughter by the shoulders.

"*So!* What are you thinking?" she hissed, panicked. "You can't say that. You shouldn't let them hear you say that!"

And Sofia's mother was right. She really shouldn't have.

••••

People have no respect these days. There are exceptions, of course, but by and large, they ought to be ashamed. This trend goes beyond the long celebrated, *demonstrably effective* methods of love divination in the superlative northern city of Dushagorod, but we can begin there as a practical example.

When the state launched the love divination campaigns in earnest, citizens took to them like a sea cow takes to a cove of shallow, algae-rich water. The Culture and Heritage Museum could offer proof of that if those vile liberation groups hadn't gone into hysterics over the thing, resulting in the entire wing that housed Repop artifacts being yanked and placed into storage. Because while one goal of the love divination renaissance was to encourage citizens to pair up and produce offspring—to bring our population's war-ravaged numbers back into a healthy range—it did much more than that.

The war that preceded the Repop was devastating to the human psyche. It was utter chaos, beyond what anyone of Sofia's generation can understand. It was impossible for anyone to predict what would happen in the next hour, much less the next day, so citizens lived moment to moment, never being so bold as to assume the next would come. They could hope for nothing, plan for nothing. There was a sheet of glass between the present and the future that began stippled and semitranslucent and gradually turned more and more opaque until they could not even make out the dark shapes beyond it.

In this context, the approved love divination methods—Toggle Tab, Dancing Rind, and Paper Crocus—provided citizens with what they had long been missing. They offered certainty where the war had brewed festering doubt, clear answers amid constant precarity. They suggested—no, they *promised*—a future that citizens had not dared to imagine.

And, yes, they brought dramatic population growth. Just as we had hoped.

Now the population remains stable and the Zalaltdinovan Law is no longer in effect, so women of breeding age are welcome to take and take their fill of Dushagorod's resources without giving a bit back. But love divination remains fairly popular. According to last month's census, 68 percent of couples met using one of the three approved methods, and another 4 percent using the one unapproved method, which we will broach shortly, though we do not relish giving further publicity to that cultish stuff. Five decades after the final shells exploded, after the fever of war mercifully broke, citizens continue to cite those qualities of certainty and clarity as their reasons for choosing love divination today.

From our perspective, they remain as relevant as ever. For the purpose of organization, compact family units are ideal.

Which returns us to the topic of respect, and how Sofia Kuzmin—with her infuriating right-side upper para-angle dimple that comes out when she smiles, that comes out when she *taunts us*—has absolutely none.

So here is what ungrateful Sofia does. (Dushagorod does not observe a standardized Gratitude Index, but if it did, she would unquestionably rate in the negative levels.) Here is what ungrateful, insolent Sofia Kuzmin does, and just see if you can believe it.

She bypasses the most premium, most efficacious Paper Crocus method, and she goes directly to the Ropes.

It's worth pausing to appreciate Paper Crocus, which finds its roots in the classrooms of school buildings since demolished to fine rubble, in whose place we raised, brick by brick, the city's modern learning centers. Before laying their foundations, our builders found thousands of paper crocuses sticking up from the rest of the war's remains: chalky debris, shards of brittle polycarbonate wood desktops, textbooks blown apart so thoroughly that neighboring chapters had no hope of ever finding each other, shoes melted to vinyl, so very many fragile little bones.

For people like Sofia's parents, Paper Crocus is the last resort, the scrimped-and-saved-for option, the prayer cast in the loudest, most urgent voice. The price for a single appointment is steep—steeper since the paper shortages exacerbated by ongoing tensions with the far west. Of the approved methods, this involves the highest level of customization and thus the most labor and talent on the part of the divinator. At the time of the last census, there were only two practicing within Dushagorod city limits, and four others scattered around the surrounding territories. Each must be proficient not only in love divination, but also in the arts of chirography, paper folding, path charting, and that specific regional style of puppetry that utilizes only the pointer fingers and thumbs.

The divinator begins with a single square leaf of paper, which she must be careful not to tear or crease incorrectly at any step of the process; even the most successful divinators cannot afford to keep a stock greater than forty leaves at a time. She performs a series of confident folds—the exact number and placement are not public knowledge—transforming the flat square into a three-dimensional paper bloom, then marks its petals with various signs and symbols. By hooking her fingers into the four tented spaces in the underside of the flower, the divinator effectively drives the crocus throughout the appointment, opening and closing its mouth lengthwise then widthwise then lengthwise again in keeping with her client's answers.

For instance, the divinator puppeteering the crocus would have said: "State your first name for me, carrot-darling."

And Sofia would have answered: "Sofia."

The divinator would then have repeated it back to her, letter by letter—"ess," opening the crocus's mouth lengthwise; "oh," widthwise; "eff," the first way again—until she had, reaching the end of Sofia's name, arrived at the crocus's final orientation.

At which point, she would have said: "Now your last name for me. Slow and clear."

And Sofia would have said, if she knew what was good for her: "Kuzmin."

And the divinator would have counted the number of letters in the name Kuzmin—*one, two, three, four, five, six*—and opened the tab marked with an elegant "6" to reveal Sofia's soulmate's name.

Or else the name of an object or animal that was phonetically similar to her soulmate's name, like a tam-tam for Timothy, or else a moth for Timothy, or else one of those teeny, skinny-legged prey crustaceans for Kirill.

Love divination is not an exact science. It is a lifting of one of the many veils worn by that clotheshorse Destiny.

This is how it most likely would have gone, had Sofia done things the way things ought to be done. Instead, tired of watching her parents drop their every coin into her bottomless well of illegibility, tired of listening to her sisters titter, "So-So!" (and at the same time not wanting to rob them of their turns at the tilting soda tab), sensing in some deep and unexplored place that she had caused her family enough trouble, and sensing too that she needed—*needed*—some sort of assured future (before death, that is, which is the ultimate future this world guarantees us all), Sofia waited until her family was asleep, then snuck through the feral, lawless night to the underground quarters of the divinators of the Ropes.

••••

Before we talk about the Ropes, let us remind ourselves: A wave of change has fallen over our fair city of Dushagorod. It has been fifteen years since the last execution. Couples are no longer required to produce an Official Match Certificate signed by a licensed love divinator during random checks performed by the city guard. The checks themselves are now almost uselessly infrequent, and after the irksome riots of last year—which, it would do well to remember, resulted in millions in state property damage—occur on a timed schedule, on the first day of each long month. This naturally puts the guard at a significant disadvantage, since citizens have time to prepare. Reports from these home visits have described calendars with red circles on check dates, the word *inspection* scrawled in a child's hand, carefree hearts over the *i*'s.

Fifteen years since the last execution, and an unremarkable one by all accounts. The typical offenses—though carried out for a longer-than-average period, we'll give her that. She was thirty-two with a 4.5-millimeter diastema between her two front teeth and hair color Indeterminate, as she, like many of her fellow dissidents, kept it shorn to the scalp to avoid categorization. She had attached earlobes, ears pierced in seven places along the rim. In them she wore curved steel darning needles, in what today's so-called countermovement scholars term a "subversion of a tool traditionally associated with women's work." Her name has been scrubbed from the system, but the liberation devils who have taken her as their hero call her Darn 'em Dolly.

Fifteen years and they still put up cloth posters every day printed with her picture and that tasteless name. The guards take them down during their daily sweeps—and there's no need to thank us, by the way; it's a service we're glad to provide to the community. Everywhere but the new anarchist district, that is. Self-governing, fu! Madness. And only the most recent of the outer zones to have fallen into disorder. They'll just have to live with those eyesores, won't they?

So, an unremarkable execution, and a lenient one to be sure. A proficient executioner, a painless technique. None of the thrilling, drawn-out spectacle of the first decades of the Repop. She had been evading her call-to-duty notices for years, and during her trial cited a medical condition that would prevent her from birthing children. But we had the state doctors examine her—exhaustively, and at our own expense, we might add—and make no mistake: She was perfectly capable of doing her part for the Repop effort. To this day it is widely believed that she had no interest in marrying a man at all.

We are lenient broadly speaking, are we not? Think of the approved love divination methods, which do not prescribe one particular partner, with whom the client may or may not feel an instant connection, but rather direct the client to a first initial, a *suggestion* of a name, so that the client retains the power of final choice. An "A" result, while narrowing the field down substantially, could yield a match with anyone from Adam to Armand. It is the ideal marriage of fate and freedom.

That was one of the first slogans Dushagorod's brilliant advertisers dreamed up for the love divination campaigns: *The Ideal Marriage of Fate and Freedom. The Ideal Marriage, Period.* The banners are so meticulously preserved you wouldn't know they waved proudly through years of sun and rain and snowstorms, and were at points torn down and doused in gasoline, at other points splattered with their defenders' blood. They're wasted now, rolled up and stacked in bins as they are in the airless museum basement. The censoring of the state's valiant struggles—*that* is what we ought to call our national shame.

We move onward now to the Ropes. The unapproved method.

It's a frightening name, the Ropes. There has been some speculation that this is by design, and that by giving the method a name so different from the state naming conventions for love divination—one so torturous in nature—its originators were able to slip it under our radar. It's true that one of the Repop's early execution techniques involved tension ropes coupled with stone weights and a tall pole structure in the town square . . . But, as you'll come to see, the Ropes method we speak of now is far and away the more barbaric of the two.

Unfortunately, the Ropes' underground quarters, located in the woefully (if predictably) impoverished and heavily littered fourth anarchist district, has circumvented our surveillance devices. So it is impossible for us to recount the traitorous Sofia Kuzmin's midnight visit in such rich detail as we have her previous appointments. However, in reviewing communications from our network of trusted loyalists, we have been able to deduce the following:

The Ropes is a brutish act. Dozens of depraved participants stand in a circle in the divinators' cramped, poorly lit quarters, their unwashed bodies pressed against one another, chanting in low, inhuman tones. From its center, one hears the slapping of the ropes against the pavement, the hard breaths of the lost citizen skipping between them.

Viewed in a more forgiving light, in many ways the Ropes operates much like the approved love divination methods: an inferior copycat born of unoriginal minds. Two thick, heavy ropes, each approximately twelve feet in length, are held on either end by a pretender to the divinator title. The illegitimate divinators manipulate the ropes so they spin in opposite directions, while the others around them chant on and on, like snake charmers drawing the foul serpent from the depths of its basket. When they prompt her, the citizen jumps into the space between the whirling ropes and continues to jump, matching their rhythm so she does not trip.

Only she must trip eventually, and that is where the love divination comes in. As she skips, the divinators—and let us add here that *divinators* in this case refers not only to the women controlling the ropes, but also to the crowd of women gathered around them, who cheer the skipper on, all recognized as divinators by the practitioners of this wretched method—as she skips, the divinators sing. And they sing a wicked, coded song:

I like coffee, I like tea—
I like the boys and the boys like me—
Or else I'll choose to play Dolly—
Eevy, ivy, over—
Tell your mama the war is won—
She had a fella when she was young—
Tell your papa the very same—
He had a gal and he changed her name—
Papa went to market to buy some meat—
Mama with the baby who's fast asleep—
Fortunes, fortunes, please tell me—
What's my sweetheart going to be?—
Doctor, lawyer, banker, cop—
Sailor, soldier, sorry sop?—
A—
B—
C—
D—

According to our trusted connections, the letter on which the skipper trips marks the first initial of her soul-mate's name.

So you see? Not so different. We take issue with its collective nature, of course, and the notion that any old hag off the street might be tempted to assume the prestigious divinator title, sullying it for those who have actually gone through the proper training. And we take issue with the secrecy and the fracas and the shameless bodily exertion and the inordinate amount of encouragement—love divination being a sacred thing that should, in its process, remind the client why they have chosen it in the first place: how very *miserable* it is to be alone. That is why the parents wait outside the office. That is why the client sits across from a solemn divinator in a near-silent room for hours, very, very still. To illustrate that a woman cannot feel on her own the joy, the union, the pleasant forward motion that is *marriage*.

The Ropes undermines all that. When the skipper trips, the crowd rushes forth, reaching their arms out to catch her on her way down. If she falls despite this, they lift her to her feet and console her, and they tend to her injuries: scraped knees and stubbed toes and raw palms where she made contact with the ground.

But with a few modifications, not so different. With the right ones, they could even register the Ropes, acquire state-approved status. Realizing our resources are many and theirs relatively few, we have on countless occasions offered to assist with the implementation. But after enough of these generous offers, we must accept that the fools are not the least interested.

There are rumors that the divinators of the Ropes were brides of the late Repop Period who originally banded together in a violent plot to kill their husbands. But this is mere conjecture.

Also conjecture is how exactly the divinators working that night managed to give a name to the anomaly of Sofia Kuzmin's situation. What's known is that as she tripped—it happened before the part of the song when the letters come in—she took one of the ropes down with her. It slipped from the spinners' hands, launching high into the air despite its considerable heft, and tumbled in a coiled heap on the ground—a heap that loosened over a matter of seconds into a shape that should not have been unfamiliar to the oft-illegible Sofia.

It was the same shape the orange peel had formed twice in the office of the Dancing Rind divinator. The same shape Sofia's breath takes when it exits her throat at an extraordinary ninety-eight kilometers per hour, mid-coughing fit.

It is not a shape that correlates with any letter of our modern alphabet.

But it is nearly identical to one specific letter in the alphabet of the dead.

The only other information we can ascertain regarding Sofia Kuzmin's final night in Dushagorod is that one of the Ropes divinators must have recognized the letter and warned her what it meant: that Sofia's soulmate resided in the realm of the dead, and that she would suffer mightily if the wrong people were to find out. As for the witch who told Sofia this, her crimes will be addressed. Deadtongue is among the 137 prohibited languages outlined in Bely and Company's series of motions toward a stronger, largely monolingual Dushagorod.

The last thing we know: Sofia has not been seen in Dushagorod since.

Sofia, Sofia, Sofia, Sofia, Sofia.

Come out, come out, wherever you are.

Our deep-dimpled, shifty-eyed sweetheart. Our dear carrot-darling. Did you know that dimples occur when the skin is pulled downward and attaches too closely to the underlying tissue? We can sort that for you, So-So. We can lift that skin right up.

No, no. We jest, of course! We only want to ensure that Sofia does not go to great lengths to meet her deceased paramour, her off-limits *amour morte*. If it could be guaranteed that she would perish first herself, then no problem. No problem! No need to worry a minute about it. But we're told there are, apparently, ways to accomplish it: to converse with the dead in their language of rotting r's and melodic vowels—yes, melodic like the right hand of an organ's funeral hymn—while keeping one foot firmly in the world of the living. To hear from the dead all they have to tell, and then return to spread their lies about us.

You understand, then, don't you? You are one of the reasonable ones? There is a great deal in Dushagorod's history that would be better for only the dead and never the living to believe. We have been careful to strike such events from our respected learning centers' educational curricula, and from the shelves of every amply supplied library and rare books store. We have been diligent in extracting them from the wagging tongues of citizens prone to gossip. Accounts of these events are comically exaggerated at best, treasonous at worst, and they have no place in citizens' collective memory.

But the dead, we cannot teach them. We cannot correct their innocent misunderstandings. We cannot control how wild and colorful their interpretations might be. Even farther beyond the reaches of our good-hearted supervision and guidance than the rogues in the anarchist districts, they're inclined to speak, let's say, too *cavalierly*. This is a benefit of supervision, is it not? And consequences. They encourage one to be more thoughtful, more *precise* with the words that one chooses. With one's shocking descriptions of what it is one thinks one has witnessed.

Now, we would be the last to minimize the impact that the war and subsequent military operations and restabilization initiatives had on the resilient citizens of Dushagorod. Any loss of life is tragic, and that Dushagorodian officials exercised immense strategic savvy, that they made impossible decisions in order to keep that loss of life to an absolute minimum, to what was utterly *unavoidable*—all this matters not to you. And what of the crop production? The well-observed fact that most plants grow taller and lusher from blood-soaked soil? Of course, this matters not to you.

Sofia: You must remember that in the first-rate city of Dushagorod, your heart's desire is not hard to find. You will meet him yet at the rotating bar or the amateur rowing club, or at that charming neojazz cafe. Forget the connection they've promised you in that dangerous realm beyond ours. We will find a nice match for you. We will make it our top priority. All future appointments free of charge. All your sisters' appointments free of charge! Your family needn't lose sleep over love or clothing or counterfeit oranges or bread on the table ever again. And you, you needn't lose sleep, either. Over your sisters' matching slender necks, the way they glow swan-white in the moonlight that streams into the bedroom you once shared. How near to the surface the vein there thrums. Remarkable, isn't it? How close our blood already is to being outside of our bodies.

This is merely a small selection of the things you needn't be distressed about.

Excuse your past divinators their clumsy, half-hearted readings. Remember that to err is human; to forgive is *divine*.

You have every tool at your disposal, and you'll find your true soulmate soon enough.

Do you hear us, Sofia Kuzmin? Have we ever spoken falsely? And if we had, would you remember?

Come home to us, darling. We'll take good care of you.

BUNNY EARS

Hannah's first impression of Colden Hills Music Camp is that, for a place with "hills" and "music" right in the name, it's too flat and way, way too quiet, and the one thing she initially thinks must be a weird rustic flute propped up against the side of the welcome cabin turns out to be just an extra-straight stick some termites bored holes through.

Not that the band-camp angle was the main selling point for Hannah's parents when they signed her up for a week of luxury bunk-bed living on the other side of the state line. The main draw for them was that Colden Hills was the most affordable sleepaway camp they could find that wasn't already booked up for the summer. The main draw for Hannah was that, well, she'd just turned thirteen, and thirteen-year-olds don't have much say in anything. Never mind that she's a compact, bony thirteen, too easy to shuffle into the back seat of a car and nudge back out, suitcase in hand, onto a dirt path two hours and half a dozen unfamiliar highway signs later.

She's not *not* into music, she guesses. She likes to listen to a song then listen to it again while looking at Lyrics Genius online, committing it to memory. The faster the words bullet at her, the better. Just, her mom gets these huge, world-ending headaches, so the screechy, halting practice of beginners, at least at their house, was never an option. Besides, Hannah's always reminding herself, a life that revolves around something called a *spit valve*? That's not a life she's going to try overhard to pursue.

The choir route, also a no-go. Her body, this body—she catches her reflection in the welcome cabin window: round face, straight lines everywhere but the pronounced slouch of her back under her stained ringer T-shirt, proof she was raised by computers. The quasi-mullet she gave herself that's somehow party-nowhere. No, her body isn't exactly what anyone would call an *instrument*.

Hannah reaches the front of the check-in line, casts her eyes back to see if the family's trusty hatchback, Miles Stubaru, is maybe parked in the shade of one of the thick-limbed trees lining the path out of here, its headlights watchful and protective, waiting to make sure she gets through this part safe. But, no. Should've known better. Can't fault good ol' Miles, of course, but ever since her parents made the announcement about Golden Hills last week, it's seemed like this moment couldn't come soon enough.

"Happy Sunday!" The woman behind the desk grins her welcome-committee grin, somehow directing every one of her teeth at Hannah while keeping her eyes glued to the clipboard in front of her, ready to scroll. "Name, please?"

"Uh, it's Hannah. Hannah Gessen."

The woman is sunburnt everywhere Hannah can see, evidence that this is week two of the camp's six weeks of summer programming: plenty of time to forget your tube of sunscreen back at the cabin, not enough time for the resulting burn to relax into a tan. But the splotchy pink's really bringing out the blue in her eyes, and Hannah notices something pungent and vegetal—after-sun lotion, probably—folding into what she's come to understand as Colden Hills' signature aromatic profile: basically, hey, what if we took a thousand of those little pine-shaped air fresheners, dropped them into a vat of rotten eggs, then stirred in the stringiest, mustiest algae east of Lake Erie?

"Gessen, Gessen . . . There you are." The woman draws a tinier-than-tiny checkmark partway down the page, then slits her eyes up at Hannah. "So you're the one who's gonna keep us *guessin'* this week, huh?"

Hannah's a blank whiteboard, an incomplete pop quiz, one of those TI-84 calculators that's like, *Error! Error!*

The woman laughs, reaches across the desk and gives Hannah's shoulder a squeeze.

"Never mind, hon. Mnemonic device. Close to a hundred kids coming in every week, I gotta do something to keep you all straight." She winks. "You'll be in Dogwood, senior girls' cabin. Take a right, cross the field, go past the flagpole, follow the signs. Real buggy out there by the water. Hope you brought spray. If not, you can pick some up at commissary tomorrow."

Hannah takes one of those memory-palace journeys, trying to recall if the bug spray did in fact make it into her bag. Surely her mom remembered. They *loved* Hannah. They being mosquitoes. They being her parents too, obviously—Hannah does that quick mental revision, feeling embarrassed and kind of guilty that her own thoughts require so much red pen.

The bugs, though. Everywhere she goes, they're drawn to her. Like she's the sun in their solar system, except they'll gladly break orbit to come hurtling toward her, totally mess up her surface terrain.

Hannah can feel the line of kids pressing in on her, and the cabin walls too, like they've collectively decided that she's taken up enough of the welcome committee's time—she doesn't have to go home but she can't stay here.

"Here, take a name tag." The woman behind the desk hands Hannah one of those red-and-white hello-my-name-is numbers. "You'll want it for the ice cream social. Happy belated, by the way. You just squeaked by. Almost had to put you in Sycamore with the little kids." She says it with fate-worse-than-death commiseration, like she, like anyone, can understand how Hannah must be feeling right now.

The woman—Hannah notices she isn't wearing a name tag herself—waves briskly in the direction of the door, finished with this particular item on the new-camper conveyor belt. Hannah turns, the stupid wheels of her stupid suitcase catching on the cabin's uneven floorboards as she goes.

When Hannah looks back, no surprise: sunburnt lady's *Happy Sunday*-ing someone new.

••••

WELCOME NIGHT

The ice cream social is . . . better named than the camp itself, Hannah has to admit, in that there *is* ice cream. Upwards of three flavors, plus rainbow sprinkles and trail mix—*trail mix*? Why trail mix?—and a bag of mini chocolate chips that got bumped at one point and half-emptied onto the floor. No whipped cream because that's just asking for germy lips-on-nozzle action and the counselors aren't trying to start a mono outbreak night one.

And people *are* being social, or social adjacent, standing in tight little circles, asking about hometowns, showing off summer vacation battle scars and shiny, white, new-this-season sneakers. Not that Hannah's an authority on what does and doesn't constitute friendly behavior. She's always joked in her own head that she wasn't socialized properly, being an only child with distracted parents and all.

Meaning the calculator-error-message thing all over again. She's supposed to have about a hundred things in common with her fellow campers, right, just by virtue of being in exactly the same place and roughly the same age? But then they look at her and every word she's ever known goes riding off into the sunset of her brain, like, *see ya, cowpoke, you're on your own.*

So here's Hannah, standing between two groups but not really committing to either, holding her arms to her sides hoping nobody notices her ballooning sweat stains, thinking massively boneheaded thoughts like: what if strawberry is just vanilla with a bad case of sunburn?

Colonel Hannah in the mess hall with the strawberry cone. The offense? Social suicide.

Finally, one of the guy counselors rolls in a TV and puts Hannah out of her misery. He doesn't look much older than some of the campers, but his name tag is way more official: printed, laminated, and hooked to a lanyard with the words MAPLE and TOMMY. Rows of fold-out chairs appear out of nowhere and the campers settle in to watch a history-of-Golden-Hills video, then a nature safety video, then a video about the camp's values and codes of conduct. There's a split-second mention of one of the founders, a local piano prodigy who went on to play the Caribbean cruise circuit, but no more is said about the camp's name and what Hannah can expect in relation to it.

Different counselors step forward to tag-team orientation, intricate tag-in handshakes and everything, so Hannah gets the sense they come back to work here year after year. Meaning it can't be *that* bad, can it? They talk about the camp's layout, kind of a backwards question mark wrapped around a small, man-made lake. The top curve, the wraparound part, is home to all the cabins, the middle part is the straight path through the flagpole field, and the dot at the bottom is this map's *you are here*—all the communal buildings, including the mess hall, commissary, and infirmary, along with the storage sheds and maintenance cabin.

Weekly schedule, themed days, mail delivery, swim tests, free time, wake-up calls, flag-raising duty, sportsmanlike behavior, *un*sportsmanlike behavior, lavatory etiquette, close-toed shoes, lights out, seconds at mealtimes, the sendoff dance at week's end—and pretty soon whatever ice cream's left has turned to fly-catcher soup and the little kids are doing all-out gotta-go dances in their seats. Hannah's sure the dam's about to give when DOGWOOD, ERIN—the senior girls' counselor and last in the line of perky undergrads—takes the stage.

"Okay, final order of business," Erin says, half weightily, half reluctantly, like she's not the *real* fun police, she's just covering for them temporarily, got it? "Prank wars." A wave of sniggers rolls through the room. "You love 'em, we love 'em. We know they're part of the culture here at Colden Hills. Just keep it good-natured, yeah? Use your best judgment. Treat others the way you want to be treated. You've heard it all before, right?" she asks herself, then answers before anybody else can: "Right."

The girls around Hannah roll their eyes and groan, while the boys farther afield begin to whisper excitedly, and no one anywhere makes any indication that they've taken Erin's words to heart. But her job wasn't to hammer anything in—more to stick it loosely to the wall with already-used Scotch tape and pray it doesn't come loose later—so as far as she's concerned, her work here is done. The counselors gather up their groups, gently rousing the youngest kids from the wreckage of their sugar crashes, and march everybody to their cabins for the night.

Because it's past dark now, the counselors issue a buddy system, and because there's fifteen in Dogwood and Hannah's social-anxiety-induced language loss includes the words for "Hey, wanna—?" she ends up being the odd girl out.

No worries. Erin guardian-angels forward, blonde braids closer to clown-wig orange in the incandescent lights outside the mess hall. She links her arm up with Hannah's and flashes a magnanimous smile. How pathetic, Hannah thinks, to be chosen by the one person who has no preference whatsoever.

They walk slowly, two by two, through the field toward the bend of the lake to Dogwood, every sprinkle Hannah ate whittling to a splinter in her gut. Somewhere around the flagpole, she disconnects from Erin, pretending she needs her arm—her right arm in particular—to . . . what? Push back the cuticles on her left hand? Adjust the strap of her admittedly unnecessary training bra? If Erin notices, or cares, she doesn't show it.

Whatever, Hannah doesn't need a buddy system. She's been just fine all this time on her own.

••••

MUSIC MONDAY

So that the camp's founder doesn't come back from whatever cruise-ship lounge he's currently playing to rain his disappointment down upon the staff for completely losing the plot, every week at Golden Hills Music Camp starts with Music Monday.

There are, again, no instruments to speak of. Not a cheapo cigar-box guitar or elementary-school recorder in sight. Instead, Music Monday consists of what feels like fairly nondescript programming: a breakfast of rubbery eggs, followed by a somber flag-raising ceremony made more somber when one of the flag's corners touches the ground and one kid on duty has to break the news to the other kid on duty that now they're for sure both going to hell, followed by generalized running around in the vague pattern of a kickball game, followed by a lunch of rubbery meat. The thematic element comes in the afternoon, in the form of an all-camp bonfire meant to give campers an introduction to Colden Hills' time-honored singalongs.

A big fire in broad daylight is a puzzling choice, especially brutal since the morning's swim tests had to be postponed after the county issued an algal bloom warning for all lakes in the area. It's eighty-five and climbing, but at least the smoke seems to be keeping the mosquitoes at bay. All day, Hannah has been minding her own business, pretending to be absorbed in the act of thumbing X's over the red bites that keep popping up all over her calves and arms. The second an "X" fades, she uses her nail to dig a new one in its place, like she's the groundskeeper of some disgusting, probably disease-ridden garden, and don't even bother trying to get her attention—this is a full-time job.

The campers are halfway through their third cheerful rendition of "Herman the Worm," a song about a worm who eats all the other worms in his family. Hannah's mouthing the words—because we're in puberty-voice-crack territory here and she's not *crazy*—when she hears it.

A girl from her cabin, Sammy, she thinks, and a boy she recognizes from Maple, looks like a Dean—but then again, doesn't every boy you're sure won't give you the time of day kind of look like a Dean? They're in the row in front of her, leaning over a stack of Polaroids and snickering.

Hannah's heart drops. She put herself to bed early last night, not because she was tired but because, with how narrow the mattresses are, how treacherously high the top bunks, that's the one time a person can be seen alone around here and guaranteed no one's going to feel sorry for them. When did she cross over from not at all sleepy to dead-to-the-whole-world asleep? She has a dim recollection of white flashes saturating the air like sheet lightning, wonders what photos she's drooling in the background of, or worse—are her cabinmates this cruel?—maybe even the subject of. Bad enough that she's a loner, worse that she's the baby of the cabin.

She tries scooching her seat forward before remembering what they're all sitting on are these colossal oak logs that aren't going to budge a bit.

Not-Dean throws her a bone when he lifts one of the Polaroids, waving it in Sammy's delicately freckled, neatly lip-glossed face.

It's a candid, or pretending to be. In it, two girls are sitting cross-legged on the cabin floor, one painting the other's nails a glittery aquamarine blue. Josie? Leia? Everyone'd ripped off their name tag as soon as they'd come in from the ice cream social, like it was the uncoolest of uncool accessories. Sammy's in the corner of the shot, clearly having snuck in at the last moment, the only one acknowledging the camera is there. She's standing behind the manicure recipient, holding two fingers behind the girl's head in a "V" that makes Hannah think of *peace, maaan*, or the shape of one of those old-school TV antennae.

Hannah scans the rest of the photo, breathes a sigh of relief when she's a no-show after all. But then:

"You never hear of the 'bunny-ear kids'?" Not-Dean's voice is scolding, a little too sharp to be strictly flirtatious.

Sammy scrunches her nose, shakes her head no. Hannah feels herself getting pulled in. She wants so desperately to be part of their too-old-for-camp-songs club that verse seven or eight of "Herman the Worm," in which Herman cannibalizes his grandpa, begins sinking into the murky background.

Not-Dean clears his throat, preparing to step into the role of veteran camper showing a newbie the ways of the world.

He asks, "Remember the camp map? Backwards question mark, all that?" Sammy nods. "Well, a question mark doesn't just stand on its own. It has to come *after* something. So picture the sentence that came before it. Any sentence, but it's gotta be a question." More nodding—Sammy's what Hannah's school guidance counselor would call an *active listener*.

After a minute: "So? What's your sentence?"

"My sentence?" Sammy looks surprised.

"Yeah. I told you to picture it. What'd you pick?"

She smirks, charmed by her instructor's more interactive style of lecture. "Okay, my sentence is . . . 'Does Ben really think I believe in ghost stories?'"

Ah, so it's Ben then.

Not-Dean-but-Ben takes his turn in the back-and-forth smirk battle Sammy started. "Good. Now picture that whole sentence backwards, and picture where that last 'S' is, to the right of the question mark. At the top of that 'S' is the town cemetery—you might've passed it on your drive in. And at the very middle of that 'S' is where the bunny-ear kids live."

"Cemetery, *spooooky*." Sammy twirls her long, fine hair, which Hannah's come to suspect is surrounded by some magical humidity-repelling force field. "So what's the deal with the bunny-ear kids? Are they a competing camp or something? Do they actually have a working archery range or is it just as janky as ours?"

"Not exactly." Either Ben's eyes go fully dark, or he just tilts his head so from where Hannah's sitting the camp-fire's no longer reflected in them. Yeah, that's the better, safer explanation. "Legend has it they're kids who went to Colden Hills, just like us, a long, long time ago. Only, the unthinkable happened. Their parents never picked them up when camp was over, so they just had to . . . stick around."

Sammy scoffs. "Like the counselors wouldn't call home for them."

"The counselors *did* call home, but no one picked up, or someone did pick up but still never showed. Anyway, eventually, the counselors leave too. They have whole lives outside of Colden Hills they gotta get back to."

Hannah feels the skin on the back of her neck prickle, suddenly feels exactly zero of all the degrees Fahrenheit it is out here.

Sammy goes on, deliberately, "But whoever's in charge wouldn't just leave kids here. That's, like, *child abuse*, isn't it?"

Ben shrugs. "Counselors are only a year or two older than you and me, remember. Tommy just graduated. They got their last paychecks, and a promise from some distracted mom or deadbeat dad or Richie Rich type's nanny that they were on their way. There was still plenty of food in the mess hall fridges. It wouldn't all go bad for another week."

In some far less important corner of Hannah's universe, the rest of the campers have moved onto "Boom Chicka Boom." They're doing the janitor verse—I said a *broom* sweep-a broom, I said a *broom* sweep-a broom—and every emphasized word feels like heavy footfalls coming closer.

"Then what?" Sammy's starting to look uncomfortable.

"Then . . . no one came. And the kids basically went feral. Or a nicer way to say it is, their families abandoned them, so they moved out to the middle of the 'S'—remember your 'S'?—and they made their own kind of family. And it would be nice like that, very after-school special, except for the way they got their name, the bunny-ear kids."

"Which is?"

"Well, they needed a *uniform*. A way of saying they were all in this together, and they weren't like anyone else. And also that, living out in the woods like they were, they were part kid but also part beast. At first they used stuff they found lying around, like a pair of branches or two big leaves. They'd put them in that 'V' shape and braid them

107

into their hair, or weave them in with moss or whatever. But then they'd been out there so long, they wanted something more . . . permanent. Something that felt more like an extension of their bodies."

"So?"

"So . . . next came animals, little ones that weren't too hard to catch. Lizard tails, squirrel tails were a big one. They'd never use *actual* rabbit ears. That'd be, like, sacrilege, the rabbit being their mascot and all. Only, since that stuff's a lot heavier than branches, they had to find a different way to attach it. They started sewing it right onto their scalps."

By now, Ben's story has drawn a small crowd. He pauses and chews his lip, all rehearsed, like, wait, there's more, but I'm not sure my gentle audience can take it. When no one objects, he plunges on:

"Then, when that wasn't enough, well. I told you the cemetery was nearby."

Sammy's got scared-horse eyes Hannah recognizes from Animal Planet and a look around her chin like she might throw up. "And?"

"*And?*" He waves the Polaroid again. "See for yourself. What makes better bunny ears than two human fingers? Not like the corpses were going to miss them. The kids must've figured so long as they put the dirt back where they found it, no one would be the wiser."

"Why bunny ears?" It's the girl sitting on the other side of Sammy now—called MJ, Hannah knows for sure, because she's wearing a gold chain with a cursive MJ pendant, very considerate. MJ's playing the skeptic, but the rest of the listeners, whose names aren't so conveniently spelled out, look rapt. Hannah makes a silent vow that tomorrow she'll try out the sunburnt lady's mnemonic devices, do a better job being a member of society.

"A promise," Ben says. "A threat, I guess you could call it. Because what do bunnies do best?"

"I don't know," Sammy barely breathes.

MJ steps in: "They multiply."

Ben nods, satisfied with his students' progress. "They multiply. That, and what your counselor said yesterday is true. Golden Hills has a long, proud history of epic prank wars. And throwing up the bunny ears, though obviously mild compared to the stuff we do now, was kind of a big deal back then. The prank that started it all."

"So what?" MJ's visibly annoyed. "When we do it, we're, what, summoning them? You said yourself they chose to *leave* camp. I know it's a shithole"—she gestures broadly toward the lake they can't swim in, the craft room without air-conditioning, the sheds full of rusting and hole-filled gear—"but at least there's shelter. If they left then, why would they come back now?"

Here the Maple boy next to Ben, who's been eavesdropping and can't contain himself any longer—or else it's his cue to join the act, be the grand finale—leans toward the girls with two fingers of his right hand in bunny-ears formation. Only he's got them pressed together, curving them then extending them, and he's making exaggerated alien suction noises with his mouth that make Hannah think of a rain boot being pulled out of deep mud.

"Perv!" Sammy gasps, pushing him away, and Hannah feels her face get red-hot, though she's not 100 percent sure why. At that very moment, the girl to Hannah's left—definitely not Dogwood, Sycamore probably—elbows her and asks her if she's got any gum, and Hannah has to say no, because her parents have yet to deposit money into her commissary bank, which means she's stuck with whatever she gets in mess hall, no special treats like freezer pops or Big Red.

The Sycamore girl turns away, disinterested, and when Hannah rotates back to the conversation in front of her, it's devolved into playful shoves and speculation about the end-of-week dance. Hannah drops her eyes, feeling all the way thirteen.

Midway through the counselor-led call-and-response of "The Green Grass Grew All Around," she answers MJ's question from earlier in her head. Why *would* the bunny-ear kids come back?

Because bunnies never stop multiplying.

And cemeteries only have so many bodies.

••••

TRAILBLAZING TUESDAY

Over a breakfast of soggy waffle sticks and twelve carefully portioned-out grapes, Hannah learns that the bunny-ear kids aren't the only thing you've got to worry about at Colden Hills. No, what you've got to live in absolute fear of, bite your nails to the quick about, sweat through your flimsy mattress each night over, is the very real possibility of getting your period underwear run up the flagpole.

One of the veteran Dogwood girls, Olivia, is regaling the table with stories of prank wars past. Olivia looks like she could be Miss New Jersey Teen U.S.A.: *Baywatch*-high terry-cloth shorts, some actual topography beneath her tank top. For a mnemonic device, Hannah pictures her doing a practiced pageant wave with a green olive stuck on each fingertip.

"Shaving cream s'mores is a classic," the older girl says. "It'll probably be one of the Maple guys, since if anyone's shaving, it's them. They'll offer to make you a s'mores, super gentleman-like, and when you're not looking they'll squirt Gillette between the graham cracker and chocolate where the marshmallow should go."

The girls wrinkle their noses and laugh, but Hannah can tell every one of them's thinking the same thing: that they're in the clear, that they'd never let it happen to *them*.

"Hot sauce in your Kool-Aid, same idea," Olivia goes on, "except anyone can do it. Maple likes to recruit the Oak boys to do their dirty work, but the really little kids are mostly spared. Leave them to their innocence and boondoggles, you know? Hm, what else . . ." She stirs a butter knife through her miniature tub of syrup. "Vaseline on the toilet seat, saran wrap over the toilet seat, mud in the toilet. Sensing a theme? Those ones they mostly do to each other."

A chorus of *ew-yuck*'s and *no-way*'s chimes around the table. Hannah eyeballs her carton of chocolate milk like who even knows what's in there anymore?

"If you see a bunch of ants on your bed, don't freak out. They're probably just chocolate sprinkles. Same goes with ants *in* your bed. That'll be the old sand-in-sleeping-bag gag. Anyway, whatever it is, try to play it cool. Don't give them the satisfaction. As soon as they see it bothers you, you're an easy target."

The underwear up the flagpole, though? Whole different animal. Unless you have your name embroidered on the front, that one's not a personal attack. No one can *really* know they're yours. Even the guys pulling the prank probably don't have a clue. They wait to raid your cabin when no one's home—assignments are posted on the mess-hall window, so it's public knowledge who's on wakeup-call duty or trash duty any given day—then they rummage around from suitcase to suitcase, duffel bag to duffel bag, till they find a pair incriminating enough. Sometimes the underwear itself is mortifying: plain, loose, and grannyish. Or, on the other side of things, too sleazy: what you'd categorize as *panties*, whale tale and rhinestones, trying too hard.

More often than not, though, it's the stain they're on the lookout for. A fresh, red Rorschach, big enough to be noticed from thirty feet down.

It's not a personal attack: it's an attack on all girlkind. It's the reason the Dogwood counselors started keeping a discreet stash of pads and tampons in the topmost compartment of the tackle box beside the cabin door, and the reason the Maple counselors started dropping the "boys will be boys" line into every conversation, so it's nice and worn-in when they have to deploy it big-time. It's the reason if a girl bleeds through her underwear, she'll wear that same pair the rest of the week, like swallowing a key or sewing a secret love letter into your jacket's lining. Because the boys can't find it if it's on her person.

For all forty-five minutes of morning free time that day, Hannah's bent over her suitcase reevaluating every life choice she's ever made that's led her to her current selection.

It's all shoved in the top mesh compartment, all the same: white cotton with scalloped edges, a dainty 3D rosebud at the hem. The kind somebody's mom spots at the department store, thinks "How *sweet*," and buys in packs of seven. One pair is lightly stained, yes—an old, persistent stain dozens of washes haven't been able to get out—and Hannah flashes back to the excruciating conversation from around that time, about keeping a monthly calendar and being a *young lady now*. Another pair, though unmarked, has a clump of thread unraveling around the leg. She shoves both into the bottom of her pillowcase and exhales for the first time this century.

It's a relief to disappear them like that, actually. Like all the girly things that Hannah's not really about.

Her tomboyishness has always been a sore subject with her parents. They can't go a week without making some comment about her short, usually unbrushed hair, her preference for baggy cargo pants from the boys' section over tight, bedazzled skinny jeans. Her absolutely lethal allergy to the Frankensteined monstrosity that is *skorts*. You'd think they'd be used to it by year thirteen, or at least grateful she's not stretching their already near-translucent budget with non-necessities like makeup and butterfly clips.

The trouble, though, is they wanted a girl. She knows that. Not just a girl but a *real* girl, a *girl* girl, like Olivia or Sammy. Barbies, manicures, giggly sleepovers, the works. And having girl*friends* was part of that, obviously. She'd already gotten the message, but then, a couple months ago, something her parents said made it painfully clear.

She was on an expedition to the bathroom, having bravely left her post at the family's shared computer midgame, when she passed her parents' bedroom, the door cracked slightly open.

Yearbooks had been distributed at school that day. Hannah's mom was sitting on the bed, Hannah's copy open on her lap.

"Am I going crazy?" her mom was saying. "Look at this." She jabbed her finger at one of the pages. "Really *look*. I thought when we first got her yearbook photos, sure, there was a resemblance. Obviously, they're related. *Were*, whatever. But now, seeing her next to all these other kids—I don't know. It's like she's his identical twin, a whole decade later."

Hannah's dad spoke slowly, like tiptoeing through the minefield this absolutely was. "You don't think it's just . . . the hair? The clothes? That, plus her being a late bloomer?

It doesn't help that she's almost the same age as he was when, you know." He paused, cleared his throat of anything coming up that he knew better than to say. Then, softly: "We've talked about this. She's her own person, Patricia."

Hannah's mom slumped her shoulders. "I don't know, Dave. *Is* she? It's getting worse the older she gets. And it's not just the superficial stuff. It's the way she . . . holds a fork? Have you noticed? With her whole fist? It's like being with his ghost."

There's no shortage of anxieties for the seventh grader willing to entertain them, and with all of them tugging constantly at her attention, either Hannah hasn't thought much about that night since, or she's relegated her thoughts about it to such a deep, subconscious crevice of her brain that her conscious self would need spelunking gear and a cave map to ever find them.

But something about the prospect of a week spent boarded up with fifteen strangers is reminding her how much of her time outside of Golden Hills she spends alone. Never mind that by now her cabinmates don't seem like strangers to one another. Hannah's seen friendship bracelets exchanged, and three of them even made matching tie-dyed shirts during crafts block.

Worse, Ben's story about the bunny-ear kids is glomming onto that loneliness in the weirdest way. Yesterday, when he told it, Hannah figured those kids' parents never picked them up because they were *bad kids*. Like, keying teachers' cars, lawn-mowering over the neighbor's foot, accidentally-on-purpose lighting the classroom gerbil on fire level bad. Spiteful and uncontrollable, so that their parents had no choice, after countless attempts to improve the situation, but to send the kids to Colden Hills and make it a lifelong sentence.

Bad kids don't get to go home. That's the only explanation.

Except now, Hannah's wondering: How much would it *really* take for your parents to want to be rid of you?

Hannah's an only child, yes, has accepted this as a main, load-bearing pillar of her identity. It's the thing she's been longer than she's been almost anything else. But what if what she *really* is, to her parents anyway, is the kid sister who, with every passing year, reminds them more and more of their dead son?

Hannah can't shake these thoughts, and Trailblazing Tuesday passes in a haze of water-balloon tag, sloppy joes, and doubt.

She's still caught up in them when mail from home gets passed out in the mess hall after lunch, and of course she comes up zilch. *Of course*, because it's only Tuesday, *duh*, and for her to receive a letter today her parents would have had to send it the day they dropped her off. And it's okay if they didn't miss her that soon.

But will they miss her eventually? Will they miss her, like, ever?

She's still lost in those thoughts when she gets lost, *actually* lost, during the day's main event: a sunset hike around the still-potentially-contaminated lake. She gets separated from the group just as the sun sinks below the tree line, the sky around it a radioactive orange. She's only lost for four or five minutes before Erin, with her rescue searchlight of bright blonde hair, appears in the small clearing. Not even long enough to qualify as lost, really—more like briefly lagging behind.

But it's enough time to feel ashamed, because how does one even get lost on a trail around a lake? Just follow the sounds of the burping toads, the water. Hannah's not the spoiled kind of only child, the kind swaddled from birth in parental attention, so she's got to be the self-sufficient kind. The kind that's straight-A's at being alone.

And she *is* that—though maybe dock a few points off her final grade for failing this particular wilderness test.

Only, if she lets herself admit it, she's always had this nagging feeling, ever since she was little. That, somehow, she wasn't *meant* to be doing this whole thing solo.

She feels it again that night, by the lake. The presence of someone or something there with her. It scurries into the brush as Erin approaches, making too much contact with just about everything to be something as careful as a deer, as small as a possum or raccoon.

It's only four or five minutes, but it's enough time for Hannah to be outed too. Like if an apex predator is out casing the joint and homes in on one undersized gazelle that's separated from the rest of the herd—and not just separated, but *pitiful*, crying like a little baby about it?

The predator's going to remember that, right?

Going to mentally tag, for the real hunt, this sniveling, susceptible animal.

••••

WET & WILD WEDNESDAY

Halfway through the week, because there is some justice in this world after all, the county health officials clear Golden Lake for recreational activities.

And because, scratch that, on second thought, there's absolutely *no* justice in this world *whatsoever*, Hannah gets her period.

It's days early according to the little calendar she half keeps track of in the back of one of her spiral notebooks. Probably summoned it with the underwear-under-the-pillow thing. She remembers the spells the kids at school cast to make snow days happen: wearing their pajamas inside-out, flushing ice cubes down the toilet, sticking white crayons in the freezer overnight. More often than not, one of these works, the odds in eastern Pennsylvania being pretty good to begin with. The other popular one is sleeping with a spoon under your pillow, which suggests to Hannah that this spot is home to, like, some *tear* in the fabric of the universe through which magic, the good and bad kind, can pass through. She should've known better than to tamper with it.

She finds reinforcements in her bag, thank God. Turns out her mom *did* remember to pack those. Spared a very public trip to the cabin tackle box, Hannah feels an overwhelming swell of appreciation for her parents, like how could she ever have questioned their love for her?

She readies herself in a bathroom stall, gets dressed there too, while the rest of the girls are stripping down, helping each other with straps and tags back at the cabin. In her one-piece swimsuit off the sales rack, Hannah's the most flat-chested she's ever been. The vertical stripes pull her proportions in all the wrong directions, so she comes out looking more surfboard than teenage girl.

She wraps her towel around her chest protectively and, in the solitude of the girls' lav, takes a series of deep, measured breaths. It's all wet rust and mildewed shower curtains, but for this moment, it's her turf and hers alone. She thinks, okay, brain, time out, huddle up, and kicks off a pep talk about how it's already Wednesday and so the game plan is this: get through swim tests, get through field day, get through whatever else Colden Hills throws at her, then go home and never see or talk to or even think about any of these people ever again. Hands in, go team. She's reminding her brain that one week can't last *forever*— unless you're the bunny-ear kids, of course—when the lavatory door swings open and the Dogwood girls flood in.

"Did you bring one?" one of them asks, giddy. "It's okay if you didn't. You can borrow mine. My sister does it *all* the time."

It's Sammy, MJ, Yume, and Jeanette—Hannah rattles through her mnemonics for each—in a swirl of colorful tankinis and cacophonous flip-flops. They're walking like on some top-secret mission, and through the gap in the stall door, Hannah soon sees why. A bright pink razor blossoms from each girl's palm, and MJ, bringing up the rear, produces a can of vanilla-scented Skintimate. Hannah recognizes the swooshy banner and yellow-to-orange gradient from the pharmacy aisle, though her mom would never buy it, insists her dad's shaving cream is cheaper and does the job fine.

One by one, like dancers in a can-can line, the girls throw a leg up on the rim of a sink and begin to shave.

There's no mirror in Hannah's stall but she's the exact color of canned beets and she knows it. She's acutely aware of her legs now, virgin ground untouched by any blade, and especially the part below the knee, which, because the fates are cruel like that, happens to be both the hairiest part *and* the only part visible beneath the bottom edge of the bathroom stall. She tries to console herself: from this angle, if she squints, it looks more like dried mud, like she slid during a rainy game of kickball and it smudged and hardened. But then she reaches down and, yep, that's hair all right.

She swears she can feel a burning pressure *inside* her follicles, like the hair is growing faster than her body can handle. Like animal fur, the thought occurs to her. Or another tick on her parents' looks-just-like-her-brother checklist.

Even if her legs didn't suddenly feel like they were on fire, Hannah wouldn't be able to stay there for long. Bathroom math is a delicate thing: if you're in and out too quick, gross, guess you didn't wash your hands—if you take too much time, gross for different reasons. She might not be the type people naturally pay attention to, but the girls are bound to notice her eventually.

Hannah briefly considers evaporating her corporeal form through the rafters and letting the clouds over

Colden Hills absorb her, like in the precipitation cycle she learned about in science class last year. In the end, though, she settles for dropping the towel to her waist, twisting the lock, making a big show of using the soap dispenser, and walking briskly out the door.

The morning's swim test is uneventful on the one hand, excruciating on the other. Uneventful because she's a competent enough swimmer that breaststroking to the buoys and back is the most hilarious joke. Excruciating because, after that, she's got to sit on the shore with the other kids, air-drying like so much forgotten laundry and waiting, and this is when all her usual symptoms come out in full force.

The thing about her current circumstances, though, is it's impossible to know whether her pounding headache and bone-deep exhaustion really *are* Aunt Flo rudely knocking, or dehydration setting in after all the sun she's gotten, or night after night of the restless sleep of bunk beds, or severe computer withdrawal, or whatever disease she's probably contracted from the algae bloom or mosquitoes by now. Or just, you know, the consequences of racking her brain so hard about why she still hasn't gotten a letter, still hasn't had money deposited in her commissary account, and how her parents' hushed conversation months ago might factor into all that.

If she'd gotten to be part of that conversation, she might've said: How can they think they're the only ones who miss him, the only ones who've been deprived? At least they got to *know* him—for thirteen whole years, too. How dare they keep depriving her of him now? She must've been a toddler when he died, doesn't remember. How different would their relationship be if they let her in?

How different would her *life* have been if she'd had that kind of companion?

She feels that tug again, like someone's waiting in the bushes. Watching her or watching *over* her, she can't be sure.

Anyway, your brain's like any other part of your body: you work it too hard, it's going to get tired. That explains the cottonheadedness Hannah feels when Erin calls for cabin check-in, and the spots that swarm her vision when she stands up too fast to go.

It's obvious enough that Erin gives Hannah a pass to skip the rest of the "wet and wild" portion of the day—there are canoes being hauled down from the storage sheds, pool noodles that look like a rottweiler got to them—with orders to head straight to the infirmary. There's only one lifeguard on duty, Counselor Tommy, to ninety-something kids: a ratio that doesn't exactly support knowingly letting a sick one go off into the water, wobbly and weak.

The infirmary is just across from the mess hall and indistinguishable from the other cabins, except for the relative lack of windows and the white banner with a red cross nailed to the front door. Inside is the woman from the welcome desk, her bare shoulders more healthy-human-skin-colored now, less surface of Mars. She greets Hannah with an enthusiastic:

"Gessen!"

It makes Hannah feel nice and liquid, grateful to be remembered.

The woman's wearing a name tag now. HELLO MY NAME IS: Tess.

Tess has Hannah lie down on a cot and thrusts an extra-large water bottle at her, saying by the time Hannah walks out of here, this had gosh darn better be empty. She sticks a thermometer under Hannah's tongue, a stethoscope on her back above where her swimsuit scoops. She brings out one of those blood-pressure cuffs that feel like an anaconda hug and lets Hannah choose which arm. There's only one other kid in the infirmary, and he's at the end of the row of cots, facing the wall, so for the first time in a long time Hannah feels like she can *relax*. Tess gives her a couple of Tylenol and soon everything starts to lag, until finally, mercifully, Hannah powers down.

When she wakes, the other kid is gone.

"Seems like you were in sore need of a nap, kiddo," Tess says. "Clean bill of health, though. Except all those bites. They're really going after you, huh? Even with bug spray?"

Hannah scratches her arm absently and nods. Leaves out the bit about not being able to buy spray, due to her parents having completely forgotten about her, wanting her to be dead to them to match her actually dead brother.

Tess frowns sympathetically. "I'll give you some calamine lotion. Unlucky about these ones"—she taps two fingers against the center top of her forehead—"but apply this a couple times a day and I bet they'll be gone in time for Friday's dance."

Hannah reaches for her own forehead and, true enough, finds two enormous welts forming there, about an inch and a half apart, almost but not quite hidden by the first baby wisps of her hairline.

Where a smarter girl would've grown bangs to conceal exactly this kind of problem.

And where—Hannah feels a bolt of lightning course through her—bunny ears would sprout from.

••••

THRILLING THURSDAY

The plan was zip-lining and ropes-coursing, trust falls off wooden platforms built around the trunks of trees, but the sky cracked open in the early morning and after that the rain wouldn't let up.

Hannah has a hard time imagining that a ropes course built by the Colden Hills people could be any definition of safe, but Counselor Tommy insists their setup—located past the cabins, all the way at the tippy-top of the question mark—is *totally legit*. Not that she'll find out now. While the field takes on the consistency of a massive chocolate milkshake, everyone's relegated to the mess hall, where the counselors announce the backup plan: campers in two groups, one in charge of making decorations for tomor-row's dance, the other putting together an impromptu talent show.

Hannah feels a knife twist in her gut at the mention of a talent show, decides to blame it on a particularly nasty cramp. She practically teleports to the side of the room designated for Team Decorators, passing kids mur-mur-bragging about their knack for celebrity impressions, or how fast they can do the clapping cup game. The only semi-talent Hannah can think of is her knowledge of all the cheat codes in *The Sims*, and rattling those off hardly counts as entertainment. No way she's going to get up and perform in front of everybody on a *good* day—and that's when she doesn't have a pair of Mount Vesuviuses protruding from her forehead.

The bites got worse overnight, even with Hannah smothering the calamine on twice as often as prescribed, in addition to her usual ritual of thumbnail X's. From afar, they could be mistaken for your run-of-the-mill period zits. She can't decide if that's better or worse than the other versions of the truth: that mosquitoes really *are* obsessed with her, or that—she thinks this part more quietly—the bunny-ear kids are.

Either way, she's not looking forward to the fresh swarm of bloodsuckers bound to be drawn out by the rain. Everyone else is talking about how they're just so glad the heat broke, and puddle jumping's for babies but all right sometimes, and maybe there'll be a nice rainbow when the clouds clear.

"Double rainbow!" Ben's friend, the one Sammy accused of being a pervert, is shouting from the other side of the room. Hannah recognizes the video he's quoting—it's been making the rounds since the beginning of the year. "Double rainbow! *Whoa-ho-ho!* All the way across the sky!" He's made for the talent-show group, all bugged-out eyes and hands sweeping in exaggerated arcs so the kids nearest him have to duck to avoid getting whacked in the face. The real surprise is Ben's not with him, is instead leaning over a rectangular table near Hannah, casually flipping through the construction paper the counselors laid out.

Hannah doesn't give herself time to think. Just fluffs her hair over the bumps best she can, picks up a bottle of puffy paint—because you don't show up at someone else's house empty-handed—and marches over.

"Hey." So far, so good. Then, so she doesn't have to hear him admit he has no earthly idea who she is: "I'm Hannah. Dogwood."

Ben looks up, brows raised. "Hey, Hannah. I'm Ben. Maple." He takes the puffy paint she's holding out to him for some reason. "You decorating too?"

"Yeah," she says. "I don't really have a talent."

He laughs. "Me neither. Unless we can hold a food-eating contest. My mom's always complaining about how much me and my brothers eat. Except judging by what I've seen here"—he tips his chin toward the kitchen—"Colden Hills is clearly under some tight rations."

Hannah perks up. "You have brothers?"

"Two. Older. One's in his second year at Penn. You?"

Hannah's pause is too long for so straightforward a question. "No," she says finally. "Nope. Only child."

"Lucky." Ben grins. "When you've got brothers, and you can't be the biggest or oldest, you gotta be the quickest. That's why I can eat so fast. Fifteen years of training. If you don't get to the food first and get your fill, they'll finish it off before you can take a bite."

He sits down and starts cutting the construction paper into many-colored strips. At a neighboring table, kids are making construction-paper stars and hand turkeys, while counselors blow up balloons and try to fashion them into the beginnings of an arch. Every so often, one breathes deep into a balloon and emerges with a squeaky *Alvin and the Chipmunks* voice, sending the other counselors into a giggling fit. At one point, there's a muffled shriek, followed by high-fives and laughter—Hannah assumes someone's hot-sauce-in-the-Kool-Aid trick went off without a hitch.

When Ben has accumulated a pile of strips, he slides them across to Hannah, along with a half-used glue stick, the kind that goes on purple but dries clear. "Well, fellow child laborer? These decorations aren't going to make themselves."

Hannah feels the morning's tater tots churning inside her, but forces a smile, starts on her part of the paper-chain factory line. Five loops in, she says, "You're good at scary stories too."

"Hm?" Ben's back on strip-cutting duty.

"Oh, I just mean—" she stumbles. "For the talent show. If you did want to do something. Storytelling's a good talent." When the crease in his forehead doesn't smooth out, she explains, "I heard you, Monday. At the bonfire?"

"Oh-hh. Right. The *bunny-ear kids*." Hannah's taken aback by the mocking note in his voice, his sideways smirk, so different from the solemn posture he maintained in front of Sammy, MJ, and the others.

"You don't believe it? That they haunt Colden Hills?" She works to keep her tone neutral. What made perfect sense in the confines of her head feels ridiculous flapping out there in the open air between them.

"*Believe* it?" Ben pushes another two or three dozen strips toward her side of the table, then puts his scissors down and sighs. "Listen, don't tell your friends this. I know rainy days are pretty much tailor-made for ghost stories, but I'm not really in the mood. I've been waiting for the ropes course all week."

Hannah's brain catches on the word "friends"—Ben files her and the other Dogwood girls into the same category? Boys really *are* stupid. She misses something about Ben's family being very into *American Ninja Warrior*, then unsticks herself in time to hear:

"The bunny-ear kids aren't even special to Colden Hills. My brother told me about them, and he never went here. He heard the story during initiation week at his fraternity. And then my *other* brother said he'd already heard it too, a long time ago. At soccer camp. *Youth* soccer camp."

"It's been around that long?"

He nods. "*All* around. A true urban legend."

Just then, three Maple boys swoop down on their table and, without acknowledging Hannah at all, drag Ben to the corner of the mess hall, where a group of them are drawing crime-scene chalk outlines of their bodies on butcher paper, over-the-top blood splatter and everything.

Hannah finishes the paper chains in silence, mulling over what Ben said.

So the bunny-ear kids are just another Colden Hills prank, a rinse-and-repeat from the same book of pranks and tall tales used by all guys everywhere? Another thing for the Maple boys to laugh about while tallying hits in their cabin at the end of the night? Talking about "You should've seen her *face*, man," while Counselor Tommy listens in, pretending to be reproachful when he's actually totally proud?

But also: Ben said the story went beyond Colden Hills. That didn't mean it didn't *start* here. People take stories and retell them all the time, right? Could be something horrible happened at Penn, and at that youth soccer camp, and people just pinned it on the bunny-ear kids because it feels good to give the villain a name, feels even better to give it a face you recognize. It's not the bunny-ear kids' fault, really, but once those people decided their evil thing looked like the bunny-ear kids, it couldn't look like anything else ever again.

Just like her parents' idea that Hannah is identical to her long-gone brother, more and more so every day. How's she supposed to undo that? What good would all the frilly dresses and acrylic nails in the world be, when they've already made their minds up about her? Worse, when it's two against one?

If they don't pick her up Saturday, it won't even be the first time. And she *was* wearing a frilly dress, *and* nail polish, at least one of the times they forgot. A piano recital, at the upscale performing arts center downtown that's approximately 90 percent mahogany. She was nine. It was her first and only recital before her mom broke the news that, sorry, Han, it's not good for the headaches, and we're never going to be able to afford a piano, so how would you practice anyway? Hannah would've come to the same conclusion soon enough. Her unsteady "Twinkle Twinkle" was pathetic compared to the Bachs and Beethovens of the other students her age. She figured her fingers were just made for a different set of keys.

Similar memories slideshow through her mind, unwelcome. Hannah waiting in the school parking lot on a day she had to stay late for a makeup history test, the janitors already gone, the sun low and lazy. Hannah waiting outside the Barnes and Noble five hours after her mom had dropped her off, two hours after their agreed-upon meeting time. At one point, a young employee of the Starbucks inside peeked his head out, asked if there was someone he could call. When Hannah shook her head no thanks, he brought her out a pity Frappuccino.

How long have her parents been trying to get rid of her? How has she been so blind to it?

Their town's too small for them to just desert a kid in public, firehouse style. But sleepaway camp in a different state, paid for with years of holiday checks from a super rich, super religious great-aunt both her parents tacitly hate—basically blood money? They must've really wanted this if they were willing to endure the smug look Aunt Lucy'll be wearing the next time she visits, having reviewed her bank statements, knowing they finally cashed in.

Even yesterday, Hannah was *so* sick. Surely Tess or Erin or *someone* called her parents, gave them the full run-down of her symptoms, and still they didn't come get her? Didn't even ring up the camp landline, apparently, to check how she was feeling today.

How sick, how hurt, how scared would she have to be? Or are humans one of those species that are more likely to abandon their young the weaker they get?

"*Ow!*" The pain starts at her fingertips and seismic-waves up the length of her arm, ricocheting like it wants to be sure to hit every single nerve ending on the way. Jeanette, of the silky-smooth Skintimate brigade, is standing next to Hannah, a hammer in one hand, the other hand clasped over her mouth.

"*Shit*," Jeanette whispers. "I'm sorry. I'm supposed to wear glasses, but, you know . . ." She waves a hand over her face in a gesture that says: *but the moneymaker, you understand.*

Hannah doubles over, clutching the pointer and middle fingers of her right hand like the more layers of defense she can put up between them and Bone Crusher Jeanette, the better. They pulse violently against her left palm, blood protesting.

Hannah and a few others were hanging paper chains along the back wall. It was a simple tape job most of the way, but then there was this weird squishy felt section, like the surface of a pool table, that Hannah assumed was for acoustics. Dampening the chatter of all those kids so, what, the local squirrel population doesn't call in a noise complaint? Between that and the almost-windowless infirmary and the sloped cabin floors campers joke you can practically ski down, it's clear whoever architected this place was a madman. Anyway, Jeanette got the okay from one of the counselors to put nails into the felt wall, so long as she tried to find the holes already there from past years, and Hannah was holding the loop of the paper chain real straight when—

Erin jogs over with a first-aid kit and a bag of frozen stir-fry. Jeanette shrinks into the background to, Hannah can only assume, locate her next victim. Ben sits up from where he was lying on the butcher paper, getting the dead-body treatment, but most of the other kids barely glance in her direction before going back to their alternative rainy-day fun.

Hannah musters up the strength to look at her finger-nails, which are purpling already.

••••

FIELD GAME FRIDAY

By seven the next morning, they've fallen off. The skin underneath is so deeply bruised it looks like Hannah tried to draw on a pair of replacement nails in black Sharpie, and in some places it's peeling, as if air, to it, is some corrosive substance. Hannah stays in bed as long as she can, listening to Dogwood wake up around her, the girls babbling about lemon juice highlights and the unlucky puke green of their pinnies and what they're wearing to tonight's dance. Yume's snapping pictures with her Polaroid, trying to use up her film before the week's end, and Olivia's speculating that the Maple boys have been sneaking into the office and stealing her mail, *again, just like last year*, which is especially annoying because she's expecting a letter from her real-life boyfriend, and not just any letter, but the R-rated kind.

Hannah feels safe and out of sight in her top bunk, the same way a cow stuck in a tree is safe from rescue because people, sane people, don't think to look up there. Then Jeanette, AKA Thor, God of Thunder, peers over the edge of the mattress, hands up to show that Hannah can rest easy: she's not wielding her mighty hammer this time.

"Morning," Jeanette says tentatively. "How are you feeling?"

Hannah can tell Erin put her up to this. She does a quick scan of the cabin and, yep, there's their counselor, one eye on the day bag she's packing and the other on this lousy reconciliation-in-progress.

"I'm okay," Hannah lies, tucking her arm under the covers because she doesn't feel like trying to explain why the nails fell off so quickly, or why the bruising has started to wrap around the tops and backs of the fingers, and on the pointer finger is spreading down toward the second knuckle. "Just tired, is all. Didn't get much sleep."

That part isn't a lie. Last night was worse than the others, and the others weren't anything to write home about—not that writing home is an option. Hannah can't be sure if she slept at all, if the shapes she saw in the night were dreams or waking thoughts run rampant or hallucinations or real, flesh-and-blood things.

There was a menagerie of beasts: hawks, elephants, jackals, goats, bear cubs, and, yes, rabbits too. Only when the cameraman in her mind panned out, she saw they were harmless: mere shadow puppets pinned to a wall. Another zoom out brought the sick realization that it wasn't *one* hand making each animal, like she expected, but *many*. Because each hand was missing between one and three fingers, all of them had to work together, combining what they had left to make sure the shadow animal got all its parts.

Branches, two by two, floated up to her, clumps of hair, skin, and viscera dangling from the ends. Some invisible drummer flicked them against her arms and legs, up and down and up and down like her body was a xylophone, like she was nothing but some children's plaything.

When she woke, or didn't *wake* but continued *being* awake, now with other awake people around her for perspective, she found the scratches on her forearms, as if all night she'd been running through an endless forest, whipped by every tree limb from here to Vermont.

Hannah always prided herself on being a sound sleeper, despite her parents' monologues about all the screen time being bad for her REM. She was sure a certain time of night was none of her business.

Turns out she was right.

"I'm okay," she says again to Jeanette, who looks plenty convinced already—she did what she came here to do, no need to put a debate team together about it.

"Good," the other girl says, patting the sheet over Hannah's hand with a little too much enthusiasm. Hannah winces. "Get ready then, huh? We're leaving for field day any second."

••••

Hannah's forced to play red rover and partner relay, but Erin lets her sit out for the more rough-and-tumble games. While the other campers do crack the whip, throwing their bodies back and forth till they send the kid at the end of the line flying, Hannah sits under a tree and, with her good hand, picks at the dark hairs sticking out from the bottom of her pants leg. The bites on her forehead throb urgently. They rise half an inch off her face now, and are hot to the touch, and in the rhythm of their throbbing she hears an order.

Once everyone is good and warmed up, the counselors set out orange cones and sun-faded bean bags for the field day special: capture the flag.

It's what the athletic kids have been waiting for, because they get to show off: sprint into enemy territory, outrun any defenders, and return to their side a hero. It's what the peaceful kids, the dreamers, have been waiting for too, because all they have to do is get tagged into another team's jail and they get to sit in the soft, wet grass watching the passing clouds morph into jellyfish and profiles of famous figures till a teammate rudely appears to liberate them.

And it's what Hannah's been waiting for, because in four-way capture the flag there's so much commotion that it's easy enough for one measly thirteen-year-old to slip away unnoticed.

Especially because Erin's in charge of the Dogwood girls. And is Hannah that, strictly speaking, anymore? Was she ever? A *girl*?

She runs the length of the straight part of the question mark, then partway around the backwards curve until she arrives at Dogwood. She never was much of a runner outside of Golden Hills, was always out of breath by the third lap of the fitness test's timed mile. But something's come over her now, some raw animal instinct. Wildebeest run a marathon every day—isn't that what her science teacher said during their unit on Serengeti ecosystems? They don't get tired, and even if they do, they don't stop running. Because? Better tired than dead.

Besides, being a crummy runner, that's in her other life. Everybody knows camp's something else: a second chance, a place to try to answer all of your first life's *what if*'s.

Without its campers, Dogwood is a *sight*. Gone are the girls' overlapping voices, the warring aromas of mineral sunscreen and coconut-scented tanning oil, the flashes of Yume's camera, bright enough to blind—and without them, Hannah can finally *focus*. She feels her senses sharpen. Her ears prick at the rustle of a leaf against wood clear across the cabin, the almost imperceptible plucking of a spider in her web. Hannah's nose twitches when the breeze comes through the open windows, carrying the expected medley: air freshener, the rotten-egg smell she's learned is caused by a not-necessarily-dangerous amount of sulfur in the water, petrichor from yesterday's rain. And something else. Something . . . living. Warm and sour; salt, onions, and copper. It reminds her of the time they went to Newport for her mom's birthday and Hannah got stuck in the tiny hotel elevator for forty minutes, with six other people, and her parents weren't two of them—they had gone down to continental breakfast while she was still asleep. She never could forget the suffocating stench of those bodies, twice her height, pressing in on her, and the way her parents looked sitting at the table together after, splitting a cherry Danish. Like a complete thought on their own.

Like they were better off without her. Wouldn't have noticed if she'd stayed in that elevator the rest of her life.

These are the nuances, of course, the scents she can pick up if she concentrates her new powers hard enough. The dominant smell in the room is that of sirloin steak left to spoil in the sun. She glances down at her pointer and middle fingers, black past the first and largest knuckle, and inflamed, like something inside is hot, too hot, and trying desperately to shrug the skin off.

With her left hand, Hannah flips the metal clasp on the tackle box, accordions out the compartments, and reaches past the complete Carefree and Always product lines to what she came here for: the needle-nose pliers, the spool of fishing line. She looks around for a ziplock and, coming up short, thinks to grab the old pair of period underwear she thrust into her pillowcase earlier in the week. No need to be picky: she just needs something to wrap them in when she's done, so they don't get lost before she has time to reattach them. And the underwear's already ruined—what's a little more gore? This way they'll be perfect when the Maple boys find them, a shoo-in to get pulled up the flagpole for the final prank before everyone goes home. Yeah, once she's through with them, no other bloody underwear'll stand a chance. She'll save every Dogwood girl the humiliation. So who's the hero *now*?

Hannah won't be there to see it, but that's okay: it was never for her. She understands that now. There are places where she doesn't belong.

And places where she *does*. Ben said it himself: after their parents abandoned them, the bunny-ear kids made their *own* kind of family. The thing about the old gag is this: you can't give *yourself* bunny ears in a photo—you need someone beside you. It's a given. You need a friend. It takes at least two.

She'll bring them this sacrifice as a talisman of her devotion, proof she's willing to destroy a part of herself to become something new. But she can't do it all alone. Because of the placement on her head, and the fact that she'll be missing two pretty crucial fingers, she'll need their help to sew them on. Her first pair of bunny ears. Well, her first real, *official* pair, not counting the bites. Which were just the kids' way of tapping her, she's guessing, selecting her for their team.

Again Hannah, supposed only child, feels that profound ache at her side, like there's meant to be more there—something or someone—that all her life has been absent.

What will *she* make of what she's got left?

When she leaves Dogwood, she's not so much running as hopping, tracing the curve of the backwards question mark till she finds the clearing where she got not-lost on Trailblazing Tuesday—where she first felt their nervous eyes upon her. If she's visualizing Ben's map correctly, it's the closest she's come to the home of the bunny-ear kids, and the closest to Colden Hills they're willing to meet her. If there wasn't a state park in the way, she'd be able to see straight through to the town cemetery, where, legend has it, they like to go foraging.

This near the lake, the top layers of ground are still dense, squelching mud. Hannah scoops up a handful and rubs it on her face, her arms, her stained ringer tee, and her still-tender mosquito bites are instantly soothed by the cool paste. Good, she thinks, smothering the mud all over her flat chest, all through her short hair, up and down her prickly legs. *Good.* The more she looks like them, like the brown rabbits she's seen bounding across the field, the less she'll look like a thirteen-year-old boy. One boy in particular, permanently thirteen.

Once she's caked in the stuff, she unspools the fishing line and wraps it around her two dead-black fingers— once, twice, three times—and *pulls.* Better for everyone this way. Her parents won't have to deal with the constant reminder of the son they once had, taking up space in their house, eating their frozen pancakes. They can move on. And she can move on too: spare herself the wicked wait as each camper, one by one, lugs their duffel to the car, waving behind them, then ahead, at the driver's-side door already opening, at the somebody stepping out, arms outstretched to greet them, welcome them *home*. She'll have a new home now. All the brothers she's ever wanted.

Important to get a clean, straight line, so they sit on top of her head just right. Once the fishing line breaks through the skin, she'll use the pliers to crack the bone, and when it's time to position them, she'll bend the tip of one of the fingers forward, like what happens with bunnies' ears sometimes: one all cutesy-flopsy, the other on high alert.

And while everyone else is dancing tonight, in the mess hall she helped decorate in her previous life, she'll have her own dance. One of those Southern-style debutante balls she learned about in social studies. Except not because she's a *young lady* now. No, a *proper* coming out.

She pulls and pulls, and there's a brilliant supernova pain, like a million camera flashes going off inside her bloodstream, when the plastic finally cuts through. Through the static that starts at the brink of her sight and pinwheels inward, she sees them. They're here. They've kept their promise.

They've come to pick her up.

At first, it's just the one boy. He has a mop of wavy dark hair, a style that was en route to Mullet Town but took an unfortunate detour along the way. His bunny ears are the leg of a red fox, the broken wing of a songbird Hannah can't identify. He's smiling with every one of his rotten teeth. He's holding, for some reason, a *fork*, with his whole fist—and as he approaches, Hannah understands.

The fishing line isn't going to be enough. He's going to help her pry them off.

Like big brothers, for little sisters, do.

He uses his thumbs to bend the fork's tines so they're far enough apart, and it looks so easy, like either he's wild-animal strong or the metal's especially cheap and pliable, something straight out of Colden Hills' mess hall, bought in bulk. Taking Hannah's hand in his own, he positions the fork so the tines are on either side of the exposed bone. He leans forward until his forehead is touching her forehead. They inhale together, exhale together. She can detect the meat on his breath.

Then he tightens his grip on the fork's handle, and he twists.

The crack is too quiet for the volume of the pain. In Hannah's brain, acres of great oaks are simultaneously falling, an immense glacier is calving in two. Outside of it, though, it sounds more like a twig snapping—and there's her first bunny ear glistening, like a fat worm, in her new brother's palm.

The crack is quiet, but the kids have good ears, the best around, and it draws them out from where they've been hiding in the thick undergrowth. They appear, hesitantly: boys and girls her age, and younger, and older, infinitely older, with bunny ears made of stacked mushroom caps, pinecones, banana slugs, deer antlers, beaver tails, skunk tails, fisher cat tails, whole snakes with tent stakes driven through to keep them a straight line.

The crack is quiet, but the scream is not. Hannah

registers it as coming from the far side of the lake: a barn owl or a bobcat or even a mountain lion, maybe, if New Jersey's got those. She isn't sure. Wasn't really paying attention during the first night's nature safety video, and now everything's getting hazy, like she's looking at the world through the frosted glass at the dentist's office, and her head's light, and her throat's gone raw.

There's a commotion in the trees on the camp side of the clearing, and suddenly Olivia and Yume burst through. Yume's swatting at invisible bugs and Olivia's pulling burs from her terry-cloth shorts. Erin must've sent them when she realized Hannah was missing, the *pair* of them because the buddy system is pretty much a Golden Hills code. When they look up and see the crowd, the blood, the strange boy threading a large, curved needle, Yume makes a sound like she's choking on commissary pudding and sprints back from where she came.

Only Olivia stays. Because she's a veteran; she's been around. She's weathered every prank this camp has spit at her over the years, and nothing surprises her anymore. She's hardened and, stupidly, she's unafraid.

She whistles low, almost impressed. "Elaborate. Did Oak put you guys up to this?"

Hannah's new brother turns to inspect the intruder and Hannah does the same, so their eyes move as one over Olivia's ballerina-long limbs, her neatly lacquered fingernails. Then he turns back to Hannah and nods once. Hannah nods back, understanding.

She reaches Olivia in a single bound, pliers and fishing line poised. Bounds so fast that the other girl's half-amused smile doesn't have time to work itself into a yelp.

Some of the kids wear clothing so tattered it's impossible to recognize it as clothing—as opposed to long strips of bark, as opposed to flayed skin—much less distinguish its era. Most wear nothing. They hold each other tight at the elbows, refusing to stray or separate. Some are missing fingers and even whole hands. When Hannah begins to forage Olivia for parts, the bunny-ear kids help, pushing their shrieking prey into the dirt.

In the grateful, kaleidoscopic stupor that overcomes Hannah at the end, she thinks: God, how *beautiful*.

They're distinct from one another, each their *own person*, yet part of the same imperishable herd. Made whole despite what they're missing.

Beautiful, and whole, yes.

And multiplying.

SEVEN DAYS IN THE KINGDOM
OF THE MISPLACER

On my first day in the Kingdom of the Misplacer, the king explains the nuances of Brecht's alienation effect. He positions it opposite the Aristotelian effect, once the dominant school of thought in theatrical theory. The king went to a prestigious acting academy once upon a time, in a walled-off city known for its liars.

The alienation effect presents familiar situations in unfamiliar ways, so the audience, at a distance, can more critically observe them. The Aristotelian effect prioritizes self-identification, so the audience, relating closely, feels a profound emotional connection. The king misplaces his memory of this exact conversation, which we've had already, word for word, a dozen times this morning.

On my second day in the Kingdom of the Misplacer, the king loses his house keys, has to dig up the spare he keeps under the flowerpot on the far side of the shark-filled moat. He loses his wallet, his designer transition lenses, the noise-canceling headphones with the gaming mic. The king is, in general, quite forgetful. Says men have a hundred things on their minds, and kings are men to the hundredth power.

I nod, practicing self-identification. Already I want to be closer to him.

On the third day, the king misplaces my luggage. I'm meant to leave that night, the third night, in accordance with centuries-old wisdom about the proper durations of things, but without my luggage, I'm forced to stay. I search the whole castle, but only halfheartedly, while the king explains the nuances of his principles. He is: For lively debate but against war. For building a diverse and equitable crown's counsel. For the installation of a heated bidet in every single hut in the realm.

The king is one of those progressive types. He is also, it turns out, a relationship anarchist. On my fourth day, he explains the ethics of non-monogamy. On the claw-foot divan in his antechamber, he misplaces his own wife's name.

If the king misses the queen, sleeping alone in her gilded, tapestried wing, I wouldn't know it. It must have been an extraordinary academy. The king is a talented actor.

On my fifth day, he says now that I'll be sticking around, I can call him Tsar if I prefer—or Emperor, Jeonha, Pyeha? If that is, like, more in keeping with the ethnic customs of my people? I can tell he means it kindly. Part of being with a loss-prone king is finding things and offering them graciously to him. On the fifth day, his headphones under the skirts of a lesser duchess. On the sixth, the benefit of the doubt.

Mere subjects can't hope to identify with their ruler, but they should strive to be more like him. He who is the nearest soul in all the world, they say, to Heavenly God.

By my seventh day in the kingdom, I'm a loyal misplacer, having lost whatever is deemed most essential: my wits, my head, my cool, my virtue, my grip, my bearings, my fool way home.

LAST LETTER FIRST

Duri begins. "Category is . . ."

On their way to the Nova satellite colony, three hundred miles from home in Earth's low orbit, Duri and Margosha play a game to pass the time. It's an old game, one their society has largely forgotten—more sophisticated amusements are invented every day. This one is simple, boring even. It's a relic of another age, before flashy graphics cards and total-immersion headsets, before massively multiplayer networks, before the proliferation of wires and screens.

Of course, these old things have a way of coming back to us when we need them.

Margosha waits for the boredom the game promised to set in. Before launch, the pilot announced that their projected travel time was just over four days—they got a suboptimal slot, screwed up the matching trajectories, and now there was a debris field to circumnavigate—but she's certain she and Duri have been playing for months, years, decades, centuries. She longs to be bored, for that one feeling to drape a heavy blanket over her other feelings. Namely anticipation. Namely terror. Namely dread.

Drape a heavy blanket over them and kiss them goodnight. Tell them to hush, go to sleep now.

"Animals," Margosha offers, and there's that stupid shake in her voice. She thinks about blaming it on the airbus's rocky suspension, a way to save face in front of her new seatmate. But the truth is Margosha didn't know a thing about suspension systems back on Earth—or alternators, transmissions, carburetors, or spark plugs. She was always setting off her auto shop's dumbass-city-girl detector too, always getting taken for a ride. The techs could tell just by looking at her: another dumbass city girl, who'd barely passed her driving test and got a used clunker just to go with her cousins, twice a year, to the wineries upstate.

So up here in the cramped passenger airbus, everything more alien than it's ever been, feels like a bad time to start playing mechanic.

Besides, it's actually been pretty smooth since they broke through the stratosphere.

"Good one," Duri says. "Animals, animals . . ." She chews the ends of her straight black hair, considering her next move, and when she pulls her mouth away, the strands are a bright, lemony yellow. Duri must have one of those color-changing mods, Margosha realizes, the new moisture-activated one from J&J. The ads light up the buildings on her way to work each morning. Mousy-haired girls transformed while running through sprinklers. Greying women whose hair goes all psychedelic Roy G. Biv jamboree when they're dancing in the rain.

From her seat in the middle-back of the bus, Margosha can peer up and down the aisle and see plenty of mods. A few seats up, a blue tail with fat spikes flops over the armrest, before its owner, a kid who can't be out of her teens yet, reaches over and tucks it back under her seatbelt. There's an older woman sitting catty-corner with a hyper-realistic tattoo of a wolf on her shoulder, curled in a tight ball with its tail warming its snout. Suddenly, the wolf stands and stretches, seesaw-style—creaking forwards, backwards, forwards again—then begins stalking the pair of tattooed swallows flitting on the back of the woman's neck.

Margosha expects Duri to take the hint and say wolf, but instead, for her first word, Duri picks:

"Aardvark."

"*Aardvark?* They have many of those on the farm?"

"Oh, shut up." Duri laughs. "Just play."

Even though they've been breathing the same dry, circulated air since they boarded the airbus and wound up, by chance of fate, sitting side by side—and even though Margosha has told Duri a safe, small amount about her life in the city and Duri has told Margosha a safe, small amount about her own life in the rural reaches of the opposite coast—Margosha didn't think the two of them were close enough to say a thing like "shut up" to each other. But then, time loses meaning when you're hurtling through black sky, without sunrises and sunsets to hold onto. And Duri has a rough-edged familiarity about her that Margosha isn't used to. A matter-of-factness that she imagines Duri perfected during a lifetime on her farm, surrounded by Earth's more gentle creatures. Creatures

who want only what they need—food, water, sleep, sun—
and who have no talent for doublespeak, no interest in
controlling others.

"Aardvark. Ends in 'K' . . ." Slowly, Margosha traces
the long seam of the seat in front of her, then brightens.
"Easy. Kangaroo."

"Kangaroo, huh?" Duri smirks. "They have many of
those in the city?"

Margosha thinks to stick her tongue out but at the last
second pulls back. She wanted the mod that lets you program your taste buds to perceive certain flavors no matter
what it is you're actually eating: hazelnut liqueur truffles
instead of fried bologna, beluga caviar instead of a bowl
of Lucky Charms. But it's not cheap, and even with the
funding the airbus organizers managed to raise, she had
to pour all her savings into this trip.

And surely she and Duri aren't stick-your-tongue-out
friends quite yet.

So they play. It's kangaroo-ends-in-"O," then octopus;
salamander-ends-in-"R," then rabbit. Tarantula, "A."
Antelope, "E." Earthworm, "M," then macaw, walrus,
snake. At one point, Margosha gets stumped by her seventh "O" of the game until Duri cough-hints "ocelot."
At another, Duri begs Margosha to go with the full word,
"rhinoceros," instead of the shortened "rhino," because
those are the rules, or if they're not, they should be—and
besides, Duri already gave Margosha "ocelot" and she's
pretty sure there aren't any other animals that start with
"O" on their entire godforsaken planet—and Margosha,

ever the good sport, relents. Late in the game, stalling on a tricky "G," Duri suggests they should get extra points for animals that are extinct, and Margosha agrees that's not a bad idea.

Except maybe the last thing they need right now is to introduce further complications. Or to start obsessing over all the things they'll never see again.

Come to think of it, nobody's keeping track of points in the first place. Because this game is about the grace of distraction. And if winning means the end of the game, they don't want it.

To win, to really win, would be to get to Nova in one piece. To get back to Earth with what they came for—*that'd* be a miracle.

••••

"Category is . . ."

It's Duri's turn to choose. "We've done all the usual ones. How about . . . body parts? And before you ask, yes, *human* body parts."

Margosha grins. "Mods or no mods?"

Duri scans what she can of Margosha above the tray table her seatmate dropped over her lap hours ago, and on which she's since accumulated half a dozen empty bags of airbus-brand trail mix. Margosha has strawberry-blonde hair, buzzed short on one side. Lips so chapped they're cracked at the corners, close to bleeding—it's that dry in here—and two eyes the color of honey. No mods that Duri can make out. Not so much as a sharpened canine or a heart-shaped freckle, not even a harmless little piercing, grandma stuff. Strange, Duri thinks. There must be gills hiding beneath the hood of that baggy sweatshirt. She figured someone from one of the cities would have had just about everything done.

"Let's go old-school," Duri says. "No mods. The natural stuff."

"All right," Margosha starts. "Nose."

"Hm. Ends in 'E,' so . . . ears."

"Skin."

"Nail."

"Liver."

Normally, on one of her long drives into town, or to drop meat or eggs off at a neighbor's, Duri would look out of the window of her rumbling pickup and think. She did some of her best thinking gazing out at that dusty, low-shrub country, blinking up at the wisps of clouds as they crawled lazily by. Now she's sitting in the window seat of a patched-together airbus without windows, chewing her nails down to the quick. She turns instinctively to her left, but finds only a thick plate of sheet metal there.

"Rib," she manages.

She should be focusing on body parts, on calling to mind the anatomy worksheets she had to fill out back in high school, but instead she's still thinking about the last round. About animals. Duri's always been more of an animal person than a person person, and when she stares at the rivets bordering the metal plate, they remind her of the blank, wet eyes of cows.

Which makes her think of an old tradition her grandfather told her about, back when he owned the farm, when the fields were still productive and Duri was shorter than the stalks. It was once customary, he told her, for newlyweds to spend their wedding night in the barn, clutching at each other in the stalls, the hay giving their skin new texture. It was said their lust would improve the animals' fertility. Like making babies was something contagious.

And she said, "Grandpa, *ew*," and her grandfather chuckled in his quiet way, scrambled her not-yet-modded hair.

Which makes her think of something her mother once told her: after the last of the animals go, it won't be long till the barns fall. One depends on the other. It's the barns that give the animals shelter, and it's the heat of the animals—spreading out to the walls, the ceilings and foundations—that keeps the barns standing upright. Without that heat, the materials will grow cold and brittle and start to cave in on themselves. Soon, her mother warned her, hundreds of thousands of acres on Earth will be nothing but fields of crumpled brown carcasses, and the barns keeled over with them.

And in the fields, among the dead: all the children playing.

The airbus's temperature control is out, and the little hairs on Duri's arms are bright, lemony yellow with sweat. She tries to do superpower mind games on the rivets, bore through them to open windows to whatever lies beyond. She has this nagging feeling that this will all be over soon, and this is her one real shot to see the stars up close. Even though she gets that's not how space works.

Whatever body part Margosha says next, Duri doesn't register it. Instead, she tells Margosha about the barns in her part of the world, how they freeze to death when they're no longer useful, done being vessels for something warm inside.

Margosha is lost in thought, making a crinkly tower of the bags on her tray. Finally she says, "It's funny. In the city, when the buildings are empty—it doesn't happen often. There's always somebody up late, or up early. Always a few of those yellow squares still on. But when it does happen, when you do manage to find a building that's totally barren, it's the opposite of what you're saying. It's almost better for being empty. It feels somehow . . ." She grasps at the air in front of her, as if trying to pluck the right words from it. "Somehow . . ."

"More alive," Duri says, and her heart trills, imagining.

••••

They take a break to play hangman, then tic-tac-toe. One of the airbus organizers seated at the front walks down the aisle to distribute another round of water bottles and trail mix. She hands Margosha and Duri a pair of small, thin blankets folded in squares, and Margosha is momentarily overwhelmed by the kindness, the enormous risk the organizers must be taking in championing such a controversial project. Duri rolls the blanket up, shoves it in the space between her cheek and the airbus's metal wall, and falls asleep.

Margosha eavesdrops on a conversation between the spiky-tailed girl and her seatmate about how stars are born when great clouds of dust and gas called nebulas collapse. The spiky-tailed girl's neighbor asks something like, isn't it kind of beautiful how the nebula sacrifices itself to bring the star into existence? And the spiky-tailed girl, young and bitter, retorts: isn't it pathetic how the nebula has no choice? Margosha pictures her own body disintegrating, swirling pain on a colossal scale, until nothing but the hot core at its center remains. She knows someone somewhere would call that beautiful, take pictures of it, print them in textbooks.

The wolf tattoo on the catty-corner woman's shoulder, having caught one of the swallows, pins it proudly between its paws and howls.

Its owner, surprising Margosha, promptly howls back, and it's clear that they do this all the time, their duet ringing, comfortable and pure of tone. Duri wakes, and gradually the rest of the passengers on the airbus join in the howl. Margosha thinks she sees one of the organizers smile.

The howling reminds Margosha of the youth sleepaway camp her parents sent her to every summer upstate, and the songs the campers sang while marching to their assigned cabins or to the flagpole at sunup, obedient little soldiers in training: calls-and-responses and songs in the round.

And the green grass grew all around.

It reminds Duri of the stories passed down to her, of real soldiers with their own versions of the chorus howl. Energetic voices in unison as the Humvee rolled into battle. Crystalline hymns as the dead were lowered into the ground, their babies being born the very same minute, bathed in light for the first time on the other side of the world. One in and one out, the census numbers perfectly level, indifferent.

Ghosts shout-singing, *I'll be a ranger the rest of my life.*

When the racket dies down, Duri begins. "Category is . . ."

Margosha wishes the howl wasn't over. She liked the way she and Duri sounded shifting in and out of harmony. She wonders if, maybe, wanting the same thing, being willing to travel three hundred miles through Earth's atmosphere to get it, means they do understand each other well enough after all. They understand each other better than anybody, don't they? Gone chasing the things they're not allowed to have.

"Regrets?" Margosha ventures cautiously.

The women have grown accustomed to speaking in code. The game is just another way of doing that. Even though the airbus organizers promised them that they can speak freely now, that they're safe here—from the moment the hatch went down to the moment they touch down on Earth again, they're *safe here*—it's an awfully hard habit to break.

Margosha is on a performing athlete visa, Duri is on a temporary agricultural worker visa, and one is every bit as bogus as the other. The organizers who secured the project's funding also arranged travel documents for every passenger aboard, and by all appearances they knew what they were doing. The airbus flies steadily despite being a bit in disrepair, and the documents look pretty convincing. When the uniformed men at the departure dock reviewed them, they gave clipped, perfunctory nods before waving the travelers on to the next stages: vitals check, extensive cavity search, then baggage scan.

Five years ago, both Margosha and Duri could have traveled under legitimate medical treatment visas, but since the recent mods policies went into effect, everyone has had to get a little creative. Select treatments were moved out of the medcare column, where they had previously sat for more than a hundred years, and were lumped together under the new body modification column, then under the *voluntary* body modification column soon after that. Which has turned out to be convenient for some, less convenient for others, since at the same time vol-mods were declared entirely subject to government approval. Meaning they're evaluated on a case-by-case basis, permitted or denied.

There were protests, for a time—cries that they were all regressing dangerously into another, darker century. But lawmakers insisted that the past was worth returning to: *These old things*, they said, *have a way of coming back to us when we need them.*

Duri's color-changing hair is a piece-of-cake level-one vol-mod—J&J rigged it so most of their cosmetic mods are—and the prowling, animated wolf tattoo is a level one-point-five. The latest out of Prada is a fatty tissue transplant to the heels and balls of the feet that allows the brand's loyalists to endure the shoes for more consecutive hours. It debuted at level two, but was upgraded to level three when one unintended side effect became apparent: the springy transplants improved the wearer's ability to sprint short distances. The mod's opponents dubbed it "the escape advantage."

Levels four through six get into the experimental mods, and those heavier-duty ones that call for some prerequisite training. J&J's injectable tans and sunscreens got cleared as entry levels, but their offshoot, an injectable camouflage, is never going to drop below level six, ensuring the military holds a monopoly on it.

The procedures Margosha and Duri were seeking when the organizers found them and offered to help, plucking them from their lives thousands of miles apart, are categorized as level sevens: the highest level currently assigned. By design, level-seven vol-mods are harshly stigmatized, and they remain virtually impossible to get licenses for on Earth.

Nova is another story, one everybody's heard. The colony broke away two decades ago, when Earth started becoming a truly intolerable place to live and the wealthiest of its citizens realized that they did not, in fact, have to tolerate it. Only the most well-off can afford to stay on Nova permanently, expats in their peaceful, progressive society orbiting Earth. But people like Margosha and Duri, and the rest of the passengers on the airbus, can pay the satellite a brief visit. For a price.

What Margosha wants to modify is there's a baby inside her that she doesn't want to be there.

What Duri wants to modify is the fact of her body being able to carry babies at all.

The four days in the hot, crowded airbus will be worth it, the organizers remind them again and again, to arrive at the plush Nova clinic, with its simulated gravity, its sympathetic doctors, its pillows stuffed with the last of Earth's real goose down. There'll be some discomfort. Not pain, never pain—only *discomfort*. Nova doesn't recognize mod levels or license requirements, but rumor has it the colony does share Earth's penchant for calling things something other than what they really are. All the level-seven mods get sanitized, labyrinthine names to match Nova's sanitized, labyrinthine environment: fetal tissue evacuation, absolute uterine transfer, breast tissue alleviation. Pudendum reconstructive therapy, from the Latin *pudere*: to be ashamed.

Still, in comparison, a sanctuary.

"Regrets?" Margosha repeats softly.

Duri is silent for some time, staring out of her not-window at the not-arid not-land not-outside. At long last, she replies plainly, "None."

Margosha agrees quickly: "None." Even though it means losing the game. Because if she were playing by the rules, she'd have started with "E." It would have been so easy. If the game were more important, she could have said any number of things: "Eavesdropping," or "Ending it," or "Everything."

But instead she says it again, with more force this time, "*None*," and the twin cracks at the parched corners of her mouth split open.

••••

"Category is . . ."

Exhausted from the hunt, the catty-corner wolf is snoring loudly, a pile of tattooed bones and broken wings forming a jumbled graveyard at its feet. The crackly-voiced pilot announces that they're very close now, everyone should make sure their seatbelts are fastened—he'll let them know when it's time to brace themselves for final descent.

"Wishes," Duri finishes.

Earlier, while playing tic-tac-toe, the *O*'s made Margosha think of empty cavities: subway tunnels after the trains stop running, holes in tree trunks, vacant bellies, cracks in sidewalks. Hollow spaces responsible for holding nothing, free to simply *exist* as they are. The *X*'s made Duri think of the way people get buried sometimes, with their arms crossed neatly over their chests. Because the person preparing the body wanted the dead to appear penitent when meeting God. Or just because it made it easier to fit the corpse inside the box.

When they played hangman, Duri drew a single straight line for the middle part of the hanged man's body. Margosha was grateful, even though the truth—a circle middle with a stick baby inside—would have given Margosha an extra guess. It meant that Duri couldn't tell what Margosha really had under that baggy sweatshirt, or that even if she could, she wasn't the kind to commit another person's secrets to paper. In the end, Duri drew a couple of little shoes at the ends of the hanged man's little legs, so Margosha got the extra guesses anyway.

"Wishes, wishes . . ." Margosha murmurs. "Well, I've heard Nova has a great view of Earth."

"*The best in the galaxy*!" Duri knows the tagline well. She's seen the ads, too—they're inescapable. She might not get them full-res on the side of a skyscraper, but they come through just fine on the tiny smart screen she keeps in her kitchen and turns on once a day to check the weather and the progression of dust storms across her county each morning.

Margosha smiles sadly. "Then my wish is for Earth to be better to us from a distance."

Duri nods. She knows exactly what Margosha means. She reaches over to the tray table, where Margosha is nervously drumming her fingers over the gulch cut half an inch into the plastic where the cup is supposed to go, and she takes Margosha's hands into her own. Again, Margosha marvels at Duri's shamelessness, her willingness to feel something and act on it right away. The way Duri's eyelashes are turning a bright, lemony yellow and she's leaving her hands right where they are, isn't even bothering to wipe the tears away.

Margosha sticks her tongue out at her new friend. They're nearly there; they'll get there together. She licks the split corners of her lips, tastes blood.

••••

It happens faster than anything. Fast as these things happen sometimes.

It happens before Duri can take her turn in the game.

Before she can put together that she's been thinking about death, about nooses and hanged bodies and burials, for a reason.

Before she can realize that the way she's been holding Margosha's hands, it's with the same combination of firmness and gentleness she used to cradle the cows on the farm as they died. How do you make steel latticework of your fingers? How do you keep a body from coming apart and at the same time give the soul the space it needs to float up off the ground?

When the airbus organizers come down the aisle this time, they're not holding packets of trail mix or water bottles. They're not squeezing the passengers' shoulders. They're not wearing their calm, reassuring expressions anymore.

They're wearing the kind of vests Margosha sees every day without exception and the kind Duri sees on the special days she goes into town. The vests the armed guards wear while patrolling in front of the government buildings, in front of schools and grocery stores, post offices and corner markets, medical clinics and law offices and drugstores.

The organizers of Project Storm Port, of the airbus meant to ferry Duri, Margosha, and the others to safe-haven clinics on Nova, are carrying stun guns and zip ties, and rolls and rolls of military-issue restraint tape. They cover mouths and eyes, bind arms, legs, talons, and tails, methodically working their way down the narrow aisle. The passengers in the first rows are too taken aback to do anything but go compliantly, but the others, witnessing the sudden change in the organizers' demeanor, are screaming, flailing, shooting up from their seats. With nowhere else to go, they stampede in place, in this windowless metal tube gaining speed toward a destination they now understand is very different from the one they had set out for.

The organizers are close now, and Margosha and Duri can just make out the blocky white letters across their vests:

OFFICER.

NOVA INTERPLANETARY CORRECTIONS.

The wolf on the woman's shoulder awoke at the first commotion and now, sensing danger, snaps wildly and snarls. It bucks and bites, defiant to the end, while the officers struggle to contain it to the surface of the woman's skin, one long, sticky strip of black tape after another.

Duri is frozen, astonished. She can't believe she's been so naive. People from the cities, like Margosha, sure. But *her*? No. Her county was one of the first to incite citizen militias to enforce the level-seven mod bans in their own communities. Self-appointed bounty hunters lurk in the shadows back home, snatching shoppers as they come out of drugstores and rifling through their bags. Hackers tap into personal networks, monitor order histories. Groups of men follow groups of women down the street, waiting for them to separate when they reach their cars.

It should've always been a possibility in her mind for Nova to be not paradise but prison.

Duri looks at Margosha, in her two eyes the color of honey, and reads in them, in an instant, a million urgent things. Namely rage. Namely wrath.

And something else—something strange.

Something like satisfaction.

As Margosha begins her transformation, both women think, not for the first time, that here and on Earth, they really are regulating the wrong things.

Margosha got the Deere vol-mod last year. Rated level five for commercial machinery. She and her cousins, fellow city girls, were taking their biannual tour of the wineries upstate when she saw the ad in a gift shop. The auto cashier spit it out to her along with her change and a coupon for a local reds tasting class. It was Deere's first foray into cosmetic mods, designed to mimic the manufacturer's line of combine grape harvesters, only on a much smaller scale: the scale of the human body. It was meant for family vineyards that didn't have much ground to cover and whose owners couldn't afford the bigger external equipment. And it was recalled almost immediately—while the ads were still running—because the mod had a tendency to clog and overheat, and because it came with a non-negligible risk of permanent disfiguration.

Margosha got it for a steal. The shop couldn't wait to be rid of it. Practically gift wrapped it with a bow.

She never expected to use the mod for its intended purpose. What's she know about tractors and combines? Half the time she can't get her own little sedan to start.

But it sure has helped her feel safer walking home alone late in the city, when the men at last turned out their sickly yellow squares and the buildings, fed up, spit them out. Every night she thought, if the men *had* to look at her, why couldn't they do it the way they looked at the stars? The harmless admiration of some remote, unreachable thing, more dream than anything. But no. She was, to them, all too attainable.

The Deere mod helped her feel safer then.

Here, too, it'll do just fine.

Margosha's mouth stretches wide, wide, then wider, ripping apart the scabs at the corners that never heal quite right. Gears snap into place and sprockets turn somewhere at her center. Her lips stretch out to her jawline—ends in "E"—then to her ears, and steel blades, painted Deere green and yellow, erupt from her gums and begin to rattle and whir. Before the combine's face can overtake the rest of her, reconfiguring her eyes into plate-glass windows, Margosha throws Duri a don't-you-worry wink.

The blades start their sputtering and churning, and the liquid trickling down Margosha's grill balances out to equal parts fuel and blood. The Nova officer nearest the hungry machine clutches her useless roll of tape and tries frantically to backtrack up the congested aisle. But the airbus is packed with the hopefuls Project Storm Port baited, and they do all they can to get in the way.

Margosha bears forward and begins to harvest.

By the time they dock at Nova Interplanetary Corrections Facility, Duri's moisture-activated hair is more yellow than black, and more of a deep, syrupy red than yellow at that. Chunks of flesh and bone decorate the airbus's walls. The passengers have yanked off one another's bindings and stand ready at the hatch, mods out and confiscated stun guns in hand. The pilot is pinned against the cabin door, blubbering about how he has *daughters*, and don't his daughters need their *father*, the sharp spikes of a scaly blue tail pressing triangles into his throat.

The wolf, freed, howls, and the others howl back.

Duri thinks, as the hatch clicks open and the passengers pour out onto a world woefully unprepared for them, that Margosha is merely continuing the game they started. The simple, boring game they've been playing on and off for the past four eternal days of their doomed road trip: last letter first.

They are, technically, still on wishes. Last Duri can remember, she said something about wanting a good, solid meal—the trail mix had been getting tiresome, not even being the kind with chocolate.

Which makes it Margosha's turn.

The cheering and baying, the sounds of Margosha's inner mechanisms patiently digesting the officers, overwhelm the echoing shuttle bay. And while Duri can't quite make out what her seatmate says, she figures she can guess well enough.

MEL FOR MELISSA

This isn't one of those dystopian varsity survivalist sto-ries. I know they're popular again because my students are talking about them. I do this icebreaker game the first day. Easy prompts like "What's your favorite TV show?" because "What's your favorite book?" feels too much like a pop quiz in a writing class, and they all freeze up searching for some impressive title, what they think I want to hear, instead of what's actually true. So I stick with the TV question, and lately everyone's answer is *Yellowjackets*.

You know, varsity team's plane crashes en route to nationals; cue struggle to survive in the remote wilder-ness as chaos and savagery ensue. Another addition to the you'd-think-they'd-act-like-a-team genre, shot through with that specific brand of cutthroat reserved for teenage girls. When my kids, a mix of nervous freshmen and zoned-out seniors taking their last elective, described the plot of *Yellowjackets*, I said it sounded like a modern *Lord of the Flies*. At which point one of them piped brightly that they hadn't "seen" that one. Which, fine. I haven't seen *Yellowjackets* either. Still can't bring myself to watch it. So I guess we're even.

The icebreaker feels a little juvenile for a college course, but as far as I know all the grad TAs do it. It's funny how little those first-day games have changed since my own grade school days. The common one then was alliterative epithets: every student came up with a descriptive word that started with the same sound as their first name. Jolly Jerry, Cheerful Cheryl, that sort of thing. It was supposed to help the class commit everyone's name to memory.

Today I can look up adjectives that start with "K" and there are dozens to choose from—kind, kingly, keen—and that's before you factor in the hard *C*'s, like clever or courageous. But back then we didn't have smartphones, and put on the spot and Googleless like that, I could only ever think of one thing. So for the first few weeks of every class those days, everybody called me Killer Katherine.

It's ridiculous if you know me, more ridiculous if you knew me then. I was the girl slouching against walls, walking with my head down to camouflage my way-ahead-of-the-boys growth spurt. I was painfully shy, embarrassed by everything. Would've crawled into a locker and stayed there till the 3:02 p.m. bell every day if I could've.

That's one reason I loved being a Lady Panther, and despite everything I'm going to write here, I did love it. Coach Canfield opened our eyes to the idea that it might be good to be tall, to be loud, aggressive, a performer. She said it all the time: we had to have that *killer instinct*.

It was nothing like *Yellowjackets*, from what I've heard of it. We didn't loot the corpses of dead passengers for ponies of vodka and half-eaten bags of airline peanuts. We didn't "feed off each other's insecurities," like that circu-lation-nothing *Star Gazette* article suggested; there was no cannibalism, metaphorical or otherwise. We didn't hunt each other for sport. We didn't even sleep with each other's boyfriends. We were a sisterhood with sisterhood rules. We had in-jokes about the assistant coach's new mushroom cut, diss cheers our opponents wished they could've thought of, bowls and bowls of Mrs. Krakowiak's red-sauce pasta every night before home games.

People want blood, though. Always have. As if the grade-two concussions, screeching foot-long floor burns, dislocated fingers, and gruesome ACL tears weren't enough. People want carnage. Sorry to disappoint. The only one who saw anything like that was Mel. And, weirdly, out of all of us, she's the one who turned out all right.

For two years during the latchkey aughts, the Lady Panthers varsity volleyball team gave me purpose. Gave me routine, and built-in friendships, and a place to be after school that wasn't my boring, empty house. The Panthers gave me family—but that's too Vitamin C's "Graduation" song, isn't it? Anyway, what the Panthers really gave me was "Kat."

Coach Canfield wasn't an easy icebreaker kind of person. The first day of my first hell week, she strolled into the locker room and shut the door softly behind her. Then she had us go around and say our names.

Seems like a no-brainer, but that's when I learned you could in fact be wrong about a thing as foundational as your name. Because when the first girl—who I would later know as our fearless leader and team captain, your typical bossy setter with hands for days—introduced herself as

Brianna, Coach slapped her clipboard lightly against her thigh a few times as if considering her options, then said, simply, "No."

Coach was a short woman, 5'5" if you were being generous, shorter than all of us but the setters and liberos. Every day without exception, she wore a short-sleeved polo in one of those thick performance fabrics, tucked into a pair of men's slacks belted tight around the waist. She always carried a clipboard, but because none of us ever saw a piece of paper attached to that clipboard, we assumed she kept the plays in her head and just brought the clipboard along as an accessory, the way that now, even though I don't drink, I grab a beer first thing at parties just to have something to do with my hands. Coach Canfield never sat down as long as I knew her. She never raised her voice. She never slammed doors.

We were in awe of her, and we were terrified of her—but not the way the *Star Gazette* reported it. We were terrified of the way we would feel if we were ever to disappoint her.

Lady Panthers volleyball was almost a decade past its heyday by the time I got there, but the championship banners that hung around the gym weren't faded yet, and all of us still knew someone, a cousin or neighbor or classmate's older sister, who had played during the miracle spree. Even the girls from Lancaster showed up at our gym quaking in their Mizunos. The Swedes of Western New York, we called them: tall, blonde, and lean—must've been something in the water. Don't get me wrong, we were still good when I got pulled up from JV my sophomore year.

Still competitive. But we were inconsistent, and our legacy had more bite than our actual record. There were rumors, too, that Coach was getting ready to retire, and these loomed over us as much as the banners. We couldn't let ours be the team that closed her career out on a whimper.

Coach caught a lot of flack after everything that happened with Mel, and though most of it was framed as speculation, I know it must've killed her. Her reputation, and that of the program as a whole, meant everything to her. She never got married, never had kids. The Panthers were her entire life. So even though it blew over quickly, and even though I told Coach myself not to take that reporter seriously—he studied journalism at Corning Community College, for God's sake, not Cornell—she wouldn't be consoled. I should've known better: she'd never been an elitist, and the look she gave me for my attempted joke made me want to wither up and die. But what do you say to someone when you know they're about to leave the game for good?

I want to set the record straight, that, yeah, while her rules were intense, by and large they came from a place of logic. Like her rule about our names being one syllable long. It was an efficiency thing, so we could call out to one another quickly and clearly in the middle of a high-speed play. No wasted air. No confusion about whose name was said. It was smart, really, and you don't bring home the state trophy for nine consecutive years without establishing some smart rules and sticking to them. So that's how Brianna became Bri, Caitlyn Cait, Alicia Al. Morgan was Mo, Whitney was Whit, and Allison couldn't be Al because that was taken already, so she went by Vees, a shortening of her last name, Vieselmeyer. Amanda didn't want to be called Man (who would?), so she opted for her middle name, Leigh. And I went from Katherine to Kat. And Melissa, my first real best friend, was Mel.

I went back and forth about using their real names here. Even though nobody's ever going to read this, I can't help feeling kind of guilty.

My therapist has made that point a bunch of times: that no one's going to read this, not even her, and because of that, I should look at this as an opportunity to be 100 percent honest. She says our sessions have begun to *plateau*, and if I don't make a sincere effort to *climb this hill* now, the next *mountain* will be even taller. Her geological metaphors don't track, and that's only reason five of, like, five hundred that I don't really trust her.

She told me her patients, especially women "around my age," find it cathartic to write their experiences down on paper. What I thought to myself but didn't say out loud was that I'm pretty sure good therapists don't waste expensive session time blabbing to patients about other patients.

Anyway, cathartic? I'm not sure. Mostly I wonder what Coach would think of therapy. Sometimes I'm sure she would scoff at the idea and say something in her unnervingly quiet, all-knowing way about willpower and battling your demons on the court. But then I second-guess myself, because that sounds less like her than like a salad of the famous TV and movie coaches I still carry around in my head: the Eric Taylors, Tony D'Amatos, and Jimmy Dugans. How about all my fictional mentors being dudes, by the way? A lot to unpack there, as my therapist would say. Probably Coach would take one long, indecipherable look at me and tell me that, yep, therapy seems like a damn good plan.

The other rule that got a lot of attention in the press, if you can call the *Star Gazette* the press, was Coach's rule about weight. It was a sophisticated calculation for someone like me, who nearly flunked precalc sophomore year and after that gave up any hope of a proud girls-in-STEM future forever.

The rule was this: take the number of inches you are over five feet, multiply that number times three, and that's the number of pounds you're allowed to weigh over one hundred.

It's kind of complicated, I know. Let me put it this way: I was 5'8" when I joined varsity—the roster said 5'10", but every high school athlete knows roster height's its own thing, an intimidation tactic not remotely concerned with the truth. So at 5'8", I was eight inches over five feet, which meant I could weigh, at maximum, one hundred twenty-four pounds.

One hundred twenty-four pounds was my assigned weight, and I had one month—hell week plus a grace period—to get there or I'd be off the team. After that, we'd be monitored weekly for maintenance. The first time we came in over, there'd be per-pound punishments: bleachers, suicides, burpees, and other, more creative tortures. The second time, we'd be benched. The third time, cut.

Coach was hardcore. We wanted to be hardcore. By the second day of hell week, hers was the only math any of us cared about. This was especially true for Mel.

••••

I'm tempted to quit now, to admit to myself and my therapist—yes, Dr. Abbott, I know you're going to read this—that this isn't my story to tell. Even though Mel and I became inseparable our sophomore year, what happened to her didn't happen to me. I was an innocent bystander. Or if not exactly innocent, then exactly a bystander: someone who stands idly by. You could argue that the mannequin in the basement was my part in all of it, but that would be a pretty weak argument, since it wasn't really a mannequin, it was a dress form, and it didn't belong to me, it was my mother's. And it's not like a mannequin (or a dress form) can force a person to do a thing like that anyway. The whole point of mannequins is that they're not real.

Besides, even though it happened in my parents' basement, I wasn't there. I was out watching the famous Barrington Brats, every Chemung County babysitter's worst nightmare, when Mel finally, officially snapped.

Really, it's her story and hers alone. She saw the parts the rest of us missed. That's what I told myself when college application season rolled around and I had to write that essay everyone has to write about the greatest obstacle I'd overcome. My mom suggested gently, in her new don't-scare-your-daughter-away voice, that I try writing about what happened, and I said hell no, H-E-L-L no—I wasn't touching that with a seven-and-a-half-foot volleyball pole.

Mel never did come out and talk about it, though, and by now we've all come to grips with the likelihood that she never will. After high school, she flew south to Austin and never looked back, and now she's one of those YouTube/Instagram/TikTok influencers. Hundreds of thousands of followers, meticulously curated sponcon, the filters that make your nose look narrower, all that. I'm not brave enough to follow any of her accounts, since doing so would remind her that I'm still alive, but I do check up on them from time to time, when I get too stoned and/or nostalgic. I'm not going to write her handle here and risk casting some kind of summoning spell, but anyone could find her without too much trouble. She's on a lot of those top food blogger lists, and she's a staple on Austin's morning show circuit. Her parents recently opened a fast-casual burger joint in this gated community and she does all their marketing. Kind of quaint, if you ask me, but it must be working, since they say more than half of restaurants shut down during their first year and her parents' place is still kicking. This year she published a cookbook—I think it's self-published, but I still can't believe she got a book out before me—and now you can find her on Travis County's "Top 30 Under 30."

I've had a copy of her book in my Amazon cart for seven months. I can't bring myself to buy it, but I can't bring myself to delete it either. It's wild to think, after everything, how much of Mel's life revolves around food.

Between pictures of churro ice cream cones and charcoal burger buns—what I imagine must be trending cuisine in Central Texas—she posts photos of herself. She's either thinner or less thin than I remember, and she has that trained smile where you press your tongue to the roof of your mouth against your front teeth. Pretty, flowing sundresses. Never two-piece bathing suits or crop tops. Never anything too close to the skin, that might reveal too much.

She has another account where she posts her versions of Rupi Kaur poetry. Not a lot of people know this; the two have almost no follower crossover. The poems are short, and bad, rendered in a let's-pretend-I-used-a-typewriter Courier New. But I have to admit she seems happy. That's the most fucked-up thing. That after all of it, *she's* happy, and I'm the one writing this letter to no one.

••••

Our high school had all the usual girls' teams (basketball, softball, cross-country, track, swimming, lacrosse), plus a few of the less common ones (tennis, bowling, golf). And, yeah, like I said, this isn't one of those over-the-top girls-team-goes-berserk stories. But I guess out of all of them, we *were* the crazy ones.

Part of it was that we had been brought into a situation of extremes. Even though I don't agree with everything that's been said about Coach Canfield, she definitely was extreme. It was an open secret in the athletics department that, although we weren't the winningest team anymore, we practiced harder than everyone, including the guys.

Coach's mantra was: Leave Your Bodies on the Court. The first day of sophomore preseason, she printed it out just like that on a sheet of paper and taped it over the entrance to the girls' locker room. It would've taken her less time to write it out by hand, but she printed it. She had to have the letters perfect: bold, straight, and even. No compromises. That's how Coach was.

We must've done all the typical drills. Pepper, block joust, serve and shag. They're not what I remember, though. What I remember is the conditioning.

Thousands and millions and billions of stairs.

In the school's squeaky stairwells. On the bleachers bookending the football field outside. Both feet, left foot, right foot, switch. Left foot, facing left. Right foot, facing right. Backwards. Forwards, backwards. For every missed serve, every shanked ball. If we were at an away game, Coach would find the nearest stairwell in that dangerous enemy territory and make us run stairs there. It didn't matter if we had won, or even if it had been a sweep. If there were unforced errors, we were running. Till someone puked, or fell—or in the case of Mo that one time, puked *then* fell (in said puke). Sometimes we ran for no discernible reason.

Now I live with my boyfriend in a garden apartment without stairs. We pay rent out of a joint bank account and we buy produce at the farmers' market and most of the time we feel very adult. He says the best part of being an adult is that you can eat whatever you want, whenever you want to. You can eat Cocoa Puffs five meals in a row. You can eat cold pizza for breakfast.

But I say no—no way. The best part of being an adult is no more stairs.

We left our bodies on the court every day then peeled them up after, carried our skins, floor-bruised and still sweating, to the shower stalls. We shrank our bodies till we made assigned weight, then kept counting calories in the margins of our chemistry notebooks. We quizzed each other on the numbers so thoroughly that now there are whole sections of nutrition facts labels I'll never be able to scrub from my mind. Like Kellogg's Pop Tarts: the frosted ones are 200 calories, while the unfrosted ones are 210. I couldn't believe it. Apparently it's because the unfrosted ones have a thicker crust to make up for the lack of frosting.

Can't remember my cousins' birthdays. Can't remember half of my students' names. But that Pop Tarts factoid, guess I'm stuck with it for life.

At the same time we made ourselves smaller, we stretched ourselves out, Gumbied our bodies for the roster. My 5'8" became 5'10", and even Mel—who was our starting libero, short and supposed to be—fibbed her way to 5'4". Our bodies became these uncertain things, nebulous and malleable. There was nothing concrete or fixed about them. We were the amazing, shape-shifting Lady Panthers! The edges were all fuzzy. Our bodies were negotiable, only we weren't the ones setting the terms.

Maybe Mel wanted to test that. Maybe that's why she thought she could do what she did and come out unscathed.

We were the crazy ones. We were *hardcore*. There were rumors circulating well before the *Star Gazette* ran its series, and some of them were even true.

Yes, we really tattooed *KILL* on one another using a stick-and-poke kit Al had stolen from her sister.

No, we didn't grind up someone's pet guinea pig into meatballs for the spaghetti dinner before Vestal's big tournament. And no, it wasn't a hamster either.

Yes, it was an off-season tradition to go skinny-dipping in Otisco the day the ice finally broke. (Off-season for varsity wasn't off-season for Coach, by the way. Nearly all of us spent the winter and spring months playing for the local travel team, which she ran just like she did the Panthers, but in a different, fluorescent-bulbed gym.)

What we were best known for, and what everyone at parties always asked to see, were our Lady Panthers Volleyball Victory V's.

They were Whit's idea. Or Mo's. Definitely not mine, though a lot of people would remember it that way just because it was my house we went to, to use my mother's iron.

Mom had all kinds of sewing accoutrements. When we moved to the U.S., she didn't have the kind of visa that allowed her to work legally, so she found a job working under the table as a seamstress for a small bridal company.

By the time I was in high school, she had a whole other career, but she kept half our unfinished basement as her sewing room for the odd mending job or Halloween costume she made as a favor for one of the neighbors' little kids.

There was her sewing table and trusty Bernina; dozens of tiny, tomato-shaped pincushions; the headless, armless, legless dress form standing off to the side. There was the fabric-covered ironing board and the old Black and Decker steam iron perched atop it with its flat metal belly exposed. It wasn't the nicest iron, and with the way the vents worked in our house, the whole basement smelled like the cat's scented litter. But my mom and dad were around the least of any of our parents, which made that basement the coolest place in town.

How it worked was: the point of the iron was shaped in such a way that, if you heated it up and rolled it across a surface just so, tipping it forward halfway through the roll, you would get an imprint that looked exactly like the letter "V." We practiced a few times on a potato we found growing sprouts in the corner of the pantry, then closed the blinds and threw our warmup mix on someone's iPod, loud as it would go. We decided everyone would get to choose the spot they wanted for their Victory V. A few of the girls picked their biceps, with the idea that they could kiss it for an extra boost midgame. I knew my parents would kill me if they found out—I still cover my tattoos when I come home for Thanksgiving dinner—so I looked for somewhere they wouldn't see. Because of how skimpy our uniforms were, it wasn't easy to find a spot I could guarantee would be kept hidden. In the end, I chose the outside of my hip, halfway between the waistband of our spandex shorts and their bottom hem.

The scar still hurts sometimes. Not when it's about to rain or anything like that. That would be cool—for it to be predictive, useful. No, it just hurts whenever it feels like it. Like for a long time it's been sleeping and then it suddenly wakes up.

We were the crazy ones. It's what made us good. We were practicing being unpredictable. If you can work it so the other team never knows what to expect from you, you're golden. When they know what's coming, that's when they've got you.

And, too, the crazy things we did made us believe in ourselves. If we could grimace through those excruciating seconds under the hot iron, without backing out, without crying out, what couldn't we handle?

One of my students this semester wants to be a Marine. He has this shirt that says, in one of those yelling-at-you fonts, PAIN IS WEAKNESS LEAVING THE BODY, and every time he wears it, I think of the iron.

After the girls left that day and the iron cooled down, I took it to the bathroom sink and scrubbed the tip of the plate with a dish sponge. I knew I had to get the fried flesh off the metal before my parents came home.

Leave your bodies on the court, she said.

We left our bodies everywhere.

••••

I think my therapist means well. She says her office is a *safe space*. By this she must mean that she observes doctor-patient confidentiality, or that she won't tweet the embarrassing things I tell her, even anonymized, or that she won't include me in a TikTok roundup of the ten most bizarre traumas her patients have confessed to, which is apparently a thing that some therapists do. I don't like her very much. (Sorry, Dr. A, if you really are reading this.) She just seems too nervous too much of the time, like she's worried I'm going to say something that'll cause her pleasant, neutral expression to fissure. But she's what I can afford right now.

It's one of those overused phrases. I use it too, I'll admit: I tell my students that our classroom is a safe space. I feel corny and sentimental when I say it, but between last year's supermarket shooting and this year's constant out-of-season wildfires and the ongoing pandemic and state-sanctioned police violence and governors passing anti-abortion legislation left and right and now the war, I feel like it's too much and I have to say something. Something that conveys my sheer disbelief that we're all somehow still alive in this dying world together—but in a way that's less melodramatic, you know? That allows us to maintain the appropriate distance. To not understand each other too well.

So I call our space a safe space, hoping it helps even one person. Even though I don't believe that safe spaces exist.

It's a newish term. Back then, we had no illusions that the hallways of our high school, or the Lady Panthers locker room, or even my own parents' basement could offer us a safe space. Which was an honest way to grow up, if not a kind one.

Speaking of honest. I was a mediocre volleyball player, the worst one in the starting lineup by far. I played right side, which meant I had decent hands for a tall girl and didn't have to be good at anything else. I wasn't an especially strong hitter, couldn't do a jump serve, and my ball control was so rocky I had to be subbed out in the back row. I would get in my head, too. I didn't have what Coach called the *mental game*. It didn't matter how many people were in the stands or how many visualization exercises we did beforehand, at the start of every game, I was so rattled my hands were shaking at the net. In the end, a lot of the stairs we ran as punishment were my fault. The girls wouldn't say it out loud, though. That's how much of a team we were.

Why Coach kept me around: I had more hustle than anybody. What I lacked in athleticism and natural ability I more than made up with my willingness to throw myself around the gym like some possessed rag doll. At practice, there wasn't a single play I would say die on. I remember once, we were doing a pepper drill, and because the nets hadn't been set up yet, one of the round metal hatches that covered the pole port wasn't pushed all the way down. So instead of being flush with the synthetic wood flooring, it was sticking a tiny bit into the stale gym air. When Mel shanked the ball and I ran for it, I ended up skidding right over where the pole would've been, and the tab on that little hatch took a nice quarter-inch chunk out of my thigh.

Now I'm thinking maybe that's where Mel got the idea.

I had the attitude, what Coach called the "it" factor. Even though I had to share the rotation with the second-string right side—a junior named Jan, short for Janet, who had a bum knee she couldn't turn on and a bulky knee brace that made her look like a Transformer—Coach told me I was vital to the team. She said I kept the *air right*.

I was all in. I was *devoted*. Which is why, when Mel showed the warning signs that in retrospect seem so obvious, I took them as the acts of someone as devoted as me.

Mel and I knew each other on JV, but we didn't get close until the next year on varsity. Coach Canfield deserves some of the credit for that, and the rest goes to our simultaneous entry into the world of late-2000s emo rock. Mel and I were the closest thing to the choppy-black-hair, corner-lip-piercing set that the largely preppy Lady Panthers had to offer.

I was in the parking lot one day after tryouts, trying to get the disc player in my mom's old Corolla to stop skipping over my favorite Thrice CD, when Mel tapped lightly on the stuck-half-down driver's-side window. She said, with a kind of restrained admiration, that she didn't know I drove yet, and I said that, yeah, I did, but kind of illegally: I only had my permit, but my parents had given their blessing, not wanting to get straddled with the responsibility of chauffeuring me to extracurriculars themselves. Mel said if I promised not to get us caught, maybe she'd catch a ride with me sometime, and I replied with some uncool, overeager version of *you bet*. The last thing she said before walking the rest of the way to where her dad was waiting (in his gleaming white BMW X5, by the way) was that she liked the song I had on, but "Stare at the Sun" was better.

Mel's parents were loaded. It's how they managed to successfully open their first restaurant in the middle of a pandemic, and it's why I always begged to go to her house after practice all those years ago. It was in the nicest and quietest part of town, with six bedrooms, a heated driveway, and a bright green lawn some contractor had rolled out like a carpet runner. It was all brick too, so you knew it was expensive. Some other houses in town had a little brick on one section of front-facing wall and the rest was regular vinyl siding, but Mel's house had it top to bottom. It made me think of "The Three Little Pigs," and the brick house that wouldn't come down when the wolf came a-blowing. The closest thing we had to a safe space.

Mel, for her part, always begged to come to my house, which I didn't understand. Because of the pervasive litter box smell, for one; the single nineteen-inch TV, for two; and third, the fact that all we had to eat were microwavable fish sticks, while at Mel's place, it was home-cooked meals every day of the week.

Looking back on it, I understand what she liked about my house was that her parents and rah-rah older sister didn't live there.

Still, Mel's parents were super nice, and their three-car McMansion was, too. Which is why nobody really worried about Mel. And why, when I came to pick her up for school one morning, and her mom waved me upstairs—head down, absorbed in the application of her nail polish—and I walked into Mel's palatial bedroom to find her bleeding profusely onto her frilly duvet cover, I thought I must be hallucinating.

I realize I'm telling this out of order, but I don't think Dr. A can be critical of a therapy journal she's not even supposed to be reading, and God knows I'm not going to read this back. This happened sophomore year, right around Christmas. I remember because Mel's parents had put up a Douglas fir that stretched all the way to their vaulted ceiling, and my parents had brought home from Sam's Club a two-foot-tall plastic tabletop tree with fiber-optic needles that were supposed to light up in wavy rainbow patterns (except half of them were broken) and that were nontoxic for cats (which was good, at least, because ours devoured 80 percent of them within the week).

Anyway, while Mel's mom was putting the last shiny bauble on their perfect Hallmark Channel tree, Mel was slicing her boyfriend's name into the inside of her arm with a steak knife.

She and Luke had been on-again, off-again since they got together a few months prior, and if I was a good friend I would've told her how absolutely caustic they were for each other. He wasn't an evil guy. It was like when you mix two substances that aren't inherently bad on their own? They each have their merits, like bleach and vinegar, but when you put them together, boom, you've got toxic gas.

It's mortifying to think about now, the way we spent those two years basically reenacting a My Chemical Romance music video. I would tell a different, less played-out story if I could. Teenage angst stories are boring. Eating disorder stories are, too. Even I have to stop myself from rolling my eyes when a student slides one across my desk. I have to be careful to separate out the "cliché" in bright letters on the backside of my forehead, slam-dunk it into the recycling bin of my brain so it can be turned into something better, more constructive.

If that makes me a bad teacher, fine.

If that makes this a bad "story," same thing.

I lost fifteen pounds in the month after tryouts and Mel lost twelve, but her change looked more dramatic on her much shorter frame. All the reckless things we did after, we did out of some kind of attempt at reclamation of our bodies. (You like that, Dr. A? That one's for you.)

It was Mel's idea to become blood sisters during free period in the girls' bathroom one afternoon, dragging our forearms back and forth across the raspy edge of the hand dryer's metal nozzle.

It was my idea for us to go home with the army guys we met at the homecoming bonfire, who were older than us, but we didn't know/ask/care by how much. It was Mel who said okay when they asked if we wanted to watch them play a first-person-shooter game whose name I can't remember, and it was me who laughed when they said their platonic ideal of a date was to shoot a gun and shoot a load at the same time. I didn't know what it meant until I learned what it meant. I remember the sounds of low-stakes grenades over my shoulder. I remember Mel at practice the next day, pulling her kneepads up over the rug burns, her expression part wince, part smirk. The inside joke we wore on our faces.

Army Guy Night happened during one of Mel and Luke's short-lived breakups.

The jagged *LUKE* she cut into her arm did, too.

It wasn't the first rash thing she'd done to distract herself from—or draw herself further into—her heartbreak, but it was the most literal, and the scariest, and the hardest to clean up.

While Christmas music played from the entertainment center downstairs, I helped Mel pull on a long-sleeved shirt, then grabbed her backpack and walked her gingerly to the Corolla parked out front. Instead of going to school, we drove to the nearest CVS, where I bought a roll of gauze and a Vitamin Water with the last of my babysitting money, and I made her drink the whole bottle in the parking lot while I bandaged her up. I played Top 40 instead of Thrice, thinking the situation called for something light and poppy, even though she was right: "Stare at the Sun" was better, was the very *best*. I told Mel that if she ever needed to do something like that again, if she really couldn't help it, to use a house key or something. The side of a library card. The sharp corner of a rock. Or to do it on her leg, where the skin was thicker and where she had a chance of hiding it at practice. I knew what I was talking about. I did that stuff too, a lot of us did. But unlike Mel, I didn't mean anything by it. There was just some stuff in me I needed to get out. It wasn't a death wish, I told myself. It was a pressure release valve.

What Mel and I could agree on, though, what I think we all could agree on, was that it felt good to add something to our bodies instead of subtracting. A crosshatch of shallow red lines, or a shitty stick-and-poke tattoo, or a V-shaped brand from a steam iron, or a hickey that took two weeks to heal. Or Starting Line lyrics scribbled in gel pen in class, or a girl's wet mouth, or a boy's rough hands. Or our jersey numbers in permanent marker on our biceps for all the fans and haters alike to see.

I was number 21, by the way. Of course there was a running joke that I should've been number 10, but that belonged to Vees, and to her sister before her.

That day in the CVS parking lot, I made Mel promise never to touch a steak knife that way ever again, and she, all scared eyes and wet Thrice-fan mascara, agreed. Then she said something I'll never forget, something she asked me not to repeat to anyone.

I've kept that promise, and I'll keep it still.

Even though she didn't keep hers.

Not by a long shot.

••••

My second year on the team, it was obvious which of us had played for Coach before and which hadn't. Word got around about her intensity, but you couldn't fully understand until you stepped on the scale for your starting weigh-in. Shuffling into the locker room that first dreaded day of preseason, duffel bags over our shoulders, we surveyed one another, taking in what the summer had done.

Bri in particular was unrecognizable. Naturally slim, she now resembled one of those science-lab skeletons, and her signature butt-length hair had been shorn to a bob that barely grazed the top of her jawline. It was a mystery to me. She'd always said her hair was her best feature, and she liked to hold the tip of her long braid between her teeth while she waited for the whistle to blow.

Later she told us that she was worried about making weight. She thought it'd be a close call, and she figured without the hair she'd be at least a pound or two lighter and guaranteed safe. She said Coach had appointed her team captain that season, and it was up to her to set an example.

That's what the air was like going into my junior year on the Panthers. And there was nothing I could do to make it right.

I thought I saw Coach the other day. At the criminally expensive grocery store I only go to when I'm picking up wine to bring to a friend's place, because it has a better selection than my corner store. She had her back to me, same haircut, a little greyer, and was wrist deep in a bin of organic tomatoes, leisurely feeling around. Different decade, different city, and she was still as judicious as ever. I felt sick and snuck into the aisle with the exotic trail mixes to hide.

Except when the woman turned, she was another person entirely. She had a face full of makeup and a phone pressed between her shoulder and ear, and she was talking into it blazing fast in a thick Brooklyn accent.

She wasn't Coach. Or, in the way of ghosts, she wasn't, and she was.

I've put it off long enough, haven't I? I've talked around it long enough. Dr. A would ask, who am I protecting? Dr. A would insist I'm not doing myself any favors.

But my problem with Dr. A—my biggest problem, that is—is that she's 100 percent committed to finding an answer. *An* answer. One root cause, a direct correlation between what happened and what made it happen. Between what happened and why I'm the way I am today.

Except anyone who knew Mel, knew her as well as I did, knows that what happened can't be traced back in a single neat, dark, unwavering line to Coach's rules and our assigned weights system. Our principal tried to do it, so did our guidance counselor and our parents—they were all tempted by that one straight line. But I suspect the truth is splintered and combinational, a massive web that spans hundreds of pages, drawn by many hands in invisible ink.

There was our weigh-in math, sure. And there was Luke, too, now in year two of their middle-school-science-fair-volcano of a relationship. There was Mel's sister, Stacy, who didn't go by Stace because she wasn't a volleyball player, she was a cheerleader, and she was *really* a cheerleader: tidy, bubbly, uncomplicated. She made those movies about stereotypical high school cliques look like hard-hitting documentaries. There was something about Mel's chemistry, too, that we didn't have the language for then, and that I'm sure Dr. A would supply the language for now if I ever get stupid enough to ask.

There was also the fact that, that year, the new assistant coach ordered the wrong spandex sizes for every single person on the team. Coach blamed it on a clerical error, a new hire still learning the ropes, but we were quietly suspicious. All of us had gotten exactly one size smaller than what we'd requested on the order form.

And there was the fact that—whose bright idea was this, anyway?—we decided to wear our jerseys and spandex only, no warmup pants, skin all out, all day, every day of Spirit Week at school.

And finally: the dress form my mom kept in the sewing room part of our basement. A floating torso wrapped in coarse fabric the same off-white as the gauze from CVS, with tripod feet where there should have been legs and a brass-colored knob where there should have been a head. Since my mom had quit sewing, it stood bare, a handful of forgotten pins embedded at the chest and waistline.

As it happens, it was exactly Mel's height.

I know, I've put it off long enough.

For years after, I had these terrible nightmares. Or *nightmare*, rather—the same one again and again. In the nightmare, I'm in my bed in my parents' house, only my bed's been moved down to the basement, and dream-me wakes up with my teeth chattering, because the basement doesn't hold heat well. At the foot of my basement bed, a shadow appears, and I try to scream, but I can't scream, and I try to get up and run, but I'm glued to the mattress.

I'd beg in the dream for someone to come, but the only one coming for me was the shadow, and it would come closer and closer, and gradually it would take the shape of a human being. And its waist was so tiny, it looked like it was wearing one of those old-fashioned Victorian corsets made of—what is it? Whale bone?

Of course, it doesn't sound very scary on paper, but back then, when I woke up—*really* woke up, in my real bedroom, outside of the dream—my mouth would feel sore and taste full of pennies. That's because I wore this wire-front retainer and one of the wires had come loose, but I was too busy and afraid of dentists to go in and have it mended. The loose wire dug into my gums if I didn't set my mouth just right, and I guess those nights I must've been gnashing my teeth, or close-mouthed screaming or something, because every time I woke up, my mouth was pooling with blood.

Once, my dad saw the blood on my pillowcase and I told him it was my period. Which doesn't make any sense if you know how sleeping and pillows work—and besides, because of the way we were dieting, most of us hadn't gotten our period in months. But if you know my dad, or if you've known any dad ever, you understand why he didn't ask questions.

Okay, I've put it off long enough.

By late October of my junior year, with the twin pressures of postseason and States steadily mounting, we were all one bad weigh-in, one failed history exam, one quasi-breakup or disparaging comment about our skirt choice away from falling apart completely. We didn't talk about it after, still haven't, but I think it's safe to say everyone felt that way. It's just that Mel got there first.

I knew Mel was volatile, unpredictable, not to be trusted with herself and others. I knew that better than anyone. But it also made her exciting to be around. I feel guilty for saying that, but it's true.

She kept her promise for a while, at least, after that emergency-first-aid morning in the CVS parking lot. Ditched the really sharp objects and in their place took to giving herself paper cuts. Her arms and legs, her stomach. Her fingers were totally covered. But you had to get real close to see them. Even then, unless you had a magnifying glass, you might miss them. You'd have had to slip directly into her skin.

She asked me once if I remembered those paper dolls that were popular when we were younger, the ones that came in booklets, that you had to tear along the perforated lines. The rest of the booklet was filled with paper outfits: ballgowns and rompers and business suits edged with these little rectangular tabs. All you had to do was punch out her outfit, fold the tabs over her body, and dress her up.

I said, yeah, Mel, I remember.

She told me she wanted to be one. I said, one what? She said she was jealous. I said, jealous of what? She told me she envied the way you could turn them sideways, that's all. The way you could turn them sideways and they'd practically disappear.

She'd cut it close consecutive Mondays at Coach's weekly weigh-in. Another half-pound and she would've gotten her second warning and risked being benched during the most important stretch of the season.

We all wanted to be paper dolls at one time or another. To be Barbie dolls, automatons, to be dress forms and mannequins. We didn't want our thighs to touch. We didn't want our upper arms to wobble. We didn't want our fat to fold over the tops of our low-waisted jeans. We wanted to be made of paper or plastic or beige cotton stretched taut over a torso frame. We wanted our materials to hold their shape without our constant vigilance, the way a doll weighs the same one year and ten years later, a collectible doll the same a hundred years after that. If we had to have mouths, we didn't want them to open. If we had to have necks, we didn't want throats inside. We were so tired of ourselves, of the upkeep our bodies required. Tired of the feeding and fluctuation, which is one way to say—if it's not too melodramatic—that we were tired, sometimes, of being alive.

It is too melodramatic, of course. But, hey, once an emo girl, always an emo girl.

The day Mel carved herself away in the same basement where we'd done our Victory V's, my dad was at a conference in Tucson and my mom was visiting friends in Philly, and I was stuck at a babysitting job in Barrington Estates, which was the second-nicest neighborhood in town, after Mel's. I'd expected to be there only a couple of hours, the length of a Saturday matinee, but then the parents decided to go for ice cream at Peaches Market and I had to hang around with the twins. I'd made plans to meet Mel at my place, but I figured she'd keep herself entertained. She knew about the key we kept under the flowerpot, and the trick to getting our finicky remote to work. She knew where we put the feather-on-a-stick toy that could coax the cat to come out and play.

This was two weeks before States, and three weeks after my dad won a fancy Japanese steak knife in a raffle at a company potluck. Despite never being much of a cook, he was really proud of it. It was one of the most expensive things we owned, at least by square inch-age. He even bought a magnetic strip and mounted it above the stove.

Later, Mel admitted to everything. I couldn't believe, when we visited her at St. Joseph's, how very lucid she was. The nurse had warned us that she'd be groggy from the pain meds, and we'd all seen *Grey's Anatomy*, so none of us were prepared for how clear her eyes were, how steady her voice. We were only allowed to go in three at a time, so as not to overwhelm her. But she didn't seem overwhelmed. And she told us all the same thing.

She told us how she'd arrived at my house half an hour before we were supposed to meet and plucked my dad's prize knife off the wall, admiring its wood handle and hammered steel. How she'd gone up to my bedroom next, pulled a spliff out of my desk drawer where she knew I kept them, and sat on my bed, the knife on her lap, taking heady inhales to settle her nerves. How she'd marched then, with fresh resolve, down the stairs to the basement, and stood behind my mother's ancient dress form, and lined its waist up with her own. And how, finally, she'd carved a thick slab from her waistline, through the epidermis then the dermis then the yellow subcutaneous tissue, starting right where her body began to curve.

Or tried to. The knife didn't make it to the other side. She passed out part of the way through, then woke up and crawled behind one of the storage shelves before passing out again. When I eventually showed up, it took me a minute to find her. The first thing I noticed was the pool of red on the concrete floor, and my cat—who was always so goddamn picky, we had to rotate his wet food every other week to keep him interested—my cat, right there, lapping happily at the blood.

Mel's parents took her out of school, obviously, then spent a fortune on a six-month stint at a rehab center in the Hamptons. Soon after, their big brick house went up for sale, and through whisperings at school I was able to pick up that they'd moved an hour east to Endicott, a featureless, blue-collar town much like ours, where nothing noteworthy happened. Their volleyball team consistently ranked toward the bottom, but I thought a good libero could turn that around. I checked their roster the following year, but Mel's name wasn't there.

The Panthers' season was cut short. The athletics department scrambled to find a new coach for the next fall, the fall of my senior year, but few of us had much interest in playing. Those of us who did were subjected to their parents' instant-veto privileges: no child of theirs would go the way of that poor Melissa girl if they had anything to say about it. The program has been cursed ever since. They're lucky if they win a quarter of their games, and the turnover on the coaching staff is the worst in the Southern Tier.

Mel, though. She's good, she's fine. She stages glamour shots of Nutella crepe cakes and Korean beef tacos and all these things we wouldn't have even dreamt of eating, and I have to forcibly stop my brain from jumping to math out the calorie count. She has a sponsorship with Blue Apron. She has a sponsorship with Breville Air Fryer. She has sponsorships with luxury swimwear labels, but she never wears their bikinis—instead it's all one-pieces, low-cut and brightly patterned against the anemic tile around some pool, the plush cushions of some exclusive rooftop bar. She's leggy and she's smiling, and she has a bluebonnet tattoo on the inside of her arm where the Luke scar used to be. She's holding a sunset-colored cocktail, she's holding a teriyaki slider, she's holding a skewer of barbecued lamb kebab, and each cube of meat is wet, sticky, glistening, cooked for the second time by the hot Texas sun.

And me? It's been more than a decade. I'm an adult, and adults get over things. They have new life experiences that plaster over past life experiences. They move on. They overcome. They go to the farmers' market. They spackle the holes in the walls.

Now when I'm asked, in half-hearted interviews conducted by understaffed online lit mags, what's my guilty pleasure, I say that I don't believe in that, that I don't take *guilt* in *pleasure*, which is something I read once that I liked the sound of and not something I actually believe.

When I'm out to eat with someone and they marvel at a menu item they've deemed particularly unhealthy, same thing. I say, evolved and haughty, that I don't believe anything we consume to nourish our bodies can be in any way bad for our health.

Now, on bad days, when my therapist tells me to remember that we are, all of us, born within just a few pounds of each other—

Now when my boyfriend tells me he eats when he's hungry and he stops when he's full, what's so complicated about it?—

When he and I weigh almost exactly the same and he's four inches taller, six if we're going off my real height, not roster—

When he gets caught up doing whatever he's doing, a fantasy football draft or back-to-back meetings, and without noticing he skips two meals and eats for the first time, pan-crust Domino's pizza, at five in the evening—

I realize that, as much as I love him, we will never understand each other.

Now when I talk with my dad, one of our awkward once-a-month phone calls, and he asks how I'm doing, am I keeping well, going to the gym, is there a recreational volleyball league in our new city, would I think about joining, and I called *him* to talk about *his* health because he's fucking *sixty*, and he only wants to talk about me—

Now when I tell my students, fully becoming the woo-woo creative writing teacher they always expected, that one way we might think about it is that our bodies are only vessels *carrying around the writers inside*—

Now when my friends take me shopping at Arc, and while they're thumbing through the clothes racks, I'm keeping studiously to the housewares section, I'm pretending I need another novelty teapot, I'm not looking at mirrors—

Now when I look at this stack of paper, all the pages I've added to pages, horrified by what it is I've done, and instinctively try to calculate how much it all weighs—

Now when any of this happens, I don't think about Mel and the dress form in the basement. I don't think about the weigh-ins, or the headlines in the paper hell-bent on taking Coach Canfield down. (And isn't that growth? Some kind of plateau-getting-over?)

What I think about is this specific picture that Facebook surfaces to me every so often, in one of those "Can you believe it's been however many years?" features. One of those fond remember-whens.

It's a picture of a few of us from the JV team, mine and Mel's freshman year. We're posing for the yearbook around this weird iron structure, a fixture in the high school's poorly maintained courtyard. Me and Whit and Vees and Mel, none of us particularly close then, but assembled haphazardly by the yearbook's harried photographer. You can tell we weren't really friends yet, because I had on this fake puka shell necklace and nobody told me to take it off.

We're wearing soft, swishy shorts just like the girls on the basketball team, and if it hadn't been fashionable to roll them up a bunch at the waistband, they'd be long enough to cover our kneepads. We were as happy as we look. I think so, anyway. We thought mostly about the game: learning the plays, having fun, forgiving ourselves and one another. Not immediately getting into position for sprints any time one of the tippers accidentally grazed the net.

I would learn to hate this picture: how frizzy my hair was that day, my bad luck at having the photo taken during my last week of braces. When I first got it back, though, I liked it. And now I like it again.

We were happy. A Pop Tart was just a Pop Tart. A Pop Tart wasn't something that attached itself to and ruthlessly fed on the still-developing parts of your brain.

It wasn't Coach's fault, or it wasn't only Coach's fault. But I guess if you don't pin it all on Coach, you've got to find someone or something else to blame, and then everyone and everything becomes a potential target.

It's beside the point now, and we probably couldn't appreciate it then, but the extra-brutal part is: we were already *so thin*. In the picture, we're still growing. Every second we're growing. Between the shutter click of this photo and the next one we're growing, every molecule in our bodies concentrating its efforts on our gradual becoming. We're shooting up, the pencil markings on the wall tell us. We're reaching for our final form, preparing to take up every inch of the space allocated to us. Soon—soon!—we'll do it. We'll spread ourselves out luxuriously. *Greedily*.

But we're so slight, too. So nearly nothing.

So at risk already of disappearing.

THE FLOOD, THE TUMBLE, THE TALONS,
THE TRICK

———

No one in Grigory's life would have called him a cheat. He lived in a modest apartment on the north side of town, the last remaining bachelor among his merry friend group. He was candid and clear-eyed, and a mostly frugal spender, save for his one weakness: tiny, unfinished sketches by famous artists, which he bought at Ainsworth Auction Palace several times a year. They weren't cheap, but they were as cheap as it got for the works of a famous artist, and so for one or two thousand dollars, plus the cost of framing, Grigory could point to a wall and say, "That's a genuine so-and-so," from his Cubist phase, or plein-air period, or time spent ruminating on chairs and sunflowers. Many of the sketches were unsigned, but Grigory was serious about his collection and would produce a three-ring binder filled with certificates of authenticity if asked.

No, no one in Grigory's life would have called him a cheat. Which is how you can be sure he was a very good one.

Twice a week, his friends came over to play cards, kissing their wives on the cheeks *goodnight*, their children on the foreheads *goodnight*, and casting sheepish glances at the unwashed dishes in the sink, the baskets of unfolded laundry—because game nights at Grigory's tended to run long, and would take those willing clear into morning. Most played out of a sense of tradition, spurred on by the old logic that it was a healthy thing, good for the spirit, to find respite in the company of other men, whose only demand of you was to know whether you'd play or fold. Some, of course, joined out of need. There was money involved, and during different seasons the men would be hoping to finance a new suit, or a family theme-park vacation, or a part replacement for a finicky lawnmower.

Grigory didn't much need the money. He had only himself to think of, he hated to travel, and excluding his collection of semi-valuable sketches, he was the furthest thing from a spendthrift.

Grigory had another motive.

Grigory played to win.

So when she washed up in his basement after the rains, long silver hair soaked through and heavy as rope, water beading off her many hard, teardrop-shaped scales, Grigory had two competing thoughts in his mind. The art collector in him thought, *Wow, what a masterpiece.* The card shark in him thought, *Now, what a trick.*

••••

When she washed up in his basement, she was part girl and part not, and half asleep. She'd cruised this route countless times, knew the rivers and tributaries like the creases in her front paws: this creek fed into that stream, which fed into that river, which would in due time spit her out into that lake. After the fifth waterfall, you were out of grizzly country, and it was more or less safe to go on autopilot. Only, she'd failed to take into account the heavy rains, brought on by a subset of her cousins partying too extravagantly in the wake of another cousin's recent coming-of-age ceremony, dancing and drinking, wrestling and singing as the moon and sun swapped places again and again in the sky.

Her kind governed all the world's precipitation, and they held this responsibility in the high regard it deserved. But they also had an indulgent streak, and some were still young—a few thousand years at most—and occasionally they forgot themselves.

So the days-long bender brought on the rains, and the rains brought on the landslides, and one particular landslide swept through the north side of one particular town, rerouting the creek so it flowed directly through the back half of Grigory's humble property, the flooding transforming his carefully landscaped yard into a sodden marsh. And had she not been half asleep, letting the current take her as it pleased, she would have used her powerful tail to steer herself straight, her powerful claws to hook onto the bank and hoist herself out of the water.

Instead, she woke just as she was tumbling through Grigory's basement window, glass tearing through pockets of unprotected flesh. She thrashed about in the foot of floodwater, all this foreign wildlife—storage bins and boxes of power tools and camping equipment—cornering her on every side. She briefly mistook the floor fan for a great and regal egret, thin-legged and partly submerged as it was, standing sentry over the dark, musty landscape.

At first, the man seemed curious, and not altogether unkind. He brought a red canvas bag down from one of the shelves and pulled from it bandages and various ointments. He ran a hand over her scales, seemed to be checking for damage.

"Are you the kind that breathes fire?" he asked. He took her silver beard between his thumb and pointer finger, and tugged.

She wasn't, but it was a common enough mistake, depending on which region you found yourself in, and she tried to tell him so.

He scoffed. "What kind of dragon doesn't breathe fire?"

She hadn't been this close to a man in quite a long time; her species did their best to avoid them. This one smelled like smoke and brine and damp fox and dozens of other things she couldn't place.

"Where are your wings?" he asked, tracing the length of her serpentine body. He wedged a thumb beneath one of the scales on her flank and lifted, testing, teasing. She flinched, but didn't strike him. The base of each scale was lousy with nerve endings, but he was a human, and not a very old one, and she allowed that he couldn't have known. Besides, she was in a compromised position: dazed from the fall, her eyes still adjusting to this moonless, walled-in swamp, shards of glass stuck painfully through her lips and paws, and—she was just now realizing—without the luminous orb that gave her her powers.

She felt the orb's absence as a terrible adriftness. Her paws contracted, joints rounded as if clenching its smooth perimeter, though they held nothing. Stories about her kind said they had two hearts. Now one of hers was missing.

"What sort of dragon doesn't have wings?" the man said, more to himself this time. He rifled through the first-aid kit with one hand and lifted out a pair of scissors. He kept the other hand on her torso, too close to the underbelly where the scales went pale.

"What sort of *angel* doesn't have wings?" he murmured, turning back toward her.

She was distracted, wondering where her orb had gone off to. It was a special orb, and she'd been entrusted with its care, and it would not do to lose—

When he snipped her beard off at the chin, she screamed.

••••

"You should put some cream on that, sweetheart," Grigory's friends said about the sores that bloomed in teardrop-shaped patterns across her human skin. He'd installed the cards while she was in dragon form, and however much her scales had warped and bled and rebelled then, it was a thousand times worse once she was a girl. Jammed under her skin, the cards were foreign bodies, and above them she developed raw, bubbling infections that wouldn't heal. Grigory managed to keep the worst of it hidden, but occasionally, when the collar of one of her new shirts slipped ever so slightly, the men would see.

"It's a blessing, Gory," his friends teased him. "If she didn't have a few flaws, she'd be too good for you."

Grigory called his angel Dove. She'd told him her real name, in her strange, slippery language that made every word feel as if it'd been coated in soybean oil. But at the time, the plumbers were in the basement pumping out water, and the incredibly loud dehumidifier they'd installed in the stairwell was running full force, so Grigory couldn't quite make out what she'd said. Even if he had, it didn't seem like something he'd be able to pronounce without effort. So he bestowed upon her the name Dove, after his most treasured sketch: an outline of a pigeon done in what looked like four swift strokes of charcoal, not even a dot for the eye.

As a dragon, Dove had hundreds and hundreds of scales in iridescent shades of blue and green and gold, but the eighty-one lining her back were the ones that mattered. They were the largest, each the size of Grigory's hand with the fingers spread out, and slightly more pliant than the others.

The first time he slotted the playing cards behind her scales, he couldn't believe his luck. He remembered reading somewhere that seeing a dragon was considered good fortune. But he believed in making his *own* fortune. It was how he'd come to possess his modest apartment and all the famous minor artworks inside, and how he would have his own private creek once the flooding receded. It was how he planned to win every card game he hosted from now till kingdom come.

It was an elaborate plan, but elaborate had always worked for him. Like at Ainsworth Auction Palace:

sometimes he would pretend to be the buyer for some wealthy client, or the curator for some exciting new museum, and he would drive the price up on pieces he didn't even want, just to draw attention from the ones he did. He'd learned the more layers, the more twists, the less likely it was he'd be found out.

Eighty-one scales meant he could keep a spare deck and a half inside her, and whenever he needed a certain card, she could use her ancient dragon magic to push it up.

In girl form, Dove was slender with a long torso that had too many bends to it, as if she had not one waistline but two or even three. She had four fingers on each hand and four toes on each foot, and her irises were such a light shade of eggshell blue that, unless you were standing very, very close, it was easy to mistake them for white. Her damp hair, when not tied up, dropped down to the floor, and no matter how much time passed, or how vigorously Grigory toweled her off, it would never dry.

At least there were no wings for him to worry about. Clipping her would have been quite the project.

Dove couldn't stay a girl for long. She only transformed those two nights a week when Grigory's friends came to play cards. Even so, the cost of maintaining the illusion annoyed him. He'd bought extra-long, extra-loose shirts to hide her peculiar curves, and mittens to mask her missing fingers. The day she arrived, he sheared her beard and whiskers and filed down her nails and teeth, and by the next morning it had all grown back, thicker and stronger than ever. He went through three heavy-duty hair trimmers in one week before switching to sugar waxing strips, which he had to venture onto an online beauty forum to figure out how to use.

He kept the lights in the game room low, so the men wouldn't notice the stubble that, by the end of the night, threatened to sprout along the girl's cheeks and chin.

Dove was as uncoordinated on land as she was graceful in water. It seemed she could never get used to the fact of her two legs moving independently from one another, no tail to help with balance. She bumped into walls, tripped over rugs, knocked over the trays of drinking glasses—Monster Zero Ultra with vodka—she was meant to bring to the men at the table. The stairs down to the basement were nearly impossible for her. Once the plumbers had drained it, Grigory permitted her to retreat there in her dragon form to rest.

On game nights, he used Dove's clumsiness to his advantage. When she fell, he rushed to her side in a flurry of concern, and at that exact moment, back turned to the other men, he had her deposit the queen of hearts into his palm. And his opponents would be none the wiser, too busy cleaning up the bowl of caviar the ungainly girl had spilled mere moments ago. Grigory didn't eat caviar on his own time. It was no small expense—fifty dollars a pop at Kroger, from gold-colored cardboard pallet displays stamped LUXURY—and he wanted each tin to last as long as possible. But he always put some out on game nights, because the other men coveted it badly.

He had a reputation to uphold, after all.

He was a connoisseur of beautiful things.

••••

However light the individual cards were, carrying all of them inside her made her feel full and sick and weak.

When Grigory gave her the signal—a complicated series of eye movements and subtle table taps that his friends must've attributed to mid-game nerves—she withdrew the appropriate card from between the layers of her human skin. There was wave after wave of pain in the card's excavation, its eruption through the topmost layer, then momentary relief once the extraneous matter was removed. Once the skin took its new shape, however, she felt an excruciating hollowness that wouldn't recede until the man installed a replacement card in that one's slot—in the bathtub, both of them slick with her blood—at which point she would feel engorged again, almost to the point of immobility.

She kept all this off her human face, which remained calm as morning lake water. But beneath the surface, the face of the dragon contorted fiercely, the body of the dragon within her writhed.

She felt faint. So bloated and heavy from the cards, and so very dry. She was used to being in water much of the time, and Grigory only let her bathe twice a week, on game days before the men arrived. Even then, he was in the room with her, with his wax strips and scented powders and emery boards, working to make her presentable. His hands all over her, all but her tail, which hung over the tub's rim, the tip feebly stiffening and curling. The rest of the time, he kept the bathroom door locked, so she couldn't enter alone.

Like the fire-breathing dragons he'd read about, he

guarded this most precious of resources, and she came to rely on him for it. She craved the twice-weekly baths; without them, she would have perished long ago. Though with Grigory controlling the tap, they were too short to truly restore her.

The transformations—and the heft of the cards, and the empty, stifling air—exhausted her. But she could not get comfortable in her new environment, and this made it hard for her to sleep. When she finally managed to nod off, her dreams were filled with orbs: the golden spheres in the old kumquat trees back home, the clutch of eggs her sisters guarded watchfully, the single strange glass bulb that hovered above her on the ceiling, attached to a string that Grigory pulled each morning, flooding the basement with wretched, artificial light.

She woke with her paws still clenched, as if, by gripping the air tightly enough, she could rearrange its molecules into one luminous orb.

While the men played, her human hands clenched for different reasons.

"Where are you from, sweetie?" Grigory's friends looked her up and down, admiring. "Such a unique look to you. So unusual." They took turns guessing her origins, her *composition*, but never even came close.

She would have told them herself, only she wasn't allowed to speak. Her tongue didn't shift with the rest of her, and it was fat and forked inside her girl mouth, folded up against the backs of her flat, useless teeth. Grigory knew the way she spoke, that oily edge to her words, would give them away. And she knew that—without her second heart, without nearly enough water—she wasn't strong enough to fight off one of them, much less all of them, anymore.

They asked Grigory about her skin beyond the rashes, the proportions of her sharp cheekbones to her milk-glass eyes and pert, piggish nose. They marveled that she looked, to them, so exotic. Grigory waved them off, scolded them for being dirty, lustful men. He told them to remember the children they had at home, and—he glared—the wives.

But the men persisted. "She must be one of those mixed girls. Remember Donny's lady a while back? He said there's nothing like them." They elbowed each other, vodka-Monsters clinking, eyes twinkling.

They didn't know how right they were.

••••

The dragon they called Dove was hatched in the crevice of a vast, echoing sea cave before the card game the men played was even invented. Her cousins were not *all* of the hard-partying, troublemaking variety. They did not always cause monsoons when toasting their proud legacy, did not always reroute rivers when on the verge of winning a limbo contest—these celebrations, and the swelling emotions that came with them, throwing everything out of balance. No, many of her kind were responsible, or at some point during their long, long lives had been.

Centuries ago, her more distant relations had been tasked with pulling the chariots of the world's most respected beings—diplomats and dignitaries, high-ranking politicians and kings of all species. It was nothing like the work of farm bulls and city horses. Cockatrices weren't beasts of burden; they wore no harnesses and obeyed no orders. Instead, it was *they* who steered, deciding where their passengers would go.

These days, her kind saw to it that the rain and snow were measured out carefully, keeping the crops in their proper cycles and the plants and animals of the world in good health. Each dragon was endowed with all the faculties of the zodiac: with the wide nose of a pig, the swiveling ears of a cow, the deer's sturdy horns, the rabbit's keen eyes. They carried within them ancestral knowledge, defended against threats from all directions. More than a few of her sisters had laid the eggs from which a renowned prince or princess was born.

But the dragon they called Dove had the greatest responsibility of all. One of the uncommon four-toed, she was declared strong and dexterous enough to be entrusted with a luminous orb. These orbs held the powers of omnipotence and creation, and they'd dwindled in number over the ages—falling victim to wars and diasporas—so there weren't very many left. The fewer there were, the more valuable they became. To ensure the orbs' safety, the four-toed dragons were bound to the orbs they protected, and when an orb was lost or destroyed, its dragon went with it.

Now, the dragon they called Dove had always prided herself on being one of the mature ones of her generation, one of those who could be counted on. Take the recent coming-of-age ceremony. She had paid her respects, joined in all the rituals expected of a creature of her status, then left the party at a reasonable hour, doing her part to keep things from getting out of hand. She'd left the party—it was called *moderation*—and gone on to her next destination, a drought-ridden region that desperately needed her help. She was dozing a bit, thinking a nap would permit her to arrive in fine form, when: first the flood, then the crash, then the odd little man with his skinny fingers poking and prodding where they didn't belong.

A lot of good her sense of responsibility had done her. Her cousins were probably lounging by some crystalline alpine lake, unaware of all the problems they'd caused, sleeping the whole thing off. While she was here, growing ever more depleted.

And searching, searching.

The four-toed were tied to their luminous orbs; her very soul was tethered to it. She could not leave this place until she found hers.

When she wasn't lingering around the table on game nights, waiting for Grigory's signal for her to extract from within her swollen, stinging girl body a specific card, she was in her true form in the basement, nudging her snout through box after wet cardboard box. She must have had the orb when she burst into the house, she assured herself—her claws were many, designed to hold things well. She'd find it on some dusty shelf or in some cobwebbed corner, and then she'd shoot up to her full height, and all the jacks and kings and aces would pinwheel out of her like throwing stars, and her keeper Grigory would be doomed.

Only thoughts of her orb's safe return kept her from coming undone completely.

Grigory didn't seem to know about the luminous orb. It was the first trump card she had, in the otherwise rotten hand she'd been dealt.

••••

With Grigory employing his new trick, the winnings from the first month alone were substantial, and he decided to make an exception to his usual frugality: he went out and bought a patterned silk robe. It was a deep, moody blue with rolling cotton-candy clouds and the wrong kind of dragon—the kind that flew through the air and clung to the sides of castle walls, spit flames from between its teeth the way men spit sunflower seeds. The kind of dragon that sometimes even took riders. It didn't matter to Grigory that it wasn't Dove's species. He wore the robe on game nights because he liked having his cheat right under his friends' noses, liked hearing them compliment the beauty of the dragon print without realizing what it hinted at.

He threw a game every now and then, when the winnings were small, ensured the drinks were topped off and the mood light, to keep his friends from growing suspicious.

The men often spoke like Dove wasn't in the room— though she was *always* in the room, had to be, in case a hidden high card needed to be deployed. Grigory's friends asked whether his girl had sisters. They inquired about the skin cream: had he had any luck finding a tube, and their wives probably had extra if he wanted to try it. They made vulgar comments about Dove's nails, which were tapered and long enough to curve, and had begun to poke through the mittens' loose weave. His friends said his back must look like a scratching post the lazy mornings after.

"Will you get married already?" they pried, once Dove seemed a permanent fixture in all their lives. "Or are you addicted to the bachelor life, Gory-Ory?"

Grigory told them a truth: that he had no plans to marry Dove, nor any need to. That, if they caught his meaning, he was, in a manner of speaking, presently simply *enjoying her body*. He expected his friends to understand this to a certain extent, and they did. He expected them to misunderstand it to another extent, and they did that too.

In this way, Grigory grew incrementally richer as the seasons outside his apartment changed. The water level in the creek that ran through his property dipped lower and lower, and at first he considered this another bit of good fortune: he wouldn't have to deal with the hassles of flooding again. But then, as springtime gave way to summer, the sun beat down upon the region relentlessly, without the first black cloud of a thunderstorm in sight. The grass in the backyard, once long and soft, turned yellow-brown and brittle, and the fruit on the trees rotted from heat. He told himself that at least his new Degas sketches would be protected, moisture being the enemy of all well-preserved art.

Degas' graphite ballerinas adjusted their slippers within their gilded wood frames. They stood in fourth position, raised willowy, rough-drawn arms, while everything around them withered and died.

Something was out of balance in the kingdom of the water dragons—their kind experienced the lack of one of their own viscerally, as if a vital limb torn off—but Grigory saw it as just another unseasonably warm, dry summer.

This was the second trump card she had to her advantage.

••••

Sunsets were small in Grigory's apartment, trapped and shrunk down inside four-cornered frames.

After many such sunsets without her orb, she still sensed her proximity to it. She couldn't walk straight, couldn't think straight. She had torn the basement apart dozens of times while Grigory slept, and still her heart eluded her. Then one day, emerging briefly from her post-transformation stupor, she began to suspect the orb had decided to conceal itself, in case the man should unwittingly stumble upon it.

The luminous orb did have a mind of its own—after all, it was older than its dragon by at least a millennium, and it had seen much and knew much about the ways of the world and greedy men. When she was first assigned to it, before they became a bonded pair, the orb made a habit of sinking to the bottoms of lakes and rivers, pretending to be an ordinary stone. She understood that it was testing her. Was she perceptive enough to recognize it camouflaged among the rest of the dark, smooth stones? Was she strong enough to dig it out from the others? It took many such games of hide-and-seek for her to win the orb's trust.

Why shouldn't it be the case, then, that the orb was masquerading as something else in the man's apartment, waiting for its dragon to once again retrieve it?

She listened for Grigory's snoring—somehow louder than the wheezing of all the sleeping cousins in her den combined—then crept gingerly up the basement stairs. Snuffling through the hall closet, she found delicate glass spheres painted in shades of red and green, all with a little hook at the top, giving off the smell of pine trees. There was a larger, heavy globe with three holes on one side, each hole the width of one of Grigory's fingers. She put her ear to the holes, listening for her orb's spirit, but heard nothing—not ocean, not even air. When she set the three-holed ball back down—it tired her to hold it—it rolled along the uneven floorboards and clattered into a tower of objects at the back of the closet. Afraid of waking the man, she slunk quietly back downstairs.

A different night, she found brown hens' eggs just on the brink of going bad, and marbles streaked with vibrant ribbons, and fragrant woven orbs in a low wooden bowl. On a table by the front door: a tray of bright, circular candies. She held each in her mouth for a long moment, waiting for the warmth that would mean her luminous orb was hiding inside.

During a separate search, she ventured through a door she'd not yet opened, and stepped into a cold, grey room covered in sawdust. Everywhere there were orbs: some the size of a human palm, the color of limes, but bouncy; another tangerine-colored and bumpy as the wattles of her cockatrice relatives; another checkered with black and white tiles and lopsided, as if waiting to be inflated with breath. In another room, in a high-up cabinet, she found orange bottles filled with oblong orbs. The bottles had white caps, ridged around the edges, and she tried to pinch them off, but they were too small inside her dragon paws.

The soapy bubbles clinging to the floor of the tub.

Balls of cotton stuffed into a stout glass jar.

Balls of ice in pitchers, in the men's drinks.

Balls of yarn, of jute, of gleaming metal.

But there was nothing of the luminous orb in any of them. She gnashed her teeth in frustration, wondering if she would survive long enough to find it. She felt like a kumquat with the flesh all scooped out.

Then the men's eyes, dreadful orbs themselves, moving up and down the length of her girl body, lingering on her snakelike shape, the irritations on her chin and face where Grigory had taken to attacking the hair with a seven-blade razor. For all they didn't notice, the men did pick up on the fact of her degrading. Her skin was angrier than ever, blistering red hot over the places where the cards were concealed. She was stooped around the shoulders, and she had purple half-moons under her eyes from nights of sleepless searching.

Only, the men didn't regard her disfigurations with disgust. She recognized the expression they wore on their faces, for it was one she had worn herself, whenever a lone musk deer wandered too close to the water. The look of an apex predator sniffing out weakness.

One night, while Grigory was shuffling the deck, one of the men explained to the group the concept of "ruin value." He said he'd read about it in *Architectural Digest*: this school of thought that buildings could be designed with a view to their deterioration and eventual collapse— so they would be beautiful to start with, yes, and the ruins they left behind would remain aesthetically pleasing. As he said this, he looked at the girl they called Dove.

"Nothing lasts forever," he added, "and some things are meant to be destroyed. Whether that's a building or"—his eyes drifted lower—"something else. But why shouldn't they still look nice after time's had its way with them?"

Another man, who never seemed to know what the first man was going on about, interrupted: "But aren't women like vodka?" And when the other men took him up on this—"How do you mean?"—he replied, grinning, "Even bad vodka is still vodka."

"The worst vodka in the world is still better than the best of everything else!" he said, and all the men toasted to that. It was another hot, dry night in an unending series of hot, dry nights, and the vodka-Monsters were cool relief against their gums.

All the while, the one they called Dove couldn't take her eyes off the little bowl of caviar at the center of the table, the little spoon balanced on the ceramic rim. She sat on the margins, as she always did until she was beckoned, on the side of the room opposite her keeper Grigory. The littleness of the bowl, the spoon, seemed intentional, as if to underscore both the host's frugality and the preciousness of the delicacy he served. But Grigory was in high spirits. He dipped the spoon deeper into the bowl than was typical and proudly distributed the caviar onto his plate, atop his friends' garlic crackers.

She couldn't take her eyes off them: those hundreds of tiny, green, glistening orbs.

Between the men's laughter, she heard something familiar. It started at their teeth, then grew duller, muffled.

The sound of a river stone plunking through the water's surface.

The hum of insistent, unquenchable life.

••••

The night the longest dry spell in the region's history finally broke, she was standing in her true form over the overturned game table, digging through Grigory's gut with all eight claws. In all her time on this plane, she had never heard screams quite like his. That herd of goats by the hot sulfur springs many seasons ago was close—only there was something thin about this one, unrooted and hollow. Her cow-like ears pricked and spun.

Blood splattered across the unfinished sketches Grigory had framed on the walls of the game room. She didn't have strong opinions about human art, but if pressed she would admit she thought they looked better like that, with a little color on them. More complete.

When she first sensed the luminous orb's presence dispersed across the beads of caviar, she felt a surge of power course through her that for months had laid dormant. It was a fraction of what she felt when the two of them were united, but it was enough for her to know what to do.

Starting in the wet grotto she'd gouged into Grigory's pale underbelly, she plucked out the sturgeon eggs that called out most loudly to her—those vibrating gently inside the coils of his viscera, trilling their ancient song. With one claw, she drew a line up his stomach, then his chest, then his neck, and the skin fell away so easily, parting like a canopy of trees for the wind. She found the remainder of the eggs gathered in his gullet like dark gems.

She no longer feared his call of *Come now, my angel*, or his careless hands probing under her tender scales. In the seconds before he died, he could only claw uselessly at his face, begging soundlessly for rescue.

And did she hear him? She did not hear him. She had grown accustomed to not being spoken to—the men's habit of talking *about* her without addressing her directly.

The men. She was surprised at how long they stood and watched their friend's destruction, crowded there in the doorway, shaking as one. The goats always darted away as fast as their bony legs would take them—the deer and the fox kits, too—whenever one of their own was successfully taken down. They understood that staying put meant watching a preview of their own fate play out moments before it happened.

When the first ball of hail hit the window, the men stirred as if from a trance and went scampering backwards, tumbling over one another out the closest door. Toward the backyard and the nearly dried-up creek, where her cousins waited.

Yes, her cousins had at last arrived, bringing the long-overdue hailstorm with them. And this was the third and final trump card in her hand against the man who had got it into his head somehow that he could collect and keep her. Of course, they had shown up a bit behind schedule—Grigory already incapacitated, no longer a threat, and she, his captive, virtually free. But that wasn't unusual for her family: she was, like she always said, the most responsible among them. The one who didn't overstay at parties but went promptly where droughts and other duties called her. The one who knew when it was time to move on.

But her cousins had come as fast as they could, and she loved them for it.

Besides, the luminous orb wasn't entirely reassembled. It pulsed on the tile between Grigory's dissected corpse and the back door, growing bit by bit as the eggs she had freed rejoined it, a partial thought still, gummy and amorphous. It seemed not all of the orb was contained in the eggs Grigory had swallowed; the men had consumed their fair share as well.

She would let her cousins help with that.

At first, when she burst through the apartment's back door, she was smaller and sicker than they had ever seen her, her scales bristled and tilted at odd angles and her silver whiskers alarmingly spare. But as she raced toward them—the men a few paces ahead, then fewer—she grew taller and her lips regained their redness, like in-season strawberries, and her beard curled to her chest, then her knees, then all the way to the ground. Her tail etched wavy patterns into the once-brittle grass, which went soft and lush when she trod upon it, and the eighty-one special scales running down her back again flashed blue and green and gold.

The frozen orbs hurtled from the sky, crashing through the newly patched-up basement window. When she stepped over the shards of glass, she did not stop to glimpse whether they held her reflection.

Her cousins tore eagerly into the men, and though they were among the common three-toed, together they made quick work of them. Afterwards, lying prone on the creek bed, the men looked unexpectedly beautiful: mouths still and eyes shut tight, skin the color of kicked-up alkaline dust. The sunlight glinting off the globules of meat and fat made their insides look full of rubies. Made the whole thing look like a gigantic geode carved out.

Ruin value, she remembered, and she felt the words reverberate in the joints of her jaw: *Some things are meant to be destroyed. Why shouldn't they still look nice?* Once she and her cousins recovered the last of the orb, they would leave the carcasses for other animals to find. Hungry vultures at one end and muskies at the other, where the men's legs dangled into the water. Everything returned to its proper cycle.

When her orb was itself again, having shrugged off the last of its concealments, she cautiously approached it. The orb radiated—and its dragon absorbed—that she had a great deal of work ahead of her if she ever hoped to regain the orb's trust. No matter, she thought; she could be patient, persistent. What was another several hundred years of hide-and-seek games to her? She had done it before.

Reunited with her irksome cousins, her orb in its rightful place between her claws, she at last left that horrid place—and if she had been some other dragon, she would have taken flight. Being what she was, she traveled by water, knowing the path out like the creases in her front paws. This creek would feed into that stream, which would feed into that river, which would in due time spit them out into that lake. As she went, she sent playing cards spewing out in long lines behind her, to grow soggy and disintegrate to faceless pulp in the current.

She did this until she'd jettisoned every last card, and with them that other thing she'd been forced to carry, the other thing that didn't belong with her: Grigory's name for her, Dove. A tribute to some artist whose pencil strokes she cared not for. A name meant for winged things, for *angels*—and she'd never claimed to be one of those.

She gave a mighty snort, angled her horns due south, and dove.

THE ADVOCATE

Jae dresses for her doctor's appointment like she's going into battle. Because she is. She's suffered her losses, walked hangdog and beaten out of every office within a thirty-mile radius of her Fruitvale apartment—what her landlords call a cottage in-law, but what is really the back two-thirds of their storage shed. Dr. Kohler got the best of her. Dr. Mahoney, too. Dr. Jain. But every appointment gets her one step closer. Every clash that doesn't kill her teaches her to be better prepared.

On a shelf she's installed on the far side of the shed, above where her landlords keep their garden sprays and broken lawnmowers, is Jae's collection of books on long-ago war games. Picked up at yard sales, borrowed from the library down the street from Dimond Slice: every book she could find on medieval jousts before the rise of chivalry. She's pored over faded illustrations of tiltyards red with blood, the sky raining splinters from shattered lances. There was the king who famously died after a fragment of wood shot through his eye, the knights skewered when an opponent's spear found the unlucky gap in their armor.

Which is why she's extra, extra careful with hers.

Jae's armor? Peer-reviewed articles from medical journals, printed on heavyweight cardstock, then cut into strips and woven into something resembling chainmail. She pulls it on a little at a time to avoid paper cuts. Over that, a coat of plates, each plate a folded copy of her medical history, going back three generations on her father's side, four on her mother's. There's a map of her moles over her bandaged left shoulder, notes on color, shape, and change in diameter over time. There's a record of medications and a period calendar taped to the outside of a bicycle helmet to make a great helm. For forearm guards, she took the logs she's kept of her symptoms since she was nineteen, blew them up to poster board size, and rolled them into tubes she wears from elbow to wrist.

Proof enough, you would think. *Ironclad.* But always the doctors find some crack, some weak point to pierce into.

Of course, Jae would rather not think of them as adversaries. Would rather not spend what little she's got left after rent money on Icy Hot, duct tape, and rush services at the local Copy and Print. But they struck the first blow, started all this. And since then, they haven't let up.

The first blow: that appointment three years ago, when Jae finally set out to get a diagnosis. She walked in without so much as a breastplate, just her insurance card and a cardigan for the lobby chill, so naive. This was before the books, before all the rewatches of *A Knight's Tale* at quarter speed, Jae pausing every fifth second to scribble in her notepad, trying to calculate the exact angle of William Thatcher's shield. She'd scheduled an appointment with Dr. Young, Jr. His father, Dr. Young, Sr., worked there, too. It was a family practice on Foothill, decorated

with photographs of father and son—Harvard graduation, skeet shooting—and kitschy plastic pumpkins for
Halloween. The little light-up ghost on the welcome
desk threw her. She didn't know then it was part of their
attack style.

Every tournament has its pageantries. In the olden days,
a knight would ask a lady for her favor, some token, like
a belt or brooch, that meant: *here, take this, survive*. For
the younger Dr. Young, it was the orange tinsel wrapped
around the base of the light-up ghost, which the receptionist kissed lightly and draped over his shoulders before
waving Jae ahead into the exam room.

In retrospect, Jae figures he was of the post-chivalry
school. Soft-spoken and kind-eyed and at least outwardly
polite, nowhere near as bloodthirsty as some of those she's
seen since. But she made every mistake an amateur can:
didn't have her paperwork in order, let him talk too long
about her diet, stumbled when he asked whether anyone
had told her she had an unusually low pain tolerance. Her
defenses were down—her defenses weren't even *built* yet—
and she didn't recognize the exam room for the arena it
was. So, after just six and a half minutes, Dr. Young ush-
ered her back into the lobby, Jae nursing a bruised rib cage
and both of them convinced the rest was all in her head.

Now, Jae knows better. She scouts Zocdoc reviews ahead
of time, researching her next opponent's strengths and
weaknesses. Is the doctor brusque, dismissive, obviously distracted, doubtful, patronizing, too quick with the
script? Do they carry their weapons high or low? She can't

trust the ratings system alone: she's been to the five-star doctors, even the five-star *female* doctors, and it hasn't made a difference. She searches the reviews for the word "seriously," as in *wouldn't take me*, and the word "listen," as in *refused to*.

She's running out of targets. At this next appointment, she'll be visiting the last in-network provider accessible by the BART and bus lines. The other passengers look at her funny when she strides on from the platform in her head-to-toe paper armor, bouncing up and down to stay limber, stay sharp. But BART fare's something she can usually handle. And when she can't, jumping turnstiles is a good pre-battle warmup. After this appointment, though, she'll have to fork over out-of-network costs—not really an option—or rent a car to get to the more out-of-the-way offices, which doesn't seem possible either, given the rate at which her landlords have been upping her rent. Or, you know, hang up her great helm. Give up for good.

It's not ideal, the storage shed, but it's home. Enough room between the landlords' pool chairs and never-used snowshoes for a small dresser that doubles as a desk and nightstand, and Jae's twin bed, which doubles as a place to nurse her wounds. It's not *so* bad, really. Her landlords are landlords. They're not fire-breathing dragons or the bubonic plague. They even agreed to move the propane tanks after she noticed a new smell, like road-killed skunk, seeping into her pillow, making her wake up dizzy and sick. And when they're not home, she gets the yard to herself, to practice her blows with their arsenal of shovels and rakes.

One thing at a time. Eventually, a better living situation. First, a diagnosis—better living.

She's running out of doctors to lose to, and she knows pretty soon all this losing is going to get lethal. So Jae figures she'd better win.

Her maps app tells her this appointment is in Daly City, in a building of medical suites that also includes a CoolSculpting spa and a place that specializes in something called hyperbaric oxygen therapy. She highlights the words on her phone screen, then copies and pastes them into the search bar. If a distraction presents itself to her, she's going to take it. It's a twenty-minute walk to Fruitvale BART when she's *not* limping, twice as long now that she is, and she's already sweating under her helmet, and her armpits are already wet from nerves and chafing in that one spot where the cardstock chainmail digs in.

Jae thinks hyperbaric oxygen therapy sounds positively medieval. The pictures are pretty much what she expects.

Everyone at the station stares like she knew they would, then they look away. There are weirder and more tragic things than somebody cosplaying as a low-budget lady knight on the Blue Line at the quietest part of day. They probably assume she's test-driving a Bay to Breakers costume, or maybe there's some comic book convention in town. Still, she's in such rough shape that a teenager wearing headphones offers her their seat by the bike zone. She says no thanks, and they offer again. She waves the kid off, straightening her coat of plates as best she can.

As the train dips under the bay and the pressure in her ears changes, Jae thinks she sees someone dressed just like her, only their armor is made of something else. At first it looks like obsidian, but when she squints, she can just make out row after row of credit cards: that new one, superpremium, super exclusive, matte black.

The other knight's armor ripples with the train's jerking movements. It looks heavy, keen-edged, and its silver markings dance in the light. Jae's crossed paths with others like her before. Last month in Chinatown, there was the armor made of plaques and medals, the figure inside it slim and muscled, but hunched over, taking stiff, dragging steps. Another time, Jae passed a knight wearing armor made of portable tape recorders. Before that, the armor was jars of powder and polished crystals, vials of amber-colored oil Jae could smell through the corks.

Always, the interaction is the same. The knights lock eyes for an instant, then break away and keep moving. No one dares stop and risk being late. They know there's at most a ten-minute grace window before their appointment slot's marked *no-show*.

Just like Jae expects, the obsidian knight nods curtly before slipping into an adjoining car—on their way, she imagines, to their own doctor's office. Their own battle. Their own long shot.

Jae holds the stanchion in one hand and fingers the bottom of her chainmail with the other. At the last minute, she sewed on a line of pages from the Wikipedia entry on Plato's wandering womb theory: this outdated but once persistent idea that all a woman's ails could be traced back to her *restless womb*—which moved about her body, bumping up against her other organs, causing all sorts of problems, even all the way up to the brain. Jae went back and forth about adding the pages. She knows to be careful using sources like that: Wikipedia and random Twitter threads and WebMD. She's made that mistake before, showed a doctor an article from a blog called *This Endo-Life with Sally.* It got her a raised eyebrow and a comment like: *Let's leave the medicine to the experts, shall we?*

It was a cutting remark, and it cut.

The Wikipedia entry is meant to be nothing scientific, obviously, but an example of widely respected thinkers getting it spectacularly wrong. A cautionary tale about being satisfied with easy answers, then two thousand years later being ridiculed by the modern medical community at large. It isn't a premium matte-black credit card on a bodysuit full of them. It isn't money, or debt, or the willingness to go even further into it. But it's something.

Jae's made other improvements to her armor since her last appointment, a total bloodbath at a bougie women's clinic in the hills of Montclair. An updated list of vaccines. An updated list of allergies. Two pages from an article in last month's issue of *The New England Journal of Medicine.* Plus, there's this story her friend's grandma once told her, about the forced pelvic massages women used to receive as treatment for what was then called hysteria. Way back when, at the behest of their husbands or fathers—manual stimulation.

Afterwards, Jae's friend told her, "I'm pretty sure that's been disproven," and "Don't listen to Gram. She's halfway to crazy." But Jae couldn't get the story out of her head, so she transcribed it into her journal, ripped out the pages, and now that's part of her armor, too.

At the bougie women's clinic in Montclair, the doctor pursed his lips and asked Jae if there was a husband he could speak with.

The train pulls into Daly City with a screech and the few remaining passengers file out, hauling suitcases behind them, clearly transfers to the airport. Jae eyes them longingly, though she knows there are battles everywhere, that leaving this city, this coast, would be no escape.

She takes the stairs to street level, putting as much weight on the handrail as she can, and immediately she regrets not checking the weather. She's lived in Oakland for so long, she's forgotten about the microclimates you get further south. It's foggy today, fat beads of moisture bordering on rain, and within minutes her cardstock begins to wrinkle and curl. She vows next time she'll remember to bring an umbrella, or better yet, have her armor laminated.

Only, there can't be a next time. There *won't*. This is the battle to win the war.

There's a reason she's waited this long to come here. Dr. Guthrie has two and a half stars on Zocdoc, dinged time and time again for bedside manner. Multiple reviews use the word "gruff," which Jae understands to mean pre-chivalry: no false cordiality or scrolls framed in the hallway, detailing codes of honor. More positive reviews admit he's "efficient," but Jae knows that just means a short fight to the death. A lance to the throat on the first run.

No amount of research could've prepared her for this particular lobby.

The first thing she sees when she comes through the sliding doors? A series of open-mouthed mannequin heads stuck high on six-foot spikes. Three in a gruesome row—their hair and lips the same color as the rest of their skin, all the dull, lifeless color of a tub of Quaker Oats. Their rubbery eyes are closed, and their rubbery jaws hang slack. Inside each silent scream, Jae can make out a too-real tongue and teeth, the same shade of beige as everything else.

They're those fake heads they use for CPR training, she realizes, torn free from the chest and airway. She remembers the dummies from high school swim: synthetic corpses spilling headfirst from the storage closet between the pool and locker rooms, like a well-placed threat. What could happen to the kids if they fooled around, didn't pull the lane lines up at the end of the class period like they were supposed to.

Jae keeps the mannequin heads in her sight. Knows they, too, are a warning.

"Hi there!" The receptionist is cheerful, greets Jae before she's even reached the front desk. He follows her gaze. "Oh," he laughs, "you like those? One of our techs, Randy, came up with it. His other job is working haunted houses."

The receptionist doesn't say anything about Jae's armor, but after he's entered her insurance information and handed her a tablet loaded with forms to sign, she notices him jotting something down on a skinny notepad, then slipping that notepad to the next nurse who passes by.

While Jae waits to be called in, she goes over her attack plan, blow by blow. Most of it comes from her books on war games. Some of it comes from a Twitter thread she read on how to be taken seriously in a medical setting. It was posted by a sympathetic neurology student in Denver, who updated her bio from *wannabe MD* to *med school dropout* in the weeks after the thread went viral.

Jae's plan is this: First, she'll present the paperwork, in the right order. She'll use the scientific terms for everything. She won't mispronounce them.

Or she'll use the scientific terms for everything, and she'll mispronounce just *one* of them, just a *little*. Because she wants to sound professional, but she doesn't want to give the impression that she considers herself *to be* one of the professionals—doesn't want to make it seem like she thinks she can do their job. Also, she doesn't want to sound like one of those hypochondriacs who spends all their time clicking between unmoderated self-diagnosis forums and symptoms lists on MayoClinic.org. That's a mistake she's made already, how Dr. Kohler managed to knock her to the ground.

She'll smile.

With exactly one-third of her teeth, she'll smile.

She'll sound informed but not cold, good-natured but not overeager. She'll be well-prepared but agreeable, deferential at all the right times. When the doctor starts eyeing the clock three or four minutes in, she'll ask strategic questions to keep him engaged.

And she'll talk about the bleeding. She'll talk about the bleeding *unflinchingly*. She'll talk about the pain that feels like a cannonball that pummels her stomach and then breaks through. She'll talk about the specific treatment she's read about: the severing of nerve endings. She won't blush, or cringe. She won't let her voice drop to a whisper at the words she's been taught to find embarrassing. Like at Dr. Mahoney's, when she stared at the pale linoleum floor and all the blood boiled up to the surface of her skin. When she talks about *those* organs, she'll talk about them as if she's talking about any other organs. No—when she talks about those organs, she'll pretend she's talking about the smooth plastic organs of a medical dummy, true to size but stock-still and dry.

Because otherwise, she might cry. And she *never* wants to cry. Not after her poor showing at Dr. Jain's, and the post-visit report in the web portal that stamped her *abnormally expressive*. Here, she won't give them a reason to declare her hysterical. She won't get written off as *exceptionally sensitive*, then prescribed counseling, or exercise, or sleep, or protein, or sunshine, or shoe inserts, or sex, or books.

Books, she's got plenty.

She'll smile.

She'll inhale, exhale, like those CPR dolls with the built-in respiratory anatomy. She'll keep her voice level, even when her opponent's lifts and dips into condescension. She'll repeat the important stuff—she read once that you have to say the same thing three times for them to even begin to register it. She'll use the phrase *quality of life*.

"Jae!" Her name rings through the lobby, that one syllable squeezed, pinched, and pulled into something she can barely recognize. "Ja-e!"

Jae returns the issue of *Women's Health* she hasn't been reading to its place among the magazines fanned out on the center table. In her head, she dog-ears her attack plan for later, when she might again need it. She punctuates it with her usual pep talk: Play the underdog you are, got it? Then *strike*.

Dr. Guthrie is not what she imagined. He's short and narrow-shouldered, with an affable expression and eyes that turn down a little at the corners, and he's only lightly armored: the standard clipboard and a white lab coat. Some hefty fabric—Jae guesses it must be flame-retardant—unbuttoned to reveal a clownishly bright tie. The roll of stickers peeking out from his pocket suggests he picks up shifts in pediatrics.

There's a tiny spot of blood on his lapel from a previous appointment. The only thing that gives him away.

Jae steps over the invisible rope separating his side of the tiltyard from hers. She hoists herself up on the exam table, smoothing her paper armor so it lies flat.

In the bone at the base of her left ear, a horn sounds.

And it begins.

"So, Jae." Dr. Guthrie is beaming, already so confident. "What brings you in today?"

She sits up straight, assumes her ready stance, and tries

to ignore the disadvantages set up for her: the disposable sheet beneath her crinkling with every movement, her legs dangling, childlike, a full two feet off the tiles.

She focuses on her target. Takes a deep breath, attacks.

Family history, symptoms and durations, past rule-outs, desired outcome. One, two, three, and four—textbook delivery, right on the mark.

Dr. Guthrie reels, takes a half-step backward. He must've been banking on a slower start: a volley of niceties about the decorations out front, or the pattern of his tie, or the weather. Quickly, though, he regains his footing and turns to counter.

"I'm sorry to hear about this"—he selects his next words carefully—"*recent discomfort.*" They're at odds with everything she's just said, and together they make her pain a small, frivolous thing, so minor as to hardly merit further discussion. "Tell me," he continues, "have you tried managing your discomfort at home with OTC NSAIDs?"

The hair on Jae's arms prickles and she's glad her armor covers it, so Dr. Guthrie can't see he's struck a nerve. Acronyms are a common offensive maneuver, along with every other kind of medical jargon deployed to disorient the opponent and remind her of the vast distance between them: he the holder of a double doctorate from Johns Hopkins, she the entry-level customer service rep at a failing startup one bad quarter away from pulling its employee insurance coverage altogether.

But Jae, she's no novice. She's seen this move before. "Thanks for bringing that up," she says, forging from each word a potent dagger. "I *have* tried over-the-counter non-steroidal anti-inflammatory drugs. Unfortunately, they have not addressed the symptoms, nor the root cause, and I have observed no improvement to my diminished *quality of life*."

There's a snicker on the other side of the exam room door, then a light smack and a fast whisper like someone's telling the first person to hush. Of course they have an audience. Whether or not the others on the tournament circuit are willing to admit it, Jae knows entertainment has always been part of it. That or the insurance reps have arrived, warhorses champing at the bit for their turn on the field.

They weren't in the lobby earlier, or Jae wouldn't have proceeded the way she did. Seasoned knights know if the insurance company and the doctors are already locked in combat, you have no choice but to fall back into the crowd of spectators—admiring nurses, glassy-eyed first-year residents—and wait for them to finish their bout. Insurance knights ride heavy-set horses dressed in cloth embroidered with company logos: eagles and hands cradling other hands. They swing battle axes and two-headed maces, thump their spurs till their horses' flanks are torn and slick. Nothing good can come of you joining that skirmish. You'll be trampled.

Dr. Guthrie frowns and runs a hand over his stubbled chin, then turns his shoulders ever so slightly, directing Jae's gaze to a tray of silver instruments on the counter. Scalpels, pliers, scissors, and a single large syringe glint in the incandescent light. When Jae booked the appointment, she checked the little box next to "consultation," so there's no need for the tray or anything on it. But there it is, and Dr. Guthrie's shoulders are saying: *Are you going to make me . . . ?* And Jae knows her cardstock's only so thick.

The flash of silver takes her back to the credit card knight she saw on the train. She wonders if, wherever that knight is now, they're having better luck. Their eyes—in the twin slits between obsidian cards—were hard, grim, unblinking. Jae can't get the shine of the whites out of her mind.

What plays better on the field: influence or intimidation, a well-researched argument or a handsome bribe? Does it matter what any of them arm themselves with? Have they ever stood a chance?

Jae's heart hammers in her chest. Her opponent isn't wearing a stethoscope, but something about the way he looks at her lets her know he can hear it all.

She wants to swallow, but doesn't. Refuses to give him the satisfaction of watching the nervous lump slide down her throat. Before she can unfold the armor she strung at her hip for this exact moment—a peer-reviewed *JAMA* article detailing successful trials of presacral neurectomy coupled with psychedelic-assisted therapy—Dr. Guthrie sneaks in an extra blow.

"Look, let's cut to the chase," he says with a sigh doused in false resignation. "I think we both know why you're here." He tucks his hands in his pockets, and she keeps her eyes zeroed on his, trying not to let on how unsettling it is being unable to see them: those big hands, and what they might be doing.

She unstrings the peer-reviewed article, holds it out. "If you'll—"

But he just gives a little shake of his head, goes on.

"You're not alone, trust me. I've had a number of first-time patients come in with similar requests. It may be tempting, the quick fix. Please understand, however, that I don't make a habit of prescribing opiate-based regimens. Really, I consider them a last, *last* resort. You're still young. You *look* quite healthy. Given the high risk of addiction, and the high risk I would in fact be supporting an *existing* addiction—"

Jae's gripping the disposable sheet so hard it rips between her fingers. Of all the doctors she's seen, all the battles she's fought, this is a new one. Dr. Guthrie's playing Mr. Responsible, Mr. Hippocratic Oath. He's accusing her of being a pill chaser, and he's caught her off guard.

But she feels the weight of her chainmail, the crest she drew on the plate over her heart and colored in with different shades of permanent marker. She feels the light pressure of the bicycle helmet on her temples, and she knows it's secure.

Jae doesn't have a warhorse, but there's something else, something stronger, propelling her forward.

Six weeks ago, one of her coworkers, a woman named Heather from logistics, died of a type-three heart attack in an emergency room parking lot. She'd been playing the circuit, too—perfecting her attacks, scouting her opponents, showing up time after time ready to fight. Looking for answers, for that win. Jae didn't know how long Heather had been in it, or how deep, until she overheard a couple of Heather's teammates complaining about all the afternoons she'd been taking off.

What Heather got struck with was round after round of misdiagnoses. That's a thing that can happen, Jae knows, since the majority of medical research studies are conducted on men. Because Heather's particular symptoms couldn't be mapped precisely over a particular condition, the doctors called it something else, something vague, and prescribed a combination of Gas-X and talk therapy.

And Heather's crucial misstep?

She started to believe them.

Heather canceled her outstanding appointments, apologized to her team for her absence, and hung up her shield and helm for good. Not long after, in the middle of a postmortem meeting about the recent shipping delays out of their West Coast fulfillment center, she made an off-hand comment about the temperature in the conference room, then clutched her stomach and fell to the floor.

At the funeral, Heather's wife put out a stack of wallet-size keepsake photos of Heather. A Heather Jae had never known: goofy smile, limbs akimbo in a hammock on some rocky beach, gulls sunning happily nearby. Jae took one of those photos home that day, and now it's part of her armor, too.

Jae's armor isn't meant to guard against lance blows alone. It's also meant to protect her, as well as anything can, against the encroaching self-doubt.

She takes a deep breath. Tries to make her face as still

as the water in that photo. "I assure you," she tells Dr. Guthrie, "that's not what I've come here for."

She masks all but the slightest quiver in her voice. But there *is* the slightest quiver, and the way her opponent straightens his tie, she knows it's too late. He's heard it.

"Yield," he says, a grin spreading across his face. The snickers on the other side of the door grow louder.

Jae jumps down from the exam table, squares her hips, and clenches her hands into fists at her sides. It's the strongest shape her broken body knows how to make.

It's international joust-speak for *not on your life*.

Dr. Guthrie glances at the clock, like he'll get extra points if he finishes her off by lunchtime. "Based on what you've told me," he says, "I'd like to monitor your symptoms and check back in another six months." This slams Jae in the chest, tearing through the plates there, and a dozen copies of her family history—her aunt's rare form of blood cancer, her great-grandmother's sleeplessness after the war—go fluttering into the air.

The roll of stickers in Dr. Guthrie's coat pocket flaps loudly, like applauding.

Jae catches her breath as fast as she can. She mentally reopens her attack plan from earlier, searching for anything she might've missed, anything that might save her:

If her opponent asks about her pain tolerance, she should slip off one of her shoes to show her tattoo, the one that stretches across the top of her foot, where the needles vibrated almost into the bone. Otherwise, she'll leave her armor on.

When her opponent ignores this, she should point to the pain scale. There's always a pain scale—the one with the yellow smiling face at the bottom and the blue frowning face at the top—somewhere in the vicinity of the biohazard bin. She'll tell it straight. She won't undersell it. By now, she understands that some opponents expect women to have a *lower* pain tolerance, because women are soft and cotton-eyed as does, frail and decorative as flowers. Others expect women to have a *higher* pain tolerance, because they themselves come from a line of Strong-Ass Women™ who gave birth without a puff of anesthetic, probably standing straight up in the middle of a lush field somewhere, then wrapped their babies in a flawless swaddle and trekked home in time to make steak dinner. Jae understands that some doctors manage to believe both of these things at once, and that none of these positions will help her any more than the others.

You have to help yourself, she repeats in her head, in her thunderous heart. *You have to be your own best advocate.*

Jae pushes the plan aside, resets for an emergency maneuver. Through gritted teeth, she says what all the blog posts on how to talk to doctors have taught her to say:

"What are my—other options?"

Dr. Guthrie, who at first seemed so mild, so unimposing, towers over her now, his eyes roiling with storm clouds. His coat, once an ordinary matte white, reflects in every thread the silver from the bladed and pronged instruments on the tray.

He smirks. "Of course, you're welcome to get a second opinion."

Jae throws her arm up, trying to deflect this off her forearm guard, but she's an instant too late, and the blow catches her on the shoulder. Her left shoulder, which is already her bum shoulder, from the visit with Dr. Mahoney, or the years Jae spent playing softball in high school, or the stranger last year who wrenched her purse away from her in the side-street dark. Her mother's voluntary mastectomy, her grandmother's undiagnosed cervical cancer, the so-called myths about *manual stimulation* all split open beneath the attack. Through what few shreds of paper remain, blood begins to flow.

"Yield," her opponent says again. And again, she sneers at him: "*No.*"

"How about this?" Dr. Guthrie's eyes spark, and Jae knows the question itself is a ruse. "I'll write you a referral. There's a wonderful physician in Millbrae. I even convinced my wife to see him." He chuckles. "He's a GP, but his background is in psychiatry. So you may find he's, *ahem,* at the intersection of your needs." He smiles with what a less experienced, more hopeful version of Jae might've called kindness, then adds, "I'm not sure if he's in your network—you'll have to call the office. Anyway, it's worth it. You really can't put a price on your health."

This final blow is more than Jae can take. It hits her on the side of the neck, through a chink in the armor, the sharp point slicing widthwise as Dr. Guthrie calmly pulls from one pocket his clipboard and pen. He scribbles the new doctor's name—another battle, *unending* battles, stale-mates and never-healed-right scars the best she can hope for—and the paper knight crumples to the floor.

She holds a hand tight to her neck, trying to stanch the bleeding. Applying pressure: that's something she learned from a popular medical procedural when she was much younger, before the dead-end job and the storage shed, before the YouTube tutorials on saddle-stitch binding sheets of cardstock, before she had any clue what WebMD even *was*. Back when whatever it is she has now was still sleeping in some lesser, hidden quarters of her body. Before it moved into every room.

Blood pools hot on the cool linoleum. Jae hurts in old and new places; her throat stings metallic and her vision swims. She tries to concentrate on something, anything. Another trick the TV procedural taught her? Do all you can to not lose consciousness. Keep both feet firmly in the world of the living. There's a poster on the far wall of three kittens dangling from a tree branch. She dials in on the bubbly text over their heads, designed to look like clouds. In the generic, neutral way of motivational posters, it cheers on the kittens, Jae, and the doctor all at once: "Hang in there!" it tells them.

Dr. Guthrie appears above Jae, eclipsing the kittens. His grin is so big, so heavy, she worries it won't be able to hold—that at any moment it might drop right off his face and land on hers, ending her truly and completely. But he only reaches into his coat pocket, pulls out his roll of stickers. He peels one off, leans down, and presses it with one thumb into the middle of her forehead.

Maybe it's a smiley face. An "I was brave today!" declaration, or a gold star.

Jae doesn't get a good look.

She misses Dr. Guthrie's pink thumb wriggling for her. Where she's looking instead is the door behind him—ajar, though in the fray she didn't hear it open—and the flash of credit cards pouring through.

The superpremium, super-exclusive, matte-black kind.

The super-quiet kind, too, apparently, since Jae didn't notice their wearer tracking her all the way from the Daly City stop.

The obsidian knight lunges toward Dr. Guthrie, and through the slits in their helm, Jae can see their eyes. War-horse-wide and wild with anger. And coal black, too.

In her haze, Jae rummages through what she can of her research, trying to work it out: Is a joust ever, *ever*, two against one? No, right? Not as far as she knows. It's one lance and then the other, starting on opposite ends of a straight line—like the left and right pan of a perfectly steady scale—then charging with all their might toward the inevitable clash at the center.

Two against one, it wouldn't be a fair fight. It wouldn't be *even*.

Though, come to think of it . . . has it ever been?

The room spins and softens at the edges, and Jae has to admit she can't recall a single rule that would allow the disadvantaged combatant a late-game reinforcement. Then again, she allows, it's a very old sport. Even if much about the world hasn't changed, maybe this one thing has.

"Bull's-eye," the doctor whispers. He's talking about the sticker on Jae's forehead, hasn't yet realized a new rival's stepped onto the field.

He lifts the clipboard over his head.

The obsidian knight is a looming shadow, swiping fast and decisively. At the sudden faint tinkle of cards behind him, the doctor's face contorts and darkens. He starts to turn, manages to get about halfway round.

When the clipboard drops, it's from a spasming hand. The broad edge bounces on one corner, then the other corner—one corner, then the other corner—before clattering to the ground.

ADJECTIVE

———

Day one at your new job, your coworker wants to know are you really an immigrant.

You brought both passports to HR. You feel ADJECTIVE about that now, but last night you were so nervous about getting it wrong, you PAST-TENSE VERB all the documentation you could think of. Two passports, plus your driver's license, plus your social security card—which your parents had to ship to you rush mail—plus a copy of your lease, plus your four most recent bank statements, plus, for some reason, your membership card for a COSTCO / SAM'S CLUB / BJ'S on the opposite coast.

It's your first job out of undergrad, the one you flew three thousand miles with a pair of overstuffed suitcases for, the one you broke up with your on-again, off-again GIRL-FRIEND / BOYFRIEND / HAIRDRESSER / THERAPIST for, maybe even for good this time. To help with the moving expenses, you sold your aging MODEL OF CAR to a mechanic, who kicked lightly at the rust and said he was just looking for something his son could learn to drive in. Said he wasn't the kind of NOUN who spoiled his kid with a Benz on his sixteenth birthday. You'd read that in this city, your new city, you wouldn't need a car.

••••

After a morning of paperwork and Reagan-era onboarding videos, your team takes you to a dim sum place up the street for a Welcome Lunch, on your calendar from one to one NUMBER BETWEEN THIRTY-FIVE AND FORTY-FIVE. Where you come from, it's impossible for eight people to finish a restaurant meal within NUMBER BETWEEN THIRTY-FIVE AND FORTY-FIVE minutes, but you think maybe things are different here. Maybe in this city, where you don't need cars, you don't need time, either.

Inside, you gnaw at the ice shards in your water while the boss orders SHRIMP DUMPLINGS / PU-ERH TEA / NOT NEARLY ENOUGH for the table and one of your new coworkers suggests a get-to-know-you game. This isn't the coworker who will ask if you're really an immigrant. This is the one with the chunky-heeled Steve Madden boots and the slight twitch at the corner of her lip like she's always on the verge of bursting INTO VIOLENT SOBS / OUT LAUGHING.

Boots' get-to-know-me fact is that she brews her own kombucha at home, on the windowsill of her peeling Folsom Street Victorian. She explains the concept of a kombucha mother, says she named hers SCOBY DOO / RESTING BOOCH FACE / BEAUTY AND THE YEAST. Another coworker talks about their inflatable hot tub, another about a run-in they had with a WILD ANIMAL WHO WOULD KILL YOU WITHOUT EVEN THINKING, AS REVENGE FOR YOUR SPECIES MOUNTING HEADS LIKE HIS ON YOUR BASEMENT WALLS the last time they went camping up north. The coworker who will later have the immigrant question for now just says that he's from Washington, DC, and, fun fact, did you know that in DC you can get booze at Starbucks? You did know about the booze—it was on every news outlet for a week straight—and you assumed he was from somewhere in the vicinity of DC. He's wearing a Washington Redskins hat with the old racist name and logo, the ones the team got rid of years ago.

The intros blur together. When it's your turn, your fun fact is that you're what some people call double-jointed. You set your chopsticks down and demonstrate, using your RIGHT / LEFT hand to push the fingers on your RIGHT / LEFT: THE ONE YOU DIDN'T CHOOSE BEFORE hand almost all the way back to your wrist.

One coworker grimaces. The boss oohs.

••••

On the walk back to the office, DC falls in step with you and says, "ADJECTIVE trick. But I expected your fact to be that you aren't from around here."

You glance up at him. He's the senior copywriter, you know, someone you should probably try to get in good with. You SMILE / FROWN. "I thought Mary already told you all I moved here for this job."

"No," he says. "I mean *here* here." He moves his hand concentrically as if stirring with an invisible whisk. "America."

You flinch. You remember now that you passed by his desk this morning on the way to HR, carrying your assorted documents in a loose pile. Four bank statements, two passports.

You've noticed that, even though they're synonymous and both technically correct, there's a meaningful difference between saying *America* and saying *the U.S.* People who say *the U.S.* usually mean the U.S., and people who say *America* mean something else entirely. Something <u>BIGGER / SMALLER</u> and harder to define. In the songs, it's always America, as if that version lends itself more readily to images of <u>UNDULATING WHEAT FIELDS / GREEN COPPER LADIES</u> and <u>WHITE PICKET FENCES / SWEAT ON PALE BROWS</u>. As if abbreviation were profane, unpatriotic.

You're always getting caught up in the nuances of words. You guess that's why the agency hired you in the first place.

"Oh, yeah." You <u>KEEP SMILING / REARRANGE YOUR FROWN INTO A SMILE</u>. "I was little when we came over, though." You <u>HAVE LOST COUNT / ARE PAINFULLY AWARE</u> of how many times you've recited this exact line.

"How little?"

You tell him, "<u>BEND THE FINGERS OF ONE HAND BACK ALL THE WAY TO YOUR WRIST; THIS IS THE NUMBER OF FINGERS THAT BREAK</u>." You are rounding down, like always.

"Oh." He contemplates this, and the two of you walk the rest of the way in silence.

"I'm curious, then," he says finally, as your group reaches the office, and the boss, at the front of the line, badges everyone in. "Do you *really* consider yourself an immigrant?"

••••

The rest of the day, around outdated phishing videos, sexual harassment videos, and a tech session with the agency's long-suffering IT guy, DC wants to know <u>EVERYTHING /</u>

EVERYTHING / EVERYTHING about you. He wants to know if English is your first language, and if English is not your first language, do you still speak your first language, and can you still READ / WRITE / RECITE THE ALPHABET / SAY THE WORDS YOUR PARENTS ONCE PUNISHED YOU FOR SAYING, LIKE BITCH, ASS, TIT in your first language, and if not, why not, and if so, at what level. He wants you to rank your proficiency according to the scale he's seen on LinkedIn: elementary proficiency, limited working proficiency, minimum professional proficiency, full professional proficiency, or native or bilingual proficiency. You try to explain that you aren't sure how to answer that. You've been in only one professional setting, and it's this one.

He wants to know if you DREAM / FUCK / AGONIZE OVER EVERY TINY DAILY HUMAN INTERACTION in that language, if you give yourself PEP TALKS / GUILT TRIPS in that language, if you think in that language before translating it into English in your head. He posits this scenario: you have a run-in with a WILD ANIMAL FROM BEFORE while camping up north, and the SAME WILD ANIMAL charges—in which language do you cry out for help?

••••

For centuries, the country where you were born has been plagued by censorship. Your cousins send cryptic HOUSE PET GIFs from tapped phones and have no word for war. You've joked that it must be cultural: your own nagging self-doubt about what you're allowed to say.

••••

Months later, a woman from another team will roll her eyes and tell you not to bother with DC. That at company happy hours, he likes to get shithouse drunk, wax nostalgic about his FRAT / PINK PANTY–DROPPER PUNCH / DEAN'S LIST days at Georgetown, and start every sentence with "Just to play devil's advocate . . ." She admits he's a great copywriter, just exhausting as a person. Tells you not to take his polemicizing to heart.

But day one at your new job, you don't yet know this. You're wearing your cleanest, SUPERLATIVE ADJECTIVE, least pilly cardigan, with the fake pearl buttons that haven't yet fallen off, and jeans—because you read that in this city, nobody wears slacks unless they're a PROFESSION THAT REQUIRES THE HANDLING OF DEAD BODIES or a PROFESSION THAT WOULD MAKE YOU PERSONALLY WISH YOU WERE DEAD. Still, the way DC looks at you, you imagine he imagines you in a permanent Halloween costume. Sparkly REMEMBER THAT DATE YOU WENT ON WITH THE ASPIRING ENTOMOLOGIST; HOW BEFORE SHE KISSED YOU, SHE TOLD YOU THIS PART OF THE BUTTERFLY, WHEN PINNED TO A DISPLAY BOARD, FEELS NO PAIN, or furry tail, or caked-on alien makeup. There's nothing you can do to avoid being a spectacle.

••••

DC's followed you into the break room with his bag of organic YOUR MOUTH FILLS WITH LAKE WATER; IN THE SECONDS BEFORE YOU DROWN, THIS DRIFTS IN TANGLES AROUND YOUR BARE FEET crisps. The office is too warm, and your head's fuzzy from all the videos, and it's <u>EARLIER, YOU BENT YOUR FINGERS ALL THE WAY BACK TO YOUR WRIST; HOW MANY OF THEM ARE NOW A DEEP VIOLET, SWELLING?</u> minutes till a fresh pot of coffee. You're not thinking straight, so you engage.

"I'm immigrant enough to not be allowed to be president."

He smirks, delighted you've taken the bait. "Well, that would be pretty unlikely anyway."

You're not sure if he means it's unlikely because you're a <u>WOMAN / WOMAN / WOMAN</u>, or if he's assuming that because you're on the copy team and have a degree in creative writing, you must not have a knack for geopolitics or international affairs, which is patently <u>TRUE / FALSE</u>. Or maybe he's just talking about the statistical unlikelihood of anyone anywhere rising all the way to become that country's head of state.

••••

The copywriters sit with their backs toward one another. Boots says it's to minimize distractions, but all you can think about is how at any moment, DC might be turned around in his <u>ERGONOMIC MESH-BACK / CORE-TRAINING EXER-CISE-BALL</u> chair, analyzing the slump of your shoulders, the antennae he has—by sheer force of will—caused to sprout from your head.

••••

At <u>NUMBER UNDER TEN THAT RHYMES WITH *ALIVE*, WHICH YOU ARE LUCKY TO BE, ALL OF YOU ARE, AFTER EVERYTHING IT TOOK,</u>

YOUR PARENTS ONCE LOVED TO REMIND YOU o'clock, the boss tells you that you should head on home, says something about not letting these workaholics keep you late on your first day. He winks at DC, his star writer, and DC lifts his chin, grinning.

The boss disappears into a conference room, open laptop balanced across one forearm.

"I have a theory," DC whispers. "Want to hear it?"

You look longingly toward the door. "OKAY / NO."

"There are only two kinds of people in this country," he says. "Indians and immigrants."

You wince. He continues.

"Either you're an Indian or you're an immigrant. Either you were here first or you moved here. Get it?"

You consider this for a moment. There are nuances you don't want to get into just as the office is emptying out, the street outside REMEMBER HOW THE ASPIRING ENTOMOL-OGIST COULDN'T FLIRT LIKE A REGULAR PERSON; HOW DURING YOUR DATE, SHE TOLD YOU WASPS MAKE THIS SOUND BEFORE THEY MATE, THE SAME SOUND THEY MAKE BEFORE THEY STING with evening commuters. But for now, you think, for the purpose of leaving, this makes a fine amount of sense.

You nod. "Sure."

"Sure?"

"Sure. That sounds right."

"Wait," DC says, eyes alight. "Are you serious?"

"What?" You feel something you thought you had a grip on floating away from you, a FISTFUL OF BALLOONS / PAPER AIRPLANE / MOTHERLESS BIRD YOU FOOLED YOURSELF INTO

<u>THINKING YOU'D RESCUED</u> lost to the wind. "I'm agreeing with you."

He laughs. Animal Encounter Guy and one of your other coworkers are huddled in a corner, testing how their proposed tagline copy sounds when read out loud. Boots is a few desks over, concentrating hard on a page of blocky text, earbuds in.

"You really believe that?" DC's leaning forward, elbows on the knees of his corduroy pants.

You say again, more <u>ADVERB</u> this time, "Yes?"

"*Really*?"

You think maybe this is one of those tests where the important thing isn't whether you answer right or wrong— the important thing is that you give your answer confidently, and stand behind it 100 percent. "*Yes*."

He peers at you, his face inscrutable beneath his Redskins cap. "So you really think *I'm* an immigrant?"

Suddenly you're not so sure about this being a test. Now it feels more like a <u>SPRINGS SNAP OVER YOUR HAND AND A METAL BAR CRUSHES ANY REMAINING FINGERS THAT WEREN'T BROKEN ALREADY; REMEMBER THE NAME OF THAT MECHANISM</u>.

He shakes his head, turns back around in his chair, and mutters something under his breath. You <u>DO NOT / WISH YOU COULDN'T</u> hear what he says.

••••

Later, your on-again, off-again <u>GIRLFRIEND / BOYFRIEND / HAIRDRESSER / THERAPIST</u> will ask, with a jealous edge to their voice, whether DC was maybe just flirting. And you'll

say no, you don't think so, but you won't be able to artic-
ulate why.

••••

It will take you a long time to learn the agency lingo: terms
like *touching base* and *blue-sky thinking* and *moving the
needle*, and how to talk to <u>CLIENTS / BOSSES / COWORKERS /
WILD ANIMALS WHO WOULD KILL YOU IN AN INSTANT WITHOUT
EVEN THINKING</u> so that they think they are the ones who
came up with your idea in the first place. There are
unspoken rules, frustrating homonyms, a vocabulary that
contradicts itself constantly and changes on a dime.

You realize how your mother must have felt, all those
years ago, coming here with a wailing daughter on one
hip and a Webster's dictionary in her pocket. It makes you
feel <u>THERE IS ACTUALLY NO WORD FOR THIS IN ANY LANGUAGE</u>.

••••

Later, much later, when you are at a different job, in a
different city, DC will reach out to you on LinkedIn. His
message will say something about an urgent project, and
that he's in dire straits, his <u>NECK / ASS; IF YOU PICK ASS, SAY IT
IN YOUR NATIVE LANGUAGE</u> is really on the line with this one,
and he needs somebody to do a translation for him. Just
a couple of pages. He'll pay, but he needs it done quickly.
By end of week. Sooner. He thought of you immediately,
from your time together at that company. If he recalls,
you're <u>CHOOSE ONE FROM THE LINKEDIN PROFICIENCY SCALE
ABOVE; SECOND-GUESS YOURSELF AND CHOOSE ANOTHER</u>.

He sends the emoji of two yellow hands praying. He

tries to butter you up. What he remembers most about you, he says, is that you were always so <u>SYNONYM FOR *EASY*</u>, <u>SYNONYM FOR *DOCILE*</u>, <u>ANTONYM FOR *WILD*</u>. You don't tell him what you remember most about him.

He needs you to do a quick translation.

You type back, with what few fingers you have left: *I'm sorry. I'm afraid I can't be of help.*

He replies: *What?* But he <u>VERB ENDING IN S</u> this. What's your <u>NOUN</u>? Why won't you <u>VERB</u> him? He doesn't <u>VERB</u> why you're <u>VERB ENDING IN -ING</u> such a <u>WORD YOUR PARENTS ONCE PUNISHED YOU FOR SAYING, IN ENGLISH NOW</u>. You were always <u>ADJECTIVE</u> like that, come to think of it. He was just <u>VERB ENDING IN -ING</u> and now you're <u>ADVERB</u> <u>VERB ENDING IN -ING</u> him. Can't you at least <u>VERB</u> a <u>NOUN</u>? Then the <u>PLURAL NOUN</u> would <u>VERB</u> and the <u>YOU'RE ON YOUR OWN HERE</u> could <u>YOU'RE ON YOUR OWN HERE</u> to <u>YOU'RE ON YOUR OWN HERE</u> for the <u>YOU'RE ON YOUR OWN HERE</u> <u>AGAIN</u> and <u>AGAIN</u>.

You shut your laptop.

You push away your desk chair.

You stand to go.

You <u>FIND THE RIGHT WORD</u>.

ANOTHER ROUND AGAIN

———

Zasha was wary of stories that started in bars. When Kevin, the cute music therapist with the elderly husky mix and the port-wine stain, invited her, he had called it a tasting room, but it was most definitely, Zasha was sure now, a bar. A broey one, too: ESPN on the flat screens, IPAs with names like Hoptimus Prime on the menu, a group of four underage-looking kids at one high-top doing shots off an actual ski.

She should've known better than to come to Logan Square on a Thursday. In terms of *story*, though, Zasha wasn't worried. She wasn't exactly planning to recount this moment to their grandchildren one day, all circled up in their matching footie pajamas, a grey-haired version of today's Kevin in the kitchen making cup after cup of cocoa.

This wasn't the beginning of a love story, she knew. It was just one of those first-and-doomed-to-be-last dates to break a dry spell.

Kevin was wearing a collared shirt with the sleeves rolled up, a snow-dusted North Face slung over the back of his chair—pretty much standard issue for Chicago's after-work scene. He looked just like his pictures on the app, right down to the needles of white husky fur poking up from his shirt's plaid fabric.

If her sister knew, she would ask if Zasha was in a boy phase now, meaning a straight phase, meaning a not-giving-their-parents-a-heart-attack phase. And Zasha would sigh and, for the seventy-somethingth time, not bother explaining that that's not how it works for her, some neat little system. Like people sleeping head to foot: one way and then the other.

But Ava didn't know about the date, and neither did their parents. They were too busy daydreaming about the wedding that Ava and her new fiancé, Jeffrey, had announced over a family video call the previous week. Zasha and Ava's parents still lived in Joliet, in the house the girls had grown up in, and Ava and Jeffrey lived in the oversized colonial they'd just bought in tree-lined Saint Charles. They could've all been in the same place within an hour, but Ava and Jeffrey did it over video because they couldn't wait, were just too excited, had to get the news out now now *now*.

Jeffrey went by Jeffrey and not by Jeff, immediately correcting anybody who even tried it. His allergy to nicknames was something that, for a long time, Zasha and Ava's parents had kept in their back pockets as a potential red flag to pull out in case of a breakup. Supporting evidence in their diatribe about how they had never liked the guy anyway.

But now that he'd proposed, in a marble gazebo overlooking Lake Michigan no less, having hired a drone to document every joyous tear in stunning 4K, Jeffrey was officially in.

Zasha wished she could have a name like Jeffrey, or, better yet, a name like Ava. Something short and sweet, symmetrical. She hated the audacity of her own name, the novelty and surprise of its first letter. The way the "Z" sliced across a page, announcing itself so loudly, then the bossy *shh* that followed, as if her name was telling everyone and everything else to shut up. Since grade school, where everything was alphabetically ordered, or reverse alphabetically when an edgy teacher wanted to *switch things up*, Zasha's name had meant she stood out. She was always the last to present her summer book report, or the first to choose a name for the class lizard, or the last to pick up her equipment tray in chemistry lab, or the first to audition for the Holly Days solo.

Never safely in the middle. Never blending in.

It didn't suit Zasha at all—not the Zasha of today, anyway. Easy, conflict-averse Zasha, who everyone could count on to go with the flow, to never cause a stir.

Ava was the strong personality of the family, despite being the younger sister, and both their parents were in their own ways brazen, shamelessly opinionated. Their father about local zoning laws and who was robbed that year at the Oscars; their mother about fracking and the use of shock collars on poorly behaved dogs. They must've split topics early on, Zasha figured, and that was how they'd managed to make it work all those years. Even so, family dinners sounded like WWE matches, with Zasha pushing a single chunk of salmon around the plate, desperate to stay out of the fray.

So when dating-app Kevin suggested a tasting room on Kedzie she'd never been to, she said that sounded great. And when it turned out to be not a tasting room but an elbow-to-elbow bar with a Malört roulette wheel in the corner, she said nothing. And when Kevin got up to get the first round, she just told him she'd have what he was having. Was she an IPA girl? Sure, she was an IPA girl.

She was whatever anybody wanted her to be.

Once, when she was much younger, Zasha had asked her parents, "Why not *Sasha?*" Even that would've been better, the curves of the "S" mellow and tensile. Her parents had looked at her like she had three eyes and explained that Sasha was a *boy's* name, short for Alexander. That was another thing her parents had strong opinions about: what was allowed for boys, for girls.

And there she was now, with Kevin; a girl with a boy, in a bar—a familiar, comfortable, no-feather-ruffling story. Maybe it wouldn't be so bad. Between them, Kevin set down two frosty glasses of his-and-hers Audrey Hopburn IPAs.

Seconds later, he was back with a basket of samosas. Zasha took this as a good sign. Ava always said a guy who didn't order food was just trying to get the girl drunk faster, was almost certainly a certified creep. A woman a couple tables over gave Zasha a dirty look, and Zasha wondered if it was because she was jealous, if Kevin was in fact the ultimate prize.

"How is it?" Kevin-the-not-creep asked.

"Great!" Zasha replied too enthusiastically, having not

yet actually tried the beer. Whatever Kevin said next was drowned out by the crackling of a microphone, after which a voice like a juiced-up baseball commentator announced that everybody should go ahead and decide on their team names now—trivia night was about to begin.

"Trivia?" Zasha choked into her drink.

"Guess so." Kevin laughed, handing her a napkin from the dispenser. "Didn't mean to spring it on you. I forgot they do it on Thursdays here. I know a quizmaster when I see one, though." Kevin nodded toward the guy with the mic sitting alone at the table nearest the bar. He did look a little out of place, wearing an oversized sport coat and shuffling through a loose stack of paper.

"*Quizmaster*, huh?"

Kevin grinned. "Don't let the lingo fool you. I'm definitely not an expert. Went to Gannon's with some DePaul buddies back in the day, but their trivia was all Cubs and Bond stuff. And we only came in second once. First place was a handle of cake-flavored vodka, so you could say we dodged a bullet there."

The mention of DePaul reminded Zasha that Kevin was quite a bit younger than she was, a fact she'd forgotten because he had a real, important, helping-people job at the big children's hospital, while she was a substitute teacher who worked three days a week and even then felt like a glorified babysitter. Plus, if his pictures were up to date, he'd dutifully kept his dog alive for thirteen years and counting, and she'd never even given it an honest go with houseplants.

"It's okay that it's just the two of us?" she asked nervously. They were already there, and she wanted to be game, since being game was more or less her whole thing. She thought about adding that to her dating profile—something like "middle name: game"—after this night was through. But she also knew trivia wasn't a great fit. She had a terrible memory, especially lately. Couldn't remember what she'd had for lunch. Couldn't remember what she was wearing without looking down.

"Sure!" Kevin lit up. "Small teams are cool. Less in-fighting." He winked. Zasha was rusty—she'd been off the dating scene for six months—but she didn't realize people were still winking. Or winking again. The gesture seemed like it belonged with her parents' generation.

She smiled back. Kevin rapped the side of his glass twice with his knuckles, like, okay, that sealed it, then hurried to grab their answer sheets from the quizmaster's table.

When he got back, he asked what she thought their team name should be.

She said she was good with whatever he wanted.

"What about O-Trivia Newton John?" It was the name he and his buddies had used back at Gannon's. A classic.

He sang a few bars of "Hopelessly Devoted to You" without Zasha even asking. He had a good voice—steady, calm, and calming—but not showy. Like his throat was coated in honey. Exactly how you'd expect a music ther-apist to sound.

She wasn't going to tell him it was her birthday.

She didn't need to hear him sing anything else.

••••

Round one was literature. Ten questions per round, three rounds per night, winner takes it all. It all being a bar logo T-shirt for every team member—probably misprints or size triple extra-large leftovers, the quizmaster joked—and a handful of drink tickets good through the end of the year.

Zasha didn't think it sounded like much: another sleep shirt with the vinyl peeling after a couple of washes, and vouchers for a mediocre bar she'd probably never return to. Never mind that they'd expire soon; it was already November. But the other patrons, rowdy despite the early hour, seemed impressed, and the lively atmosphere was contagious. It was easy to go along with, especially for someone who was used to going along.

That was part of the reason for the dating-app hiatus. Six months ago, Ava had accused Zasha of being a *relationship chameleon*. Zasha didn't think much of it at first: her sister was always reading those stupid articles about "Letters From a Recovering Relationship Chameleon" and "What Your Zodiac Sign Says About Your Style in the Bedroom" and "Five Reasons You Should Never Dry-Swallow Pills," then forwarding them to Zasha's already painfully congested inbox.

But something about what Ava said had gotten under her skin.

"Think about it, though. How many hobbies have you had over the years? And how long did you stick with them?"

They were at a coffee shop in Andersonville with a rainbow flag pinned over the doorway and a window full of viny plants. The barista had drawn a teddy bear in Zasha's latte foam, and now she was murdering it with a stirring stick while her sister conducted her interrogation.

"Exactly as long as you were dating them, right? Remember how fit you got with Ibi, that rock-climber chick? And with Marco, the hairdresser, how you shaved half your head?"

"There's nothing wrong with taking an interest in your partners' interests," Zasha muttered. "You should try it sometime." She was thinking of Jeffrey and his weird collection of computer keyboards. He'd spent most of their last family dinner talking about the custom panda keycaps he'd had shipped in from Shenzhen.

Ava threw her arms up. "Fine. Tell me you don't adapt to their personalities. Go ahead. Just say it once, and I'll believe you."

But Zasha couldn't say it. The truth was, her memory failed her—she couldn't quite put together what her sister was talking about. Or, rather, she could trace the outline of it: remembered Ibi, Marco, Loren, Kim, and the others in some abstract way, and the versions of herself when she was dating them in an abstract way, too. But she didn't get the sense that she'd really inhabited any of those selves, or those relationships. Instead, she remembered them as if they were characters distinctly apart from the events of her real life. Ibi's aunt's battle with ALS, Marco's vibrating tongue ring, were just plot points in a half-forgotten movie.

What Ava didn't know, or what Zasha didn't *think* she knew, was that one reason she didn't remember much from those relationships was that she had drank straight through them. Not always at bars—sometimes at clubs, or at house parties, or at regular houses where there wasn't a party but where there was a half-finished bottle of something clear and stiff perched on top of the fridge, just low enough for Zasha to reach on tiptoe.

Only the smallest part of Zasha was ever present. Which meant that, rock climbing and hairdressing aside, Ibi and Marco couldn't have been that interesting. Which was also probably why things hadn't worked out.

Ava must've seen the blizzard swirling in Zasha's eyes, because she tried to change the subject. "What are you up to now, during your brief layover in the land of the single?"

Zasha said nothing. Didn't want to say "nothing," and prove Ava's point.

Ava exhaled in her loud way. Everything about Ava was loud, even her breathing. She split her orange-cranberry scone in two and put one half on a napkin for Zasha.

"Sister mine," she said, making concerned eyes across the table, "I just want you to be okay on your own."

On her own, trivia-night-wise, Zasha would have been screwed. Thankfully, Kevin was basically a one-man season of *Cash Cab*.

Between questions about Hemingway's favorite cocktail and which author wrote their last novel in crayon, Zasha and Kevin did the typical first-date personal inventory. Work, Chicago, travel, Chicago, family, friends, Chicago,

Chicago, some depressing item in the current news cycle. Had Zasha been downtown to see the river go green? Kevin went every year—he lived not too far away, in Old Town. Zasha didn't think anyone actually lived in Old Town, thought it was all just parking spots and set dressing for the famous comedy club at its center. Kevin, so chipper up to this point—"Call me Kev!"—suddenly grew pensive and serious. Of *course* people lived in Old Town; it was home to a *burgeoning* community of *artists*. Had Zasha been to Second City? Kevin went with his parents whenever they came into town. His parents lived in Minnesota. He missed them a lot. Kevin grew up rooting for the Twins, but now he was a die-hard Cubs fan.

Zasha thought back to that coffee shop conversation with Ava. At least there was no chance she'd adopt Kevin's personality. Earnest, saccharine Kevin, who talked a mile a minute, filled out every line on the answer sheet, and somehow still found time to get them an order of crab rangoon. Him taking the city of Chicago on board as a big part of his identity didn't shock her. Everyone in Chicago did that, even the transplants. She'd never done it, oddly enough, despite living there all her life. She couldn't name a single player in the Cubs' starting lineup.

Being into trivia did suggest that Kevin was smart, or at least passionately into *something*. Zasha had, at different points in her life, wished she could be that way: a bold, singular statement. Instead, she was more of a blank canvas—ready to absorb whatever someone else threw on.

So, maybe Ava had been right after all. Or half right.

Maybe it was good for Zasha to take a break, reset, develop her own *sense of self*, as one of the stupid articles in her inbox had put it. Something about *thinking of the self as a carefully curated bookshelf*. Did she stand by every single volume on hers? Was she even the one to put them on that shelf?

And if her baby sister, four years her junior, hadn't decided to up and get married, to be crowned queen in Jeffrey's vast empire of light-up keyboards, maybe Zasha would still be doing just that.

Kevin, with little to no help from Zasha, ended up getting eight of the ten questions right, coming in second place after a severe-looking team called the Spark Plugs, who kept their heads close together and drank only room-temperature water with no ice.

"Always the silver medal, never the bride." Kevin smiled sheepishly and raised a toast. Zasha clinked her glass to his. One of the flat screens flickered to a story about nationally rising rates of domestic violence. The bartender quickly reached up and changed the channel to poker.

At the next table, two women were arguing about the round's final answer, a bestselling novel released earlier that year. Zasha had thumbed through a copy in the teachers' lounge at one of the schools on the west side where she regularly subbed.

"I know it's not *cool* to like the *mainstream* or whatever," one woman said, "but you have to admit it's pretty spectacular. I mean, he won the MacArthur Genius Grant. He's an actual genius."

The other woman shrugged. "I don't know. I couldn't get into it. The protagonist is so bleh, so whatever. So *passive*, is the word. I'm just supposed to read five hundred pages of her aimlessly wandering around New York City? Who's got the time?"

The first woman laughed. "So that's what this is about. That chip you've got on your shoulder about New York."

"I know I've said it before, but do we really need more of those idealized, rose-colored, there's-no-place-like-New-York stories?" She overpronounced it so the York rhymed with *squawk*. "Didn't we get enough of those in the nineties?"

The first woman finished her drink, something pale and heavily garnished. "Don't you miss Meg Ryan, though?"

The other woman sighed. "I do. I really, really do."

"Zasha? You still with me?" Kevin tapped the table between them. His fingernails were clean and tidily trimmed. Great, Zasha thought. He couldn't even have been the mildly nervous sort who occasionally chewed them down, just shy of the quick. She curled her own nails into her palms. Her eyes settled back onto his, and he smiled his gentle smile. "Hey."

"Hey," she echoed.

"You ready for round two?"

One of the two questions Kevin got wrong had to do with the ship of Theseus. The other was about that Walt Whitman poem everybody studied in high school, then promptly forgot. The one that went, *Do I contradict myself? Something, something, something, something—I contain multitudes.*

Zasha felt something dark and formless pass over her mind, then dissipate.

She wondered if she contained multitudes. She wondered if she contained anything at all.

••••

The instant the theme of round two was announced, Zasha knew someone must've told Kevin about her birthday. She couldn't imagine who, or why, and whether it was meant to be a prank or a surprise.

Worst-case scenario, Kevin had found it lurking on one of her social media accounts and was in fact a certified creep. Best-case scenario, or the most likely one, anyway: Ava. Nosy Ava, tapping into the app at some point when Zasha wasn't looking and coercing Kevin into scheduling a Thursday night date. So her lonely older sister would have something to do while Ava and Jeffrey were off venue shopping in Hawaii. Zasha swallowed around a small pit of dread.

Even though Ava was borderline supportive, in that she arched her eyebrow at the rainbow flags hanging over the coffee shops but didn't force the topic, and even once went with Zasha to a queer rights march, Zasha knew her sister had always hoped she'd end up with a guy. It would put less strain on the family, was all. Would just make things easier.

So as soon as the theme was announced, Zasha knew she'd been set up.

Because the theme of round two was? Zasha herself.

When the quizmaster boomed it through the speakers, she felt her head grow electric and light, but not one person in the bar turned to look at her. Not even Kevin.

"What is this?" she hissed at him over the mess of empty glasses. They'd mercifully switched to lagers—how many consecutive IPAs could anyone be expected to stomach?—and Zasha was just starting to sink into that warm, pleasant buzz, like her brain had found the comfiest bean-bag chair in the furniture showroom.

Kevin made a goofy expression, like, *fucked if I know.* "Must be a thing the bar does," he guessed. "A joke they pull on customers. I think it's kinda fun."

"How would they even know my name?"

He tipped his chin toward her purse. "When they ID'd us, remember?"

Zasha thought this over. She had one of the new licenses: her straight-faced photo against a blue background, opposite a washed-out Abraham Lincoln. People in Illinois were obsessed with Lincoln.

As an adult, she'd toyed with the idea of changing her name, and when it came time to renew her license again, she'd seriously considered it, even made a list of potential alternatives. She couldn't *really* do "Ava," obviously. Could maybe go by her middle name. On second thought, though, that was worse than "Zasha." If that was even possible.

"But why would they do that?" she pressed. "Wouldn't it make more sense for them to do sports or, like, *Star Wars* or something?"

Kevin's port-wine stain stretched from his right wrist up under the rolled cuff of his shirt, and in the low light, it looked like blood. Was blood, technically, she knew. Something about the tiny blood vessels in the skin swelling out of control. It was the first thing she'd noticed in his pictures, she hated to admit. The second thing she'd noticed was that he made no attempts to hide it.

"Oh, c'mon. Don't be a spoilsport," Kevin teased. Then, softer: "You're special. They noticed it. Let people tell you you're special."

Zasha flinched. He was clearly a little drunk. She was a little drunk, too. Her dad had always told her that maybe she wouldn't drink so much if she was like him, if she got what he called the *Asian flush* after a single light beer. But her mother's genes were so powerful—here he would squeeze his wife's arm affectionately—that her Europeanness had diluted his Koreanness. And thank God, as a result, their daughters had been spared.

Zasha took another sip of her lager, the color of store-bought orange juice. A part of her was skeptical, still suspected Ava had set her up for this. But the overwhelming part didn't want to cause a fuss. So she went along with it.

"Well, at least this time we're guaranteed a win."

"That's the spirit!" Kevin thumped his fist against the table, and the Meg Ryan women looked over, visibly annoyed. At *her*, Zasha couldn't help but notice, though it was Kevin who'd done the thumping.

And with their wide eyes sizing up the only other two-person team in the bar, round two began.

"Question one," the quizmaster barked, and the patrons perked up, angling their ears toward the speakers. "Easy one to start. When is *Zasha's birthday?*"

Zasha smirked. There it was, the giveaway. The reveal that this was all some twisted but possibly well-meaning gift for the night's reluctant birthday girl. If Zasha was being generous, she could imagine it as Ava's way of helping her sister get back out there, come out of her shell. Of course, Zasha would have to let Kevin in on the secret. It would be awkward at first, but she'd scrawled that date on so many check-in forms and job applications that it was all muscle memory by now—she couldn't bring herself to write anything else.

But before she could move to answer, Kevin snatched up the paper and made a defensive wall around it with his arms.

"Huddle in," he instructed. "We don't want the other teams to see."

Zasha let out a startled laugh. "Okay, but—want me to write it?"

"That's okay. I know this one."

"You *know* this one? What do you mean you *know* this one?" Her dating profile had her age—her real age, even—but not her birthday. Ava said that's how people got their identities stolen.

"Don't be like that." Kevin exaggerated a frown. "Everybody googles everybody they meet online. There's not much on you, granted. You're pretty stealth. But I did at least find that. Now, just let me think for a second. Don't tell me."

Zasha sat back in her chair. Kevin tapped the eraser end of the pencil against the edge of their picked-over rangoon plate.

It was true that substitute teachers weren't known for having a massive online presence, transient as they were, never sticking around in one place for too long. Zasha didn't like the idea of having her history out there for everyone to see, anyway. Especially if she couldn't remember much of it herself. Then again, maybe that was how normal people *did* remember, by leaving breadcrumbs as they moved through the world, building some kind of written record.

"Got it!" Kevin shot his arms up, triumphant, then left one in the air, waiting for Zasha's high-five. She peeked down at the answer sheet, where he'd written, in all caps: *APRIL 14.*

"Don't leave me hanging," he said.

"I, uh," Zasha faltered. She chewed the inside of her cheek to keep from laughing. "I don't know how to break this to you, but that's not my birthday."

"Sure it is."

"You think I don't know when my own birthday is?" This was all so ridiculous: this trap Ava had led her into. This overeager, way-too-nice-for-her man-child.

"Oh, I think you know, all right." His tone was gently goading. He reached across the table and lightly pinched the inside of her arm. "I just think our establishment's fine offerings have been hitting the spot."

He gestured toward the empty glasses, and suddenly the awareness dawned on Zasha that most of them were on her side of the table, not his. She thought they'd been keeping up with each other, but now she realized that he was still nursing that first Audrey Hopburn IPA.

But that was his problem, wasn't it? What kind of life training had he gotten at DePaul, anyway? Was she really outdrinking a kid just a few years out of college?

"I'll prove it." She crinkled her nose at him, careful that her indignation could still be read as flirting.

She fished around her purse for her wallet, then yanked at one of the plastic sleeves to get to her ID.

"Read it and weep!" She thrust her license at Kevin, pride be damned. Maybe he would find it endearing that she hadn't made birthday plans before this one conveniently presented itself. Or he'd consider her progressive. Maybe she could convince him that she'd asked her friends to spend the evening volunteering at a local shelter or food bank—to donate their time in lieu of spending it with her.

Kevin blinked, then wrapped his hand around Zasha's and pulled it down. "Yeah, right. Like I said. Don't go waving it around, though." He nodded toward the Spark Plugs, locked in a heated discussion over their own answer sheet. "Not like they need another advantage."

Zasha didn't understand. She flipped the license over in her palm and brought it into the throw of the red-shaded table lamp.

And there it was, clear as day. Clear as the day she was born.

Not November 4th, as she'd known all her life.

April 14th.

••••

Zasha dropped the ID, and Kevin moved quickly to pick it up, nearly sending his chair clattering to the floor in the process.

"You okay?" he asked, gripping one of the wooden slats at the last second to catch it. "I thought this would be good news. We're one for one."

Recovering from the initial shock, she peered at the blue numbers on the DOB line. It wouldn't take much to change them, she allowed: some whiteout, a blow dryer, a super-thin-tip marker. Ava had access to all of those things, probably. And Ava *had* had Zasha out to their new house in Saint Charles just before she and Jeffrey left for Hawaii—the first time the sisters had seen each other in a while—under the guise of helping Ava unpack, but in actuality so she could brag to Zasha about the automatic fireplace and original crown molding. At some point Zasha got dragged into Jeffrey's office, where he spent forty-five minutes showing her a series of indecipherable close-ups from his recent keyboard meetup. Ava could have, in theory, done it then.

But *why*? And wasn't forgery, like, a felony? Or was it not such a big deal if the license holder wasn't actually underage?

Everything about Ava was loud, over the top, too much. Passive-aggressive, or just plain aggressive-aggressive. Even her birthday gifts, if you could call them that. Ava, who was herself impossible to embarrass, seemed intent on embarrassing Zasha when they were kids. One year, she had Zasha's face printed onto two dozen coffee mugs and swapped them in for every drinking implement in the house. It was Zasha's most recent yearbook picture, hormonal acne and braces with neon yellow rubber bands. Ava wasn't yet at babysitting age, so she must've had financial backing from their parents, who generally found their younger daughter's stunts hilarious. They drank their wine out of the Zasha mugs for a week, the cabernet staining their lips into a bruise.

Growing up, it was always three against one. It made Zasha shrink, over the years, into her current placid, agreeable form.

And she'd stay there, she decided, for the time being. And she'd leave Kevin out of it. It was obvious now he wasn't in on this. This was between her and her sister.

In the time it took Zasha to mull all this over, the speakers had blared four more questions and Kevin had scribbled four more answers onto the round two sheet.

Where was Zasha born?

Right in Chicago, at Northwestern Memorial. Her parents had met while attending Northwestern and stayed on the north side until her mom got pregnant with Ava. Then they'd moved out to the burbs, to the house with the door her mom called red-orange and her dad said was orange-red.

But: *BOISE*, the answer sheet declared.

Boise? Zasha thought. She'd never even *been* to Boise. The only thing she knew about Boise was that thing she'd read in the news about their police chief being a white supremacist. And also that their football stadium had a blue field, and every year all these birds died from diving headfirst into it, mistaking it for water.

What was Zasha's favorite team?

She didn't have a favorite team.

WHITE SOX, the answer sheet said.

What was Zasha's favorite animal?

She didn't have a favorite animal.

RACCOONS.

What was Zasha's natural hair color?

Dark brown, like the wet sludge at the bottom of the coffee filter. The same color it was now, the same color it had always been. Ava was the one who had experimented with bleach and Manic Panic all through high school and college—shifting through pinks, purples, and blues as fast as real-life Photoshop—before finally settling on a pretty deep auburn, more red-orange than the other way around. Zasha thought it looked natural enough, though Ava always complained about how expensive it was to maintain.

As a point of contrast, as if she and her sister weren't already different enough, Zasha had stuck with her own dark brown. No doubt about it.

But Kevin had written, in big, confident letters: *BLONDE*.

Suddenly, all the lager Zasha had consumed sloshed around inside her like some great biblical flood, and she shot up from her chair, murmuring to her date, "Sorry. It's—sorry. Excuse me."

She forced her way through the packed bar, past the non-trivia crowd there for the flat screens and the chatty singles and the two-dollar discount well drinks, feeling everyone's eyes resting upon her. She followed the arrows to the lone bathroom, which was, mercifully, unoccupied.

Once inside, she leaned against a wall and breathed heavily, in and out, trying to summon the meditation advice from one of Ava's early articles, without turning the lights on. So long as the lights stayed off, everything could be just as she thought it was, and nothing had to change.

She felt her way over to the toilet and relieved herself in the dark. Flushed. Sat there with her head in her hands for a few minutes after.

Finally, she stumbled the six feet or so back to the light switch, and flipped the flickering overhead on.

It was what she'd expected from a bathroom in a bar like this: cramped, low ceiling, tile walls covered in faded stickers, a bottle of generic green liquid soap on the sink. She let her eyes adjust and roll slowly upward, from the lime-stained faucet to the Glade plug-in that had evidently run out of lavender scent long ago.

Then, eventually, to the mirror.

And there she was. No escaping it now.

Zasha with the big, bold "Z" staring back at her, steadying herself against the sink's porcelain rim. Her hair cut in the short style that Ava's articles had told her was trending in Milan.

Dark brown, mostly.

And at the roots, a bright, ashy blonde.

••••

Fuck this shit, right?

Zasha must've been in the bathroom longer than she thought, because by the time she shoved the door open, an impatient line had accumulated in the hallway outside, and the quizmaster was rattling off the answers for round two. A woman with a tattoo of a long-stemmed rose on each clavicle glared at Zasha with more venom, she thought, than a slight bathroom delay truly deserved. She staggered past, mumbling an apology.

Boise. White Sox. Raccoons. Kevin had gotten them all right. He caught her eye as she approached, gave her a little wave and a double thumbs-up. The members of the Spark Plugs were nodding at each other with satisfaction. The underage kids were thumping each other on the backs.

How was it possible that everyone in this bar knew more about her than she did?

So, fuck this shit. She didn't need to stay there and endure this, whatever *this* was. Ava was the golden child, and maybe that's why their parents always begged her to make her salted caramel pie for family dinner—they called it her famous salted caramel pie, though as far as Zasha knew, the five of them were the only ones who knew about it—and maybe that's why everyone laughed at Ava's jokes, which weren't good so much as charmingly delivered. Maybe that's how she'd found someone willing to spend the rest of his sorry life with her, to weave their lives together till there was no distinguishing warp from weft. And after they'd been dating for less than two years.

But this time, Ava had gone too far.

Zasha stormed over to Kevin and snatched her purse up from where it hung on the back of her chair. She pawed around it clumsily before slapping a couple of bills down on the table.

"This has been interesting," she said, "but it's getting late. Time for me to call it."

Kevin furrowed his brow, the picture of confusion. "The last round is just about to start, though. And I think we've really got a chance. I don't know about you, but I've got my heart set on that T-shirt," he joked.

She felt the edges of her resolve soften. There was that pull to *be cool*, to not make a big deal of it, not cause a scene. To play this *just right*, so that when it got back to Ava, the story would be that Zasha had been totally composed—alluring even. That she'd won over everybody in the bar with her good-naturedness, her sense of humor and willingness to go with the flow. It was a lesson Zasha had learned the hard way, back in grade school: don't let the bully know they're getting to you, and eventually they'll get bored and leave you alone.

Kevin looked at her expectantly. When she didn't say anything, he hesitated. "Did I do something? I didn't mean anything by it, what I said about your—" He made a magician's motion over the glasses, as if, poof, soon there'd be a rabbit inside. "No judgment, seriously. It's almost the weekend. Everybody's letting loose. If anything, *I* should catch up to *you*."

He pointed toward the bar in a gesture that said if she

agreed to stay, he'd get the next few rounds all at once, and this time it'd be the hard stuff.

Zasha held a hand up. "It's not that. I'm just tired. I have to be up early. First bell's at 7:55." She couldn't remember if she'd told him she was a substitute teacher. Either way, it was a lie. Her last sub appointment was Tuesday, supervising a group of polite, somber-looking AP biology students while they worked on their final projects without even acknowledging she was in the room. She didn't have anything on her schedule again till next week.

She wondered if she was slurring, or talking too loudly, the way drunk people did in the movies. She didn't feel drunk, not *drunk* drunk anyway, but she swore there were more empty glasses on her side of the table now than there had been when she'd left for the bathroom.

Kevin was making puppy-dog eyes. "You're telling me O-Trivia Newton John is breaking up before we finish our first tour?" Zasha imagined him later, panting, begging—hot breath on her ear, hot tongue on the bend of her jaw.

She sighed. He was cute, even though she hadn't been in anything close to what Ava would call a *boy phase* in years. She liked Kevin's light stubble, the paler streak on his cheek where hair wouldn't grow—a scar, he'd explained, from that time one of his cousins had tried to teach him how to snowboard. *And failed*, he'd laughed. She liked his cheerfulness, how easy it was to be around him. The way he looked at her without fear.

It was refreshing. Different from the way Ava and their parents looked at her lately.

A shadow moved across the back of Zasha's eyeballs. She felt it slide expertly around the curve, ducking under the optic nerve like a soldier in one of those first-person-shooter games her students were always playing on their phones when they didn't think she was looking, or just didn't care. She shut her eyelids tight, forcing the strange presence backward.

He could've been a great birthday lay, Kevin the music therapist with the elderly husky mix and the port-wine stain. Or even a date to a future family dinner, proof that Zasha had turned over a new leaf. That she was finally taking control of her life, and nobody needed to worry about her.

The dark shape swelled toward the front of her skull again—the god of migraines, or some alien tumor—and again she concentrated all her energy on pushing it back to safer depths. Her head pounded from the effort, or the alcohol. Maybe a combination of the two.

"Where you gonna go, home?" Kevin nudged her arm playfully, gathering from her silence that they were still in the window in which he could potentially persuade her. "What do you have going on at home that's more fun than what we've got going on here?"

The presence retreated, and Zasha felt the creases of her brain stretch to make room. As it dropped down into the trenches, it let out a hurt little whine.

That's when she realized she didn't have an answer to Kevin's question, just like she hadn't had an answer to any of the trivia questions so far that night.

She couldn't picture what was waiting for her at her apartment, or even how to get back. A blistering panic shot through her, and she fought to push it down. Tried to conjure up some image of a living room with a fluffy, abstract-patterned rug; a cow-spotted cat batting at the spinning disc on an antique record player.

But she didn't have a record player. Or a cat. Didn't have opinions about vinyl. Had never had a particular pining or preference when it came to house pets.

Or had she? At this very moment, she couldn't recall.

The living room was too perfect. An amalgamation of two-page spreads from a West Elm holiday catalog.

The one thing she knew for sure: if she couldn't remember the first digits of her address, or even the first steps to take to get there, there was no way she was getting home.

•••

Zasha slumped back in her seat, defeated.

Kevin beamed. "I think you'll like this round. It's supposed to be less history, geography, general knowledge. More specifics. More of a challenge." He slid the answer sheet over to her. "I'm gonna go resupply. I designate you head scribe if I'm not back in time. You want the same?" He pointed toward the graveyard of glasses.

She shook her head, dazed.

The speakers popped angrily, and Kevin was gone. The quizmaster came on to announce the start of round three.

"All right, folks, this one's for all the marbles." The

bar seemed too bright too soon, like a movie theater putting the house lights on before the post-credits scene was through. The smell of burnt grease wafted in from the kitchen. Zasha thought she might throw up.

"First question." The quizmaster cleared his throat and scanned the room, building suspense. "When did Zasha first exhibit signs of disordered eating?"

Zasha let out an audible moan. In the din of pencils and silverware and idle chatter, no one seemed to hear her.

"This one's multiple choice," he went on. "A: age thirteen, B: age fifteen, C: age nine, or D: age eleven."

Woman number one at the Meg Ryan table rolled her eyes in Zasha's direction. "I thought these were going to get *harder*."

Without conferring with her teammate, woman number two jotted down the answer, then grinned. "Okay, Amy Schneider. If you want the real deal, go on *Jeopardy* or *Millionaire*. What did you expect from Brogan Square?"

Through aching eyes, Zasha noticed a dull red flashing against one of the glasses, against one corner of the remaining crab rangoon, and for a brief moment she thought the police cars had finally arrived. Good—someone had called in this transgression, and now they were coming to take the perpetrators away. And this could go back to being a regular date.

Then she realized the flashing was coming from the sign out front, the one she had passed on the way in but now couldn't remember the exact contours of. What *was* the name of this bar? She wasn't one for calling the law herself;

she thought of the domestic violence cases on the news, how the cops were never any help. They showed up hours later, took a cursory statement, walkie static interrupting every other sentence. Didn't take their shoes off inside, so their heavy-duty patrol boots saturated the rugs with spring mud.

Even if she were to call now, she wouldn't be able to tell them where she was, much less what was happening to her. She tried to retrace the neon letters in her mind, but couldn't go too far in any direction. If she did, she'd bump into that injured thing lurking there still, softly whimpering.

Zasha laid her forehead against the table and rocked it back and forth, back and forth, willing herself to wake up.

"You okay there?"

Kevin greeted her with a glass of something amber and another of something almost black, like what she'd imagined gasoline must look like before she learned it was actually a yellowish color, could easily be mistaken for piss, or beer.

"Got you a Diet Coke." He tossed down a pair of fresh coasters and set the soda on the one in front of her.

She eyed it ruefully. She hated Diet Coke, and anything else riddled with artificial sweetener. She hadn't had it since college, when it was almost *all* she had—would guzzle it three cans at a time to quiet her growling stomach—when she was still shopping exclusively in the diet, fat-free, skim, lite, low-cal everything aisle. Diet Coke and unsalted rice cakes. She thought if she drank it now, it would taste like whole years of her life she'd rather not return to. It would taste like whatever gasoline must taste like.

Instead, she wrapped her lips around the straw, and it was fantastic.

Of course, Kevin would know better than she did what she liked and didn't. If he had brought her Diet Coke, of course it must be her favorite.

Zasha wrote "C" on the first answer line, a shot in the dark, then passed the sheet back to Kevin.

The next questions came fast, with little pause between them, as if the quizmaster had another engagement after this one, at a more upscale bar across town, and he had to hurry if he wanted to make it on time. Maybe the theme there would be British pop culture or the fall of the Russian empire, something he had studied in grad school that he could really sink his teeth into.

Or at least something more enthralling than Zasha.

He sped through:

"Which part of her body is Zasha most insecure about? Bonus point if you can also identify *why*."

"Where did Zasha lose her virginity?"

"How big, in diameter, was the pool of blood she left on the covers that day?" A dozen pencils lifted as one. "Multiple choice. A: two inches, B: three inches, C: four inches, or D: six inches."

"Has Zasha *really* been fair to her parents?"

"Two-part question. How many times has Zasha called her parents in the past six months? How many times have *they* called *her*?" The smell of grease, the sound of angled lead against cheap paper, the persistent shadows were crowding Zasha out of her own mind.

A picture came into focus on the bar's largest projector screen: an Instagram post blown up to thousands of times its original size. A figure with a loose ponytail and thin, drawn-on eyebrows, lips pinched in an expression of mock annoyance, hand outstretched toward the camera, offering the lip of a tasting spoon. The image was cropped so the number of likes—fifty-six—was clearly visible, but the username was blacked out.

"Who is *this* to Zasha?" the quizmaster asked.

Zasha sipped her soda while Kevin tapped the pencil against his chin thoughtfully, then lit up when the answer invariably presented itself to him. Each time, he leaned over to show her the sheet, his hand curled protectively around it. She just shrugged. She had no clue.

They were talking about some life she had no access to. She felt like she was at the optometrist, unable to make out even the largest letter at the top of the triangle of letters—and the optometrist kept tinkering with the lenses on the machine in front of her, but the letters never got any better defined. Just slipped further and further from her comprehension, as if beneath layers of water and stippled glass and gauze.

The quizmaster continued, steadily building to the tempo of an auctioneer. "What did Zasha steal from her sister Ava when Ava was thirteen, then leave for their parents to find?"

A pair of patrons Zasha hadn't noticed before passed by their table, carrying clear mugs of steaming hot toddies and a tray of fully loaded tater tots.

"Ooh!" one said. "It's birth cont—" In his excitement, he jostled his mug and sent half its contents arching onto Zasha's lap.

"Fuck," she gasped, remembering she was wearing a short dress with boots pulled up over the knee, and thin black tights. Too thin for November in Chicago, and too thin for direct contact with any amount of hot toddy.

"*Shh*," his friend hissed, glancing quickly behind them. "You want everyone to hear you?"

And just like that, they disappeared into the throng. They apparently hadn't noticed the spill, though a few seconds later Zasha swore she saw one of them turn back to her, face screwed into a sneer.

"Why does everybody in this bar hate me?" she muttered, dabbing a napkin against her tights.

"Nobody hates you," Kevin said in his honey-coated way. "They're just wasted. Want me to get you some ice?"

"That's okay," she told him. She looked around for the sneering man, but he was long gone.

The closer they got to the game's end, the more the atmosphere shifted from one of revelry to one of poisonous suspicion. The whispers grew quieter, the circles around the answer sheets tighter on every side. At one point, one of the Spark Plugs pulled out their phone—an ancient hulking thing that didn't even look to Zasha like it *had* the internet—and someone from a neighboring table accused them loudly of cheating. But the majority of the suspicion, Zasha couldn't help but think, was pointed directly at her.

The pressure in her head ballooned, the aspartame mixing with the alcohol and the headiness of the hops, and soon Zasha felt sedated, a cat on the vet's surgical table waiting to be fixed. The shadow inched forward again, and she felt too weak to stop it. As it got closer, it took the shape of a person—with softly sloping shoulders and wide hips—and it hobbled, as if trying to put all its weight on one side of its body.

She remembered the birth control incident, though only faintly, and the way it came together in her mind, it was something that had happened to *her*, when *she* was thirteen, and not to her sister. Ava sneaking into the drawer of Zasha's nightstand in the bedroom they'd shared since Ava was born—the one Ava got to herself for four whole years after Zasha went off to college. Zasha had it for herself first, of course, before Ava was born. But she was so young then, at the age before most memories were formed, so it was as if it hadn't even happened.

Ava sneaking into Zasha's nightstand while Zasha was at—What? Band practice? Swim? Had she ever cared enough about anything to devote whole afternoons to it?—and lifting the round plastic pack out of the drawer. Moving it to the entry table for their parents to come home to, their eyes ablaze with recognition and their throats, by the end of the night, raw from whisper-screaming. Yes, they *whispered*, Zasha remembered, in their own house, out of chagrin or some closely related species, as if the neighbors could hear through multiple layers of wall. Zasha was grounded for . . . three weeks? Maybe four?

That had Ava's name all over it. Loud, over-the-top Ava, always taking things too far. Not Zasha, the peaceful, go-along sister. Who never even wanted to catch sight of the line, much less take a step across it.

"Last question of the night!" the quizmaster called, no longer bothering to hide the repeated gesture of checking his watch. Zasha tried to re-convince herself of her passing speculation from earlier, to see if it could still fit: he'd be glad when this was all over, these birthday gigs being so kitsch, so tiresome.

"For double points," he said, "*what was it that happened to Kim?*"

The shadow lurched forward, falling heavily against the inside of Zasha's skull. For an instant, she thought someone must've driven one of the bar's branded trivia pencils directly through her forehead. She drew her breath in sharply. Kevin looked up, curious as a newborn cub.

The things further back, they were easier to remember. Bits and pieces of who she once was. The beige of the birth control pack, the chipped nail polish on the hands of whoever it was that had taken it. The tugging sensation of the rubber bands she was prescribed to wear over her braces—the force of their resistance so overwhelming, it made her not even want to open her mouth.

It was within the past six months that everything truly went dark.

The shadow knocked hard, with both hands, with *more* than both hands, making Jell-O of her frontal bone.

••••

The last thing she remembered with a new, absolute clarity was that coffee shop in Andersonville, with the rainbow flag that made her feel safe and wanted, and the plants whose vines stretched over the ceiling beams, a jungle in the middle of North Clark.

Zasha was using her stirring stick to decapitate the teddy bear in her latte foam, slicing the thin red line side to side across its fuzzy neck. Every so often, she'd lean forward, trying to catch the eye of the barista who'd drawn it.

Ava snapped her fingers in front of her sister's nose. "Too soon, Zash. And leave the bear alone, would you? You're freaking me out."

"Freaking you out?"

"It's just—" Ava sucked at the inside of her cheek. "It's just kind of *violent*, you know? I get it's not a living thing, and it's not the same."

Zasha dropped her jaw in mock disbelief. "No kidding, it's not the same. That's the thing about you, though. Something happens one time and then you see it everywhere."

"It's natural for people to seek patterns in things. Anything with a brain is basically wired to do it. Otherwise, we wouldn't learn from past mistakes and successes. And we wouldn't, like, evolve right."

"Oh, yeah? *Evolve right?*" Zasha retorted. She was already on edge, had started building up her defenses the second Ava called, saying they needed to talk. "You get that from an article? Didn't see that one come through."

Ava ignored this, doming her hands over her doll-size cup of espresso as if trying to trap its warmth. "Remember when we were kids, you went through your stealing phase? And that one time, Mom had to pick you up from mall security after you stole the piercing gun from Claire's? Not a pair of studs or a bracelet or something *normal*, but the piercing gun, which obviously someone would notice was missing. What were you even planning to do with it? That whole phase started with you—"

"I know what it started with," Zasha interrupted.

"Then all those mugs, Christ. I don't know how you got them by the detectors. And what you drew on them after—"

"Enough," Zasha said. "Please. Enough."

"Anyway," Ava continued, "patterns. I wouldn't call what happened just *some* thing, either. It was a pretty big thing, I'd say." She paused. "Especially for Kim."

Zasha didn't say anything. Ava picked at her scone, pulling out the bits of dried cranberry until the surface was ugly and pockmarked.

Finally, Ava lowered her voice and said, "She almost went to the *hospital*, Zash."

The teddy bear eviscerated in its forest of foam, Zasha had taken to bending the stirring stick back and forth, and now it snapped neatly in two. She replaced it on the little plate under her cup and cradled her temple with one hand.

"I'm not proud of it," Zasha said slowly, her voice wobbling the way it did before she cried. The wobbly voice she'd inherited from their mother, but the tearfulness—she had no idea. She could count on both hands the number of times she'd seen anyone in her family cry. "Of *course* I'm not proud of it. It was a mistake. I don't know what else I can say that I haven't said already."

"I know."

"I wish she didn't have to tell you. I wish *you* didn't have to tell Mom and Dad."

"You know that's not realistic," Ava said softly. "Kim was my friend first. Mom and Dad have known her since we were in high school. They care about her. They don't want to see her hurt."

"And what about me?" Zasha knew it made her sound like a brat, like some child who hadn't gotten their turn on the dinosaur spring rocker at recess. But she couldn't help it. "Don't you care about me?"

Ava hesitated. "Of course we care about you. But you understand, don't you? You're not the victim here. You're lucky she didn't press charges."

Zasha felt a dam within her break, the one she'd constructed over time out of a combination of shame and good sense. Kim had always called it *carceral injustice*, and preached her list of community-safe alternatives to calling the cops to anyone who would listen. "You never wanted me and Kim to work out. None of you did. You were rooting for us to fail."

Ava took a while to respond, seemed to be choosing her words carefully. It was uncharacteristic for the Ava Zasha had grown up with, who was always blurting out the first thing that popped into her head. It gave Zasha a perverse sense of hope, that maybe people *could* change.

"Mom and Dad struggle with that stuff," Ava said, "and I know that must be really hard for you. But you can't really believe any of us are happy about how it ended. We would never have wished this on her. Ever."

Zasha ran her fingers over her eyes and felt a new pressure escalating behind them, hazy and misshapen.

"I'm sorry." Zasha's voice was pleading.

"I know."

"I told her I was sorry. I don't know what happened." She swallowed. "It didn't even feel like it was *me* doing it. It didn't even feel like I was *there*."

"I know," Ava said, but she looked the way Zasha imagined she must look while listening to Jeffrey recount his latest keyboard-related exploits. The way Zasha *knew* preschool teachers looked when listening to one of their kids retell the same plotless story for the hundredth time. It was a patient, mollifying expression. Kim had probably told Ava all this already.

Zasha said anyway, "I told her it would never happen again."

"I get that. But you get why she wasn't going to stick around and find out, right?"

Zasha stared into her cup, at the islands of foam floating in the muddy brown. She was overcome with a sudden pang of longing to resurrect the slain bear. It had been sweet. Innocent. It didn't deserve it. "Yeah," she said.

"Mom and Dad won't give you the silent treatment forever, you know."

"They might."

"They won't. But Zash"—here Ava brought her face down so her eyes were level with her sister's—"I think it would be good for you to take a break. From dating, I mean. Take a breather. Step back, focus on yourself, develop some new hobbies. And, I don't know." She searched for the word. "Some new convictions, too."

Zasha scoffed.

"Think about it, though," Ava backtracked. "How many hobbies have you had over the years? And how long did you stick with them?"

Zasha was quiet.

"Remember how fit you got with Ibi, that rock-climber chick? You seemed to be really into that. Why don't you pick it up again? You don't need her to go to the climbing gym," Ava joked. "I'm pretty sure they sell individual passes."

Zasha appreciated that her sister was trying to keep the mood light, and that she had shown up at all. She knew it couldn't be easy for Ava to ride that line between her longtime friend and her only sister, then that other line between her sister and their parents, who weren't on speaking terms with Zasha anymore. They'd left a curt voicemail telling her not to bother about family dinners. It was mostly her mom talking. Her dad came on the line only briefly, his voice sad, pointed and heavy as lead. "A *drunk*," he'd said. "An *abusive* person. A person who hits her girlfriend. That's no daughter of mine."

It was the first time she'd heard either of them use "girl-friend" to describe the woman she was dating. Instead of "what's her name" or "Zasha's new friend."

"I loved her, you know," she told Ava, or rather, Ava's scone—the better option if she wanted to be spared further judgment. "I still remember what day it was. A few days after Easter. A few days before they reinstalled Sue the T. rex skeleton at the Field Museum. April 14th."

"I think—" Ava paused. "I think, you know, with the rock climbing and everything, you were always so . . . easily influenced. That's not a bad thing," she said hurriedly, when Zasha looked wounded. "There's nothing wrong with taking an interest in your partners' interests. It's a *good* trait. It's just, after enough of that, a person like that might try to . . . assert themselves. To leave a bigger impression."

Zasha winced. The word was too accurate, too physical—evocative of a dented ping-pong ball or a bruise spreading fast across the topmost layers of skin.

"I just mean, if I were to psychologize it—" Ava pressed on.

"Please don't."

Ava exhaled in her loud way. She split the scone in two and put one half on a napkin for Zasha.

"I think it would be good for us to take a break, too," she said. "Not forever, just for a while. I'm your sister. I'll always be around. But right now, I should make sure that Kim's okay. I don't want her to think I'm taking sides."

"But you are. All our friends are. You know none of them have talked to me in weeks."

Ava threw her arms up, patience evidently wearing thin. "You chose this, Zash. When you blew up at her like that, you chose this. *You.* Not me. Not the rest of us. What exactly do you expect me to do?"

The people at the tables nearest them glanced up. Ava had knocked her cup over, and her espresso leaked onto the table, then the floor. It seemed impossible to Zasha that the tiny cup could've held the volume of liquid now spreading across the blue-grey wood.

Zasha's mouth contorted. "You want everyone to hear you?" But there was no bitterness to her tone, and no pity in Ava's acknowledgment of it.

The two were silent for a long time, neither moving to soak up the spill. Finally—after how long, two minutes or twenty, Zasha would never know—one of the coffee shop's employees approached, a dish rag hanging out of their apron pocket.

Ava snapped out of it first, apologizing and leaning out of the way a full foot more than was strictly necessary.

"Give it time, sister mine," she said, after the employee had gone. "I just want you to be okay on your own."

The bar erupted: cheers and groans and fists rattling tables and thrown pencils clattering end over end. The sudden uproar pierced through Zasha's consciousness and sent that limping, maimed thing that had once been just a shadow slinking back into one of its many hiding places. But in the time it had spent in the fore of her mind, it had grown, fully formed. And nothing could ever be the same, now that Zasha had seen it for what it was.

No one was looking at her anymore. The Spark Plugs were shaking one another's hands, their lips hanging sour around the words, "Good game." The Meg Ryan team was playing footsie under the table, their hands wrapped around twin margaritas, this silly trivia business a distant, long-forgotten thought. The underage kids were packing up their bags and pulling on their jackets, preparing to head onto what would certainly be just another not particularly memorable stop on another not particularly memorable night.

Zasha's eyes refocused on the table just as one of the waitstaff arrived. He shot Zasha a thin smile, then began stacking the empty glasses and mostly empty appetizer baskets. He folded the tower of glasses into the crook of one elbow, took the baskets into that hand, then used the other to pick up Kevin's still half-full pint of beer.

Kevin was nowhere to be found. Zasha thought about telling the waiter to leave that one behind, they were still working on it. Instead, she said nothing.

She knew that in order to have a clean slate, every little thing from the old tableau had to be taken away. You couldn't simply lift out one part of your life and expect things to be different. If you wanted to be rid of something—that soiled, pointless thing you couldn't stand to look at anymore—you had to also eliminate everything else.

That's what Zasha had done.

Because any lingering trace, any crumb of cold crab rangoon, any haloed memory of that bar that hosted Friday night turtle races, that time you two got stoned and snuck into Soho House, that other time you went snowshoeing down the middle of the street during what everyone was calling the Polar Vortex—and you were going to remember. That you *had* been there after all. Overindulged, lost control. That you had given wholly into some part of yourself you no longer wished to recognize.

"I'll be back in a second to wipe that up," the waiter said kindly. Zasha looked down at the table, expecting to find bits of fried dough and spilled dip and IPA, but in their place were droplets of dark blood in a drunken line, starting about a foot in and wandering toward the wooden edge. Her hand shot up to her nose, came away wet and special-effects red.

Kevin appeared out of nowhere, with the same dopey smile Zasha had, for the majority of the night, found comforting. Something about his post-collegiate charm had suggested to her that she could be that young again, too, if she did the right things, showed the right parts of herself, slept with the right people. She pictured his apartment filled with musical instruments, and the two of them clawing at each other, crashing roughly against the piano keys. His apartment in Old Town, where people really lived.

Could be young again, or younger. Could travel back to the time before what happened happened.

Kevin slowed as he got closer, pointing to Zasha's nose with his free hand, his face all concern and question marks. His other arm was loaded down with a mass of black cotton and long tendrils of blue rectangles, the kind from boardwalk carnivals that threatened *ADMISSION*.

He draped the shirts over the back of his chair, away from all the blood.

"Victor, meet spoils." He set the coil of drink tickets on the safe side of the table with exaggerated effort, as if they weighed as much as their equivalent in bars of gold.

"What?" Zasha, still returning to herself, was finding there wasn't much of a self to return to.

Kevin pulled a wad of napkins from the dispenser, then held them out to her. The broken, exposed thing in her head told her: *Take them. For God's sake, clean yourself up*.

"What? What do you mean, 'What?'" He blinked at her. "We won."

ACKNOWLEDGMENTS

My deepest gratitude to the team at Stillhouse Press—Bodie Fox, Taylor Schaefer, Jacob Sharp, Holly Bergman, Olivia Bissell, Camille Koslo, Paul Logan IV, and Scott W. Berg—for shepherding this book into the world, and to Joe Vallese for the meaningful vote of confidence.

Thank you to my agent, Isabel Kaufman, for always getting it when I'm sure no one will, and for doing what earth signs do best.

To the editors who published these stories first, for being tireless champions of fiction: Susannah Jordan at *Cease, Cows*, Wendy N. Wagner and John Joseph Adams at *Nightmare*, Michael Damian Thomas and Lynne M. Thomas at *Uncanny*, Sheree Renée Thomas at *The Magazine of Fantasy & Science Fiction*, Z Howard and Dacia Price at *Passages North*, Jennifer Lyn Parsons at *Luna Station Quarterly*, Jessica Augustsson at *The Pelagic Zone: Uncharted Waters*, and James Yeh and Laura Lampton Scott at *McSweeney's*. And to the copyeditors, designers, cover artists, podcast teams, marketers, judging panels, and everyone working behind the scenes.

Thank you to Stephen Graham Jones for building the best reading lists and for encouraging me to take these stories that crucial step further. Thanks, too, to Marcia Douglas and William Kuskin at the University of Colorado

Boulder. And to my MFA fiction cohort, who read early versions of many of these stories and laid an anchor during the unmooring pandemic grad-school years (whose idea was that, anyway?). Double thank you to Isabel Geary Phelps for I don't know how many back-and-forths about the title.

To the Smack, my farthest-flung and nearest-feeling friends: M. L. Krishnan, Eugenia Triantafyllou, Alex Crawley, Monte Lin, Tim Chawaga, Isha Karki, C. S. Peterson, Derrick Boden, Phoebe Barton, Celeste Rita Baker, Kristiana Willsey, Rosco Lance, Gardner Mounce, Filip Hajdar Drnovšek Zorko, Millie Ho, Minal Hajratwala, and Nelly Geraldine García-Rosas. And to Neile Graham, Jae Steinbacher, and everyone who makes Clarion West all it is today.

Endless love and gratitude to my family: Mom and Dad, who let me promise when I was little that I would someday make enough money from writing that I would buy them each a Porsche. None of this without you. To Sherill, Dave, Adam, Greg, Kaily, Julia, and Stepan. To Yuri Ten, Albina Sergeevna, Anzor Konstantinovich, Edward Vladimirovich, Zoiy Michailovna, Galina Innokentievna, Vladimir Sergeevich, Ilya, Sergey, and Katya: every page I write is a failed sponge trying to soak up an ocean.

To Lady Rock, Treat Street, and the Friendship M______ Squad. To Alana for talking till we're both hoarse, and being the "Hi!" I'm always happy to hear. To everyone who's been there since Boston. To Kabir.

Thanks to Boulder for the persistent sunshine and that trail with those big stones stacked to look like sofas. Thanks to the Bay Area and its writers and artists ("New shit!"), and to punks, weirdos, freaks, and organizers everywhere. To every mosh pit that's ever caught me. To the writers who know that our work takes work—and curiosity, imagination, uncertainty, discovery, failure—and there's no shortcut through that work, no real joy without it.

Thanks to libraries and librarians, bookstores and book-sellers, coffee shops and the blessed caffeinators. Thanks to the fancy combo scanner/printers at every day job I've worked at.

To that loose brick in the low wall in Calle La Paz in Tucson that all us kids used to lift up and tuck secrets under.

Thank you, Toaster Strudels. I don't care what they say about you.

Thanks to those who read this book before it took this tidy rectangle shape, and with more generosity than I can fathom. To all readers: your time and attention are the greatest gifts, and I'll always strive to be worthy of them.

To Shapka, for being one of one, my soul in a whirling fur tornado. To Conundrum, for being the rainless cloud the gods sent down to prove they love us.

Thank you, most of all, to Tim, who makes the words clearer and the colors brighter. For believing in me sincerely, even, and especially, when I don't believe in myself—"enough for the both of us." For breaking fake rules, living every day with humor and without apology,

and reminding me what truly matters. Wherever else I am,
I'm also forever sitting next to you in that room on 24th
and Treat, watching whatever movie's projected on the
wall go from dim to sharper to perfect, feeling like we're
the last ones up in the world.

THE AUTHOR

Kristina Ten's stories appear in *Best American Science Fiction and Fantasy*, *We're Here: The Best Queer Speculative Fiction*, *McSweeney's*, *Lightspeed*, *Nightmare*, *Uncanny*, and elsewhere. She has won the Stephen Dixon Award for Short Fiction, the Subjective Chaos Kind of Award, and the *F(r)iction* Writing Contest, and has been a finalist for the Shirley Jackson Award and the Locus Award. She is a graduate of Clarion West Writers Workshop and the University of Colorado Boulder's MFA program in creative writing. *Tell Me Yours, I'll Tell You Mine* is her debut collection.